AN EPIC FANTASY ADVENTURE

ELDRITCH KNIGHT

HAVEN CHRONICLES: BOOK 2

TIMOTHY McGOWEN

ELDRITCH KNIGHT BOOK 2

AN EPIC FANTASY ADVENTURE

HAVEN CHRONICLES
BOOK 2

TIMOTHY MCGOWEN

RISING TOWER BOOKS

Fantasy / LitRPG / Gamelit

BIBLIOGRAPHY OF TIMOTHY MCGOWEN

Haven Chronicles
Haven Chronicles: Eldritch Knight

Short Stories/Novellas
Dead Man's Bounty
Exiled Jahk (https://dl.bookfunnel.com/c10uz8peaf)

Last Born of Ki'darth
Reincarnation: A Litrpg/Gamelit Trilogy
Rebellion: A Litrpg/Gamelit Trilogy
Retribution: A Litrpg/Gamelit Trilogy

Order & Chaos
Arcane Knight Book 1: An Epic LITRPG Fantasy
Arcane Knight Book 2: An Epic LITRPG Fantasy
Arcane Knight Book 3: An Epic LITRPG Fantasy
Arcane Knight Book 4: An Epic LITRPG Fantasy

The Elemental Realms
Nexus Guardian Book 1: A Fantasy LitRPG Adventure
Nexus Guardian Book 2: A Fantasy LitRPG Adventure

REVIEWS ARE IMPORTANT

Every review matters, get your voice heard.

Follow me on Amazon to get informed when my next book is released!

https://www.amazon.com/stores/Timothy-McGowen/author/B087QTTRJK

Join my Patreon for early Chapters!

https://www.patreon.com/TimothyMcGowen

Join my Facebook group and discuss the books

https://www.facebook.com/groups/234653175151521/

I dedicate this book to my family.

CONTENTS

LEAVE A REVIEW & CHECK OUT MY WEBSITE

Don't forget to leave a review!

Get an exclusive short story to read if you subscribe to my newsletter at https://authortimothymcgowen.com/

CHAPTER 1
JAMES

Several Hours After Phil was Transferred to Haven

Blood poured from James's stomach and the old white van he drove sputtered as it struggled to make it the last mile. The last few blocks looked like they'd been cleared recently, trash and other debris crowding the sidewalks. James, or Tank as he was known throughout the digital world, knew he had little time left to live. His roommate, Dave-known as Frog to most-had already died. A mix of pain and adrenaline was all that kept James from falling apart. He was used to death—that wasn't the problem—what he wasn't ready for was the death of everyone he held dear, in a single day.

"Stay on mission," James' voice sounded foreign even to his own ears. Hours of screaming and a meaty punch to his throat had all but destroyed his voice. Shifting in his seat, his one free hand doing its best to stem the bleeding he turned onto the street he'd been looking for. "Damnit Phil," a bloody cough splattered the window ahead of him. "You better have made it."

The ancient van's brakes screeched as it tried to come to a

complete stop in front of a dimly lit warehouse. The last remaining hubcap continued to roll onward well after the van came to a complete stop. James glanced at the crumpled strip of paper where he had written the address that Phil had sent, he was in the right place.

1425 West Travel St.

Pain shot through him, and he cursed, his hand moving to stem the flow of blood from the bullet wound in his side. It could have been worse, he reminded himself. Taking several careful steady breaths he looked over at what remained of one of his closest friends. Dave's eyes stared directly in James's direction, lifeless and cold. James met the dark grey eyes of his friend. There wouldn't be any more jokes, no more goofy smiles from Dave. Out of all his friends Dave had been his closest. Reaching out his hand and leaning forward James pressed his forehead against Dave's, his hand firm against the side of his head.

"Rest easy friend and may the gods greet you kindly."

Dave had been courageous to the end, driving without fear as bullets had whizzed around us. There was no greater deed a friend could do than give his life for another. James released his grip and stepped free of the van.

He ripped a sleeve from his shirt and hastily tied a makeshift bandage around his midsection. Lucky for him it stretched, not many sleeves were long enough to wrap around his enormous girth.

He was a big man, but not fat or overweight by any normal standards. Normally he'd spend at least a few hours a day in the gym, but lately his time had been spent in cage fights. It had the dual benefit of keeping him in good shape and letting him vent his rage. Most that met him would agree that he was a gentle giant, he stood an easy six foot nine and weighed a sturdy three hundred and seventy pounds of muscle.

The gentle giant routine was a carefully crafted persona James had worked on since he was ten years old. Memories of the day he had gone too far flashed through his mind and even the pain of his wound felt like a relief in comparison. His teeth clenched together until he tasted blood and he let a breath out, relaxing his jaw.

Onward and forward.

James didn't feel the cold as he approached the building. Looking up he studied the warehouse, brush and vines coated the building so thickly it was hard to spot the doors ahead. Reaching up to his ARD control device he tried to scan the building. *Oh right*, he thought, recalling that he had purposely fried his ARD hours ago to keep anyone from tracking him.

His vision swam with each step. He barely noticed the empty black hover vans or the bodies that lay on the ground in a rough line. He almost missed the gaping holes in the chest of the men dressed like special forces goons. He nearly missed it all, but he wasn't that far gone.

"I missed one hell of a fight," James muttered as he stumbled forward into the building.

As squinted his eyes as he approached a blank wall where half of a man's body, the bottom half, sat outside the building. Carefully reaching his hand forward he was surprised to find that it pieced the wall without any effort, some sort of super advanced hologram. However it worked, James couldn't even begin to wonder. With only a moment's hesitation he pushed through the barrier and made his way inside.

Ahead of him was a maze of hallways and bodies. Using the walls to keep himself from collapsing he followed the trail of the dead. He coughed several times; the air was stale and tasted like burnt toast. It was odd to him that this fluorescent lit warehouse could be the scene of such an epic battle. The pale white walls and outdated light fixtures stood at odds against high tech battle armor that the mass of dead bodies wore.

Their powerful guns didn't fit next to the random assorted pictures of oceans and lonely beaches scattered on walls.

The sound of gunfire, followed by yells and then an odd whooshing noise echoed down the hall towards James.

It would appear the battle wasn't over after all, he thought to himself as he turned a corner. Ahead were two large double doors, both had been nearly blown off their hinges. Each door hung to the frame by a single point and obscured most of his view as he approached.

Pushing past the doors he didn't bother glancing inside, to weary from blood loss to care anymore.

The majority of the room sat in darkness, the vastness of the room unseen. In the furthest corner a circle of light illuminated several computers and a tomb like object. In front of all that was a single man, his hands glowed a fierce yellow-orange and just in front of him lay the body of one of the black clad men.

The white lab cloaked figure noticed James and his hands rose.

James tried to call out to him, but instead was thrown into a fit of coughing. The heavy coughing and painful spasms dropped James to a knee just as a beam of light streaked overhead. He could feel the heat of it, and he ducked even lower. Gaining a measure of control of his coughing he yelled.

"Phil sent me here," he managed to stand and noted that the large man's hand stopped glowing.

"Aw I see," the stranger said, his voice low and booming, "I am glad that another of his team could make it. Phil has already traveled through the gate, what is your name, friend? Mine is Doctor Vikar."

James eyed Doctor Vikar as he approached. The man was a few inches taller than him, a feat no one he had ever met accomplished. His lab coat was filled with bullet holes and several red spots on the large man's shirt spoke of inflicted bullet wounds. Yet he walked as if he was in perfect condition.

"My name is James," James said, letting Doctor Vikar give him an arm to keep him up. "How'd you manage that light show?"

"Aw that," Doctor Vikar chuckled as he helped James get closer to the light. "Well, I am an ascended being that managed to do a return trip to your planet in hopes that we could figure out why your people were being forced to migrate over to Haven. More specifically, I am a member of the Paladin Order."

It hurt, but James laughed. This guy was a nut.

"So, Doctor looney toons," James tried to sound funny, but his voice was too ruined to make much of an attempt at it. "You really have a way to upload us or am I going to die while you tell me stories about dragons and wizards?"

"Lay down here," the crazed giant doctor said, placing James into a stone coffin that had wires and tubes running out of it. "I'll need to cut your clothes free but be still and I should be able to get your teleported to Haven before this body of yours expires."

Teleported? James was sure he had heard that right. Perhaps the doctor was loopy because of his wounds as well. Either way James could do nothing but watch as the man cut free what remained of his clothes and rubbed handfuls of cold jelly on him. Doctor Vikar shut a lid over him with a loud thump, it went transparent moments after shutting and

James watched as Doctor Vikar clicked on a keyboard close by.

His face seemed worried and he glanced towards James with a worried look, before turning towards his coffin. The doctor's hands began to glow and he grabbed hold of the stone coffin.

"There isn't enough power!" The man yelled. "I will do my best to give you the power required, safe travels."

The stone box began to heat up and a hint of panic tried to work its way into James head but was overruled by a growing darkness. As his vision blurred and darkened, he was sure that Doctor Vikar's entire body was glowing orange and beginning to fall apart.

He was growing very tired and wasn't sure he could keep his eyes open any longer. A mixture of blood loss and exhaustion overtook him, and his world faded to black.

CHAPTER 2
PHIL
SEVERAL WEEKS AFTER THE BURNING OF THE WORLD TREE.

P hil was not ready to face what lay behind the twenty-foot rune carved wooden door ahead of him. For once it wasn't fear of harm that held him back or fear of any one person. The power he had amassed and could now call down at will against his enemies was vast.

No. He wasn't afraid of them anymore, even if they did potentially hold even deeper pools of power.

What he feared was the public speaking that would be required of him. Beside him stood his new lieutenant and friend, Ned. He had abandoned his name along with a number of other Ah'tehetah, to the displeasure of many of the Ah'ehrans. The treefolk were grateful to Phil for his intervention and ultimately saving their mother tree, but their race was dying, and without a new influx of souls, that death loomed closer than any of them wished to admit.

Sharing a look with Ned, Phil took a deep breath and prepared to enter.

Boom. Boom. Boom.

Phil did as he had been instructed by Seph, knocking thrice

then raised his hood. From what little Seph had been able to tell him, Phil expected that both Golder and Zarrick would be in attendance. He thought back to the last time he had spoken to Golder, nearly a month ago...

"What do you mean you didn't find it," Golder said, standing far enough away that he was cloaked in the smoke that rose from the burnt ground around him. "I can see it around your neck, boy."

"I didn't find it," Phil repeated, his words stronger and more confident this time. "The Eldritch Knights will not give up their most holy artifact. And while I appreciate all the assistance Zarrick has given me these past weeks, I am not as naive as I once was when we met."

Golder laughed. "So be it." His form fading away and out of view. It was an eerie sound that continued, getting further and further away as time passed until Phil stood in the quiet of the evening.

Phil's mind snapped back to the present as the doors creaked and swung open.

Before him lay a sea of people, all sitting in a cathedral-like building with seating that ran up both sides of the curved wall. There was a staircase that led to a speaking platform that stood about half way up the fifty pace high building, making it possible for people to address the entirety of the gathered people.

Phil took each step carefully, his companion Ned, walking beside him. At the edge of the viewing platform stood six figures, one of which Phil recognized immediately as Zarrick, but Golder was not in sight. Stamping down an urge to burn him off the platform, Phil continued his ascent until he was standing in the middle of the six.

Each one represented a different Order that was recognized by the council and Eldritch Knights weren't among them. There were the armored Paladins with their flames of indignation burning hot within them. And the priests who held both light and shadow within them, a duality that often brought them under the ire of some of the other orders. And of course there were the Wizards, which Zarrick stood at the head of.

The others were unknown to Phil, but he looked them over regardless. A short stout man with black leathers, a woman in armor, and a man wearing nothing but what looked like white pajamas, perhaps a monk of some kind or another.

Phil had a prepared speech that he began to give the moment he reached the middle platform, as Seph had instructed him to do. It spoke of how the Eldritch Knights were returning, their fire once more ignited and they sought to have their place restored among the council. It spoke of great deeds done in the past, how it was the fire of the Eldritch Knights that had repelled the last great war, not mentioning it was that very war that had been caused by them in the first place.

He went on and on, citing reasons and facts as best he could from what he'd been told, all the while feeding off his inner fire to give him strength and to cool his nerves. Phil feared no man any longer, but having lost an arm he was technically weaker than someone of equal strength who had access to all their nodes.

Of course no one here would know he'd lost his arm, he'd replaced it with a prosthetic that he'd covered with armor. Sure he couldn't swing it about very well, but he could move it around enough that it would appear to anyone not terribly keen on looking, that he was in full fighting form. Golder knew better, he'd seen him the night he'd lost the arm, so Zarrick would be clued in as well.

The speech finished and they gave the response that Seph said they would, basically, retire to the waiting room and we will deliberate over the matter. She expected that it would take an hour if not longer for them to issue the denial, which would give Phil the time he needed to sneak into the library and find the books they needed.

Phil allowed himself to be led out and he took a seat outside, where they left him completely unguarded. Old pompous fools that they were, Seph had guessed correctly that they'd be too secure in their own heads to expect Phil to do anything but wait for them.

Looking at Ned, Phil smiled.

"Time to go shopping," Phil said, walking down the hall and through the winding hallways toward the library.

"It is good that you have me," Ned said, in his usual accented speech. "I have great navigational sense. I once found a fruit tree in a vegetable garden."

Phil looked up at the towering man, he looked strange with his sap removed, almost human, but his ears were different, more closely set against the head and his nose blunted. He didn't know how long Ned and his kind would last without the sap of the mother tree, but Phil had found some substitutions over the months leading up to this mission.

Turns out you could find the sap they needed elsewhere if you weren't afraid of hunting Ixanas—mutated creatures that the treefolk turned into when they stopped taking the sap or aged to a certain point. It was one of the many issues Phil would have to deal with in the coming months, especially when it came to Ned and his dozen or so warriors that had come to join my side at the Eldritch Keep.

Seph wanted to turn them away at first, but when removing their sap they showed her many runes on their flesh that she'd never seen before, so she allowed them to stay—if for studying them and nothing else, she said.

Phil knew the truth was somewhere in between, so many of the treefolk warrior caste had given their lives, turning feral and using the green flame unlike any Phil had seen before, so they did have a place at the Eldritch Keep, even if their use of the flame was different than Seph's and Phil's.

Sound echoed ahead as they walked the corridors and they slipped into a door to avoid detection. It turned out to be a small broom closet and after the footsteps passed, they continued on their way.

CHAPTER 3
JAMES

The first sensation James felt as he snapped into awareness was the sudden rush of wind followed by pain as his body collided with an unknown hard surface. The cold of his new surroundings forced his mind awake and aware.

He was in water, above him he caught sight of two globes of light. Without a second thought he used his powerful limbs to swim to the surface. His lungs inhaled the sweet salty smell of the ocean and an ache he hadn't realized had been building in his lungs faded away. The cold water had brought a sudden awareness, but James was still very confused about how he had ended up in an ocean.

As he struggled to regain a sense of what he had done the night before to end up in the ocean, a voice called out to him.

"You be needing aid, lad?" The voice came from a small boat, no bigger than James' beloved van. Standing mid boat, maybe fifty feet off, was a sea worn man with attire to match that of a movie pirate. Black tricorn hat, bushy dark beard, skin of rough leather, and even a peg leg made of polished brown wood.

"Aye, aye captain I do be needing yer aid," James struggled to get the words out while keeping afloat. Most of his attempt at a pirate's accent and speech failed as a sudden gust of wind nearly put him under the water again.

The pirate wanna-be seemed to get the idea though and his boat, that looked as worn as its captain, turned towards him. The mast of the boat was made of dark wood and the sails were stained brown, filled with small holes and rips.

It took only a few minutes for the boat to get close enough for James to feel comfortable in his ability to swim the distance. He was strong, but he'd never been a great swimmer. Just as he pulled himself free of the water his memory clicked and realization of where he was smashed into the forefront of his mind.

Haven.

He had made it into Haven! Pulling himself upright he let out a loud whoop and jumped into the air. As excited as he felt, it wasn't the right move. The moment his feet hit the wet wood of the small craft he slipped and tumbled. His body hit hard on the side of the small craft, and he fell overboard, back into the cold water.

He let himself float atop the water for several long moments, just enjoying all the senses he was feeling.

Cold, salt, warmth from the sun, it was all so real. Perhaps his rescuers hadn't been speaking nonsense? No. This was a virtual reality, a very complex and awesome one, but one all the same. He was in a video game; he was sure of it.

Letting out another whoop of excitement he grabbed hold of the edge of the boat and lifted himself free of the water. His body rippled from a mix of excitement and excursion.

"So do I get my starting gear from you...Or is there a beginning player's hub I missed?" James scratched absently at his naked backside, meanwhile the-possible very real pirate-stared at him with a scowl on his face.

In response the pirate-man narrowed his dark eyes and said, "Ah'r, ya 'it yer 'ead did ya now? Gat'er yer wits 'n cover yer bits." James stared hard at the man trying to make out what he was saying. It clicked together about the same time as the pirate threw over an even more weathered and worn long coat at his feet.

James ignored it and inspected his body. The game did a pretty damn good job replicating his body, but they missed all his awesome scars. His hands pressed against every inch of his form, bending low to touch his toes and then bending as best he could to see his backside.

He had worked hard for each and every one of those scars, but he was fairly confident he would soon be able to rack up a few new scars. A smile spread across his face as he pictured the lab with the strange coffin machine, bullets everywhere, cracks on the machine itself, and not to mention the piles of dead corp goons. He no longer felt the fatigue and pain of his several bullet wounds. His body practically vibrated with energy and strength. He could feel the strength in his arms as he clenched his fist. They'd done well capturing his previous strength, in fact-if possible-he felt even stronger than before.

Someone was talking to him, and he was totally ignoring them.

He turned to the old man. "Say again?" James asked.

"We be nearing da docks," The man sounded like a B movie pirate actor, but he was becoming easier to understand. "If ye be wanting to stay out of the 'ands of the guard, you best be swimming ter last bit. Ah'r and grab me sea coat and cover yerself, your eel be scaring me fis' away." The man chuckled at his own joke in a very stereotypical pirate fashion.

He even looked like a pirate. Eye patch? Check. Large fish-man hat? Check. Wooden peg leg? Check. The only thing that gave James pause was the odd eye color. The man's left eye, the one not covered by a patch, was a dark purple. Well, that and he was built nearly as thick as him and almost as tall.

That is saying something to be sure as James stood a wonderful 6 foot 9 inches tall with a weight of 350 pounds and a speed that was unusual for his size.

"Aye matey!" James said back to the swarthy pirate. He stood and slid the coat over his wide shoulders, a little short for a long coat but it'll cover the bits and didn't feel too tight around the shoulders. "Keep the black flag flying black beard!" Where his final words as he dove into the ocean from the side of the boat with a splash, confident now that he'd be able to make the short swim to the shore.

He was surprised to find the water, after only ten or twenty feet, to be shallow enough for him to walk on the soft sand below. Walking clear of the docks that bustled with activity and surely had the guard the old man spoke of; he made his way towards a group of seaside buildings. They looked as if they could fall over at any moment. The wood of the buildings must have been a light golden brown at some point, the tops of the two story shacks still held some of its true color, but the entire first floor of each of the buildings were stained a myriad of colors from black to red.

James stood just outside a darkened street. It couldn't be later than midafternoon, but somehow this clutter of buildings and the streets inside were dark and shady. James glanced upward and saw the cause of it. All of the buildings were connected by cords that had billowing dirty cloth over them, creating an entire section of buildings that were tented off from the sun above.

A sudden gust of wind billowed James wet long coat, shifting the tented covering as well. Several holes in the tent-like material let narrow beams of light through and so as it shifted, he caught sight of at least three men with blades out, standing down the alley a ways.

James smiled; it was time to get some loot.

Like most people that worked in tech, he was a huge fan of video games and had played his fair share. There had been a few in the last ten years that did a rudimentary full-dive experience, nothing quite as impressive as Haven, but passable. In one of the more popular ones, War and Thunder it was called, he had joined with his friends, Frog, Doc, and a few others. They had spent the first few months raiding towns and killing off NPCs(non player characters) for a quick profit.

The game had tried so hard to be realistic so each town they conquered provided vast amounts of wealth in terms of supplies, food, and gold. It wasn't until they released several patches that improved the strength of the town guards and granted random NPCs abilities that rivaled real players, that the stratagem fell apart and his team had to start doing the actual quests and dungeons.

Seeing as Haven was meant to be a, well a 'Haven', James was sure he could get away with a little random killing and looting before whoever pulled the strings caught on. Either way though, he promised himself he would look for an official quest as soon as it made sense.

Before he could make the alley, he noticed the men had taken note of him as well. It looked like they'd be coming to him after all, blades out.

His eyes scanned the area while pressing salt water from his hair with his hands. Having found what he was looking for, he stopped well before the alley where they lurked and spread his arms wide. With his coat whipping behind him he pressed his eyes closed and enjoyed the cold sea breeze. His toes curled into the warm sand at the edge of the beach and James let out an exaggerated sigh.

"Well, come on already!" He bellowed. "I haven't got all day! I know there has to be a quest somewhere in this sea-soaked city." The last bit me said loud enough for only his ears.

"You are in our turf." An oily voice said, as a scrawny man slithered from the dark alleyway ahead of Tank. "Normally I'd just take your coin and give you a mild beating, but something tells me if you are carrying coin, it's in a place I don't want to go. So, I'm afraid me and the boys are gonna have to take it from your hide."

The man's speech was cut short abruptly as James's fist connected with his face and a sickened crunch turned the man's head in an odd angle.

"You talk a lot for an NPC." James said laughing. This was his kind of game! He flexed his muscles and shook his fist out. Everything felt so real!

Three more goons, wearing clothing just as dirty and torn as the first, came charging from the darkened alley. James couldn't help grinning, and he reached down, grabbing a hold of a weather worn rock. It fit nicely in his hand but stayed there only for a moment.

He threw the rock with bone breaking force at the lead attacker. It connected with a sickening crunch square in the goon's face.

It was best that he even the odds. He knew by experience that even the most skilled fighters couldn't hope to match themselves against more than one or two people. The sheer numbers and the size of his attackers, each of them—while scrawnier than James—held a good bit of wiry muscle and stood over six feet tall, could overwhelm him.

But praise to Thor and Odin the father, his attack had given the trailing goon pause. His companion reached James and lunged forward for a vicious stab of his dagger. But James had been expecting as much, he drilled what to do hundreds of times and even done it about a dozen times out on the streets.

James grabbed the end of his large coat and rolled himself to the side, putting the coat in the path of the dagger. It caught the blade, the rough material cutting easily against the sharp blade of the dagger. James then threw his arm and the rest of the left side of his coat over the man's outreached arm. All of this took moments and would have worked better if James had taken the coat off completely, but it had worked.

The man stumbled forward in surprise and James plunged his fist into the side of his head. Another sickening crunch and the goon fell, suddenly limp.

Haven had definitely made him stronger. James had always been able to delivery powerful punches, but this was ridiculous. Either the game had started him out with an increased level, or he had just found incredibly weak mobs. He found himself absently wondering if this game even had levels or a progression system in place. He decided it didn't matter.

"Second mob down!" He cried aloud, the remaining goon had stopped a full twenty feet away. "James the Tank has leveled up! Come here so I can get more experience!" He yelled the last sentence with a growl at the final alley goon.

The man's eyes went wide, a pleasant gray color, and he turned and ran.

James laughed and slammed a fist into his chest howling

after the fleeing mob. He'd catch him later, for now it was time to loot!

A few small copper looking coins, square with large holes in them, a pair of pants that were far too tight and somewhat smelly, a length of cloth that the man had been using as a belt, and a single six-inch dagger. Everything else had too many holes to be worth taking. But he squeezed the pants over his naked lower half.

He finished equipping his new items and lifted the dagger up to inspect it. It had plain features, leather handle with shoddy craftsmanship, but the blade was clean and looked to have been sharpened recently. Or he assumed that's what it meant when the lightest touch on his finger drew blood.

"Simple Worn Dagger +1 to sharpness," James announced to himself. There were no floating names or stats that he could find for items, but he was enjoying himself. Looking down at the torn and uncomfortable pants and the belt of cloth he tied around himself to hold the dagger he said. "Shit smelling pants, -10 to Charisma."

Feeling as satisfied as he could given the poor loot, James headed straight for where he saw his next kill go, into the dark alleyway.

Standing over his most recent kill, the same man who had run from him on the beach, James couldn't help but feel a little remorse for the NPC. It had begged for its life, saying it was sorry and that it wasn't his idea, etc. Why the creators of Haven had decided to invest so much time into random NPCs like this confused him. It wasn't like they were real people.

A sudden tightness clenched his chest as memories flashed

through his mind. He pushed them aside and focused on the here and now. There was no time for the past when his future was right in front of him.

He reminded himself that he would need to find a quest sooner or later. If he spent all of his time killing the NPCs there might be some sort of repercussions in the long term. He had to consider things like this now since, as far as he knew, he was basically an immortal mind living in a computer.

But for now, the easiest way to get loot and coin would be to do what he did best. Fight. So he headed for the next dark alley, hoping to find more mobs to kill and better loot.

CHAPTER 4
JAMES

He stood in an empty alley. The stank of the place wafting into his nose, despite the small pieces of cloth that filled his nostrils. The area around him bustled with quiet life. A beggar sat at the corner; James knew by several hours of experience that this man was a lookout. The sound of laughter and yelling poured from a door not far away. There was a sign that marked it as a gathering place. It was a horned pig with an apple in its mouth and a mug overflowing with drink in its hoofed hand.

James let out a long and steady sigh. He was tired. By his count he had killed nearly twenty-five mobs and collected a tidy sum of coin. His attire had been upgraded as well. He now wore a pair of pants that nearly fit him as pants should. On his chest hung a loosely fitting black shirt with only two stab holes in it and a handful of blood that didn't belong to him.

So far, he hadn't come across a proper belt, but wore an assortment of cloth ones that did well to hide a few daggers. He'd even lucked out and found a pair of boots that fit him well enough, no socks though. The boots concealed a smaller knife in each, and his long tattered black sailors coat helped hide his last weapon, a club.

It looked no more menacing than a dinner table leg, but he had a lump on his head that could attest to the effectiveness of the weapon. So armed as well as he could be, and with a leather pouch overfilled with coin taken from his mob kills, he moved to enter the establishment.

It was like all buildings in these slums, dark wood, half covered in shit and mud, with only the bare minimum supports required to keep the building from falling in on itself. The door was different though, it was made of metal-or at least covered in it from the outside, with a small slat that could be pulled aside and just be big enough to see a pair of eyes.

The scent of meat and ale wafted through the cracks of the door and James's stomach groaned in response. Eager to be out of the cold and stank of the street, he reached up to knock on the door. Before his hand had reached it though, the slat opened, and a dark orange pair of eyes stared back at him. The eyes did a once over, and lingered for a long moment at James's coin purse that sat in open view tied to one of the cloth belts.

"Hello there," James began to say, but the slat shut with a loud snap. The sound of locks being undone and chains jingling. The door swung wide and sound, heat, and smells hit him like a wave of euphoria.

Clamping his eyes shut James savored the feelings, still amazed at how detailed they all were in Haven.

"If you have any disputes," the orange eyed man began to say, "then you take them outside or you leave in a box." His speech was the best James had heard since arriving in Haven, and so James gave him a quick once over.

His skin was a light shade of orange, matching the shades of his eyes. He wore simple clean clothing that stood out in contrast to the filth on the street and the rough worn look of the establishment. He had no visible weapons, not even a simple dagger that nearly every mob James encountered wore on their belt.

The final thing that registered for James was the man's size. As James took two steps down rickety steps, he realized the orange eyed bouncer was nearly a foot taller than him and several inches thicker around the shoulders. The bouncer shifted his weight in a way that spoke of a readiness to smash James's face if he tried anything.

"You're a big fellow," James said, reaching out and slapping the man on the shoulder playfully. "I bet you'd be a hoot in a brawl."

"Mick! Don't do it," a voice boomed from across the room. James took a quick glance and saw it was a middle-aged round barkeep waggling a finger in his direction. Looking back James realized several things in a few moments.

The first was that the large man, Mick most likely, had pulled a dagger from seemingly nowhere.

The second was that the dagger was inches away from stabbing him in the gut.

"Best not touch him," the barkeep yelled from across the room. "He gets a little upset when folks get too close."

James raised his hands in mock surrender but made a mental note to keep an eye on the bouncer. He had moved without James so much as noticing the sound of his clothing ruffling.

As quickly as the dagger appeared in Mick's hands, it was gone again and the giant turned towards the door, sitting himself on a stool at the end of the small steps.

The room was lit by a large fireplace to the left of the open sitting area. James counted five, no six, tables each with a burning set of thick candles casting the shadows of the chairs at odd angles. The room had gone mostly quiet and still as he approached.

In all, including the doorman-Mick the humongous-and the barkeep, there were fourteen other people inside. A few looked dirty and grimy, but surprisingly the majority were raggedly dressed, but clean. The bustle continued after a slight pause and James weaved through the tables to find a seat at the bar.

"What's on the menu, barkeep!" He declared loudly as he took his seat. The barstool creaked under his weight but held together. The barkeep was polishing a dirty glass with an even dirty rag but made his way over with a chuckle.

Setting his rag down the barkeep said, "Welcome to the Hungry Hog. I'm Farstil, what's your name, stranger?"

James grinned broadly. "James the Tank." He couldn't decide if he wanted to use his online moniker or just his actual name, so he split the difference.

Farstil rubbed at his chin, frowning. "James Tank." He tasted the words, leaving out the added 'the' James had used. "Seems like a respectable enough name. We have brunto wine, if you have the coin for it. Mostly we serve the stew of the day and olak ale. Stew of the day is horse meat stew, old Telf died on me last week."

James's brows traveled further up the more he thought about eating horse stew. He was familiar with the animal; they'd gone extinct a few years before he was born. But if he remembered, they weren't normally used for eating. Oh well, when in Rome.

James reached into his pocket and pulled out a handful of coins, letting them fall noisily onto the thick vanished bar. "I will take your biggest bowl and mug of ale."

Farstil's eyes went wide, but he quickly found his composure and scooped the entire pile of coins. "I'll keep the bowls and mugs coming." He announced before disappearing into a door into the back. It swung closed hard and rattled the rows of mugs and, what James could only assume, were rows of liquor.

The game continued to surprise James, he wouldn't be surprised to hear that NPCs had family and friends. They really went all out to create a seamless experience. He found himself wondering if perhaps the NPCs were actually self-aware. Would they be surprised to learn they were just computer simulations on a server farm located on the moon? The true location wasn't something that was actually known to anyone James had spoken too, but it was the best guess that made sense.

A loud raspy voice, the man had perhaps had one too many drinks, thunder over the low chatter of the room. "I hear the entire seaside gang was wiped out in a bloody mess."

"You've hit your head one too many times Gurlof, shut it!" Another voice called back, this one younger but still with a bit of a rasp. James kept his back to them, but strained his ears to hear the next response. It sounded like a woman speaking, but James hadn't noticed any woman in the bar when he'd entered.

"He isn't as off his rocker as you think," the voice said just above a whisper, James struggled to hear it. "Not only did the seaside gang get wiped out this morning, but the northerners also took a hit. No one knows who is doing the hits, but one of the survivors described a monstrous man covered in blood moving as fast as an Ascended."

At that last word the entire bar fell quiet and still. James sneaked a peak over his shoulder and saw a mix of worry and anger on their faces.

The younger raspy voice spoke again. "Those damned Ascended bastards. They think they can walk through us and cut us down for sport. I say we report it to the guards, to hell with it."

The older raspy voice broke out into an over exaggerated laugh before saying. "They don't give a piss about us. If it were up to them, they'd throw us out to join the tent city growing outside the walls."

It grew quieter after that, each table drifting off into their own conversations. James's food and drink arrived with a loud clank.

"It smells wonderful!" James proclaimed, grabbing a wooden spoon that had seen better days and digging into the food.

The soup defied all description. Not that it was a culinary masterpiece or anything of the sort, but James's hunger had reached a fever pitch and the warm broth was pure ecstasy on his lips. There were a mix of vegetables, potatoes-or some kind of similar starch-, and the meat.

Whatever it was it tasted very similar to the lab grown beef James had grown up with, maybe a tad off tasting, but overall, it wasn't bad.

He continued to eat, bowl after bowl, mug of sweet ale after mug of sweet ale. No one bothered him, and the barkeep hadn't asked for additional money yet. He wondered if he had perhaps overpaid by a large margin, but with each new mug of ale he cared a little less.

His hunger sated and his inhibitions further removed he stood and went looking for conversation. The place had filled up, each table was seating at least two patrons, and a low thrum of conversation filled the room. Sitting on a chair near the fire a man wearing a long purple coat, a fair bit cleaner than the rest of the crowd, plucked at an odd-looking guitar.

It had a long narrow neck and only three tuning pegs near the top. He played a song and sang along as it went.

Something about the rising dread of the black dragon's feast. James ignored the lyrics and focused on the instrument's music. It was a slow and depressing tune, and he loved it.

He grabbed an empty chair from a nearby table and sat to listen. The music's tone changed, and James noticed the entertainer had shifted another set of pegs on the base of the instrument. The rhythm increased as well, James found his foot padding along with the beat.

Then just as it was reaching a fever pitch the song ended. James stood and began to clap.

"Wonderful! Just wonderful!" He walked over to the entertainer to introduce himself. "My name is James, and you have to let me try your odd guitar."

The entertainer raised an eyebrow, reaching up to move a strand of dark black hair out of his face. He had strikingly green eyes that almost seemed to glow.

"This is not a *guitar,*" the entertainer emphasized the word before continuing, "it is a lude. Did you enjoy the entertainment?" He held his hand out as if expecting something.

James reached out and shook it. The man didn't seem impressed. A low creek startled James and he turned to find the bouncer looming over him.

"He bothering you, Z'Jhack?" Mack asked, a growl in his words.

Reaching into his coin purse James pulled out a few coins, then held them out for Z'Jhack.

He noticed the gesture and smiled. "Not at all, me and this

fellow, was it James? Yes, James are fast friends." With a swift motion James found his hand empty of the proffered coins.

"Sit, my friend," Z'Jhack said motioning to a space next to him by the fire.

James pulled his chair over and sat. The fire was warm, but comfortable. Z'Jhack held out his instrument and James took it.

It had a good heft to it and James gave it an experimental strum. It rang out low, the base tuner must have been flipped back. He let his fingers glide up and down the neck, finding the notes he was familiar with from his own guitar playing.

He wasn't sure how long he played, lost in the music and the moment. The instrument was elegant, but strong. How the developers had come up with such a unique work of art, he did not know, but he was glad that they had.

He stopped playing, letting it rest in his lap. It was tempting to decide that it was his now and tell the NPC to get lost. But between Mick's presence and the wonder music the NPC had played, he couldn't bring himself to act on the desire.

"Thank you," James said, deciding it was time to find a place to sleep. "You wouldn't know of a place that sells beds for the night, would you?"

The entertainer, Z'Jhack smiled. "You looking to sleep alone or with company?"

"Alone." James's answer shot out a little too quickly and his face grew hot. He wasn't opposed to the idea of sex, but he had a firm rule of *not* paying for it. "I mean, I uh don't want to spend all my coin in one place. Besides, I really do need to get some rest."

"Suit yourself," Z'Jhack said, his grin deepening. "Farstil has a few rooms open I believe. You'd have to check with him to be sure. But if you change your mind." Z'Jhack reached over and put his hand on James forearm. "I'm renting the room at the end of the hall."

James blinked.

He must have misunderstood his previous statement. His face grew hotter and he gave Z'Jhack a nervous smile.

"I'm very tired," James said, standing and handing back the instrument. "You are a gifted musician. Thank you for letting me try out your axe."

James enjoyed a hot bath, for a nominal fee, and did his best to clean his soiled and torn clothing. He laid them out to dry and slipped, naked, into his bed. His dreams came swiftly and images of a black dragon pursued him throughout the night's dreaming adventures.

After speaking with some of the cleaner dressed patrons, James got a location to a market in the nicer part of town. In truth, the streets were still muck and the stench was only slightly better, but the stalls lining the wide-open street stood out in the early morning rays of the sun. This section of the city didn't have the large tent like sheets of cloth pulling it into a perpetual gloom, instead there were rows and rows of rickety vendor stalls, smashed so close together that it resembled several wooden snakes winding up and down the street.

Vendors called their wares, each fighting to be louder than the next and creating a song of chaos. Pushing himself through the sea of people, James came to his first stop.

"Welcome to Neardren's Silks! I am Neardren and I provide only the best a man can wear!" The bulbous man behind the booth was indeed wearing silks of amber, emerald, and purple, but his merchandise looked much less spectacular.

James began to pick and sort through the neatly folded stacks of clothing and cloth material. "I need clean, well-fitting clothing."

"I have just the items you require!" Neardren declared, his eyes running over James's form before thrusting his finger into the air while shouting, 'ah ha'. His hands dove into the piles of clothing at seemingly random areas and produced several items. He laid them out and stepped back, the corners of his mouth curled up into a smile.

Before James lay a black long sleeve V-neck shirt fringed with golden colored stitches and laces that could be tightened to bring the V-neck together. Running his hand across the material he wasn't sure if it was cloth or something else, it felt soft-similar to one of the expensive t-shirts that had a mix of other materials inside-but it had a stiffness that didn't fit what he expected from such a soft outer layer.

Beside the shirt, he had set out a pair of brown slacks. They had draw-strings as well, and upon closer inspection definitely looked to be his size.

Lastly were a pair of white shorts that James realized with a grin, must be the simulations version of underwear. Scratching his chin, he began to root through the piles of cloth until he came across a thick pair of gray socks.

James took out another handful of coins, he was nearing the end of his small horde, but he could go hunt down more mobs if he needed more coin. "I will take them!"

To the surprise of the surrounding crowds James pulled off and threw aside most of what he had been wearing. No one made any moves to stop him, so using his discarded clothes as a barrier from the muck filled street, he began to dress into his clean outfit.

He started with the undergarments and socks. The feeling

of putting socks over your feet after an entire day of walking without them was nearly beyond description. It felt as though clouds had descended from the sky to wrap his feet with warm comfort. Not to mention how nice it was to have his dangly bits secured and out of sight. The ripped and disrepair of his last set had the tendency of letting the horse out of the stable all too often.

Feeling comfortable, but exposed, he hurriedly put on the pants and shirt, followed by his tattered but still comfortable fisherman's long coat. The pants and shirt fit like they'd been tailor for him. The boots he had looted fit better too, after putting on the thick socks. To finish the look, he tied the variety of cloth belts he had taken from his various kills around his waist and began hiding his daggers all over himself. One in each boot, two around his waist, and even one tied firmly against his forearm for quick access. His club hung even with his right leg, attached by a leather loop at the end.

Feeling comfortable for only the second time since arriving, James began to search out the next items he needed; food, water, more weapons, and maybe a map.

This game or Haven as they'd like to have it called, didn't seem to be very good at organized quests. So, James had decided he would get his own basic gear, then stock up on more coin by killing more slum gang mobs, before moving off to find a dungeon to conquer or maybe a princess to save.

CHAPTER 5
PHIL

P hil located the library with ease, it was a grand place with tall ceilings and more books than he'd ever seen before in his life. He passed several guards, none of which stopped him from trying to enter, only tilting their heads to him. He was looking for a restricted area of the library, but according to Seph it was merely locked and he could overload it with a small bit of his power.

So he searched until he came upon a locked room in the upper section of the library. But funnily enough, the door came right open for him, as if whatever lock had been there was defunct.

Slipping inside Ned followed closely behind. They searched book after book, finding nothing. Then he came across a tome about ascension rights, claiming that there was a way to half ascend weaker souls to an almost ascended rank. It went further to explain, Phil was reading as fast as he could but it was so damn interesting, that you could ignite these half ascended without them needing to defeat a beast.

It claimed that because their souls were weaker, the power burned through them slower, only doing minimal damage if the process was done correctly. The idea of half ascended would be a boon to Phil and Seph, perhaps they could grow the ranks of the Eldritch Knights in a different way.

"What do you think of this?" Phil asked, passing the book to Ned.

"I don't read that language," Ned said, putting the book in his side pack and out of sight.

Phil smiled at the abrupt manner of his companion and continued his search. They were burning away the time they had left and he still hadn't found the book he wanted. In fact there were several places where books appeared to be missing and he wondered if perhaps someone had taken the tome he wanted already. But no, these restricted books weren't meant to leave the library, so perhaps someone inside the library had it.

Turning to Ned, he whispered, "Take the books we've found so far and leave. Tell Seph I'll be poking around a bit more to see if I can find the missing book, but I will return soon. Do not get caught."

"I understand," Ned said, nodding his head and adjusting his cloak over his head.

Most would assume the large armored man to be an Ascended so they'd leave him alone, not even asking for papers, though they had some false papers for him just in case. The Kothar nation was getting tighter and tighter on travel restrictions as the Peasant King moved closer to their territory and threatened to start invading Kothar lands.

Seph had filled him in with much since his time with her, she was even using her old spy network again to gather new intel, saying that she was old for this, but doing it regardless. Now that the Eldritch Knight had returned, she was even looking for new recruits, sending word to some of her ancestors that she hadn't spoken to in ages. Apparently they lived on some island nation that Phil couldn't remember the name of.

Phil made his way through the library, picking up a book at random and sitting at a table beside someone else, a weathered older looking man with brilliant blue eyes. Before he could say a word, someone else sat beside the elderly man and struck up a conversation.

"Almost didn't get in," the youngest of the pair said. He wore purple flowing robes and had a pointy edged mustache, ending with a little curl.

"What's that now?" Asked the elderly man. His voice louder than it needed to be for someone so close. "Speak up Taldor, my ears aren't what they used to be."

"Oh it's nothing," muttered the younger man, pulling a book free and opening it. Then raising his voice he said, "I was just saying, it is a shame that security has gotten so tight now and not months before when those books were stolen."

"There was no proof that any books were stolen, not that those old codgers could truly catalogue this entire library anymore. Our collection has gotten a bit out of hand if I do say so myself," the elderly man said.

"Yes, while rumors are going around that old man Withers, the one you all threw out of the order a decade or so back, is up to his old tricks and it was one of his agents that stole the book. Might be that he's gathering forces, could even be thinking about striking back and getting some revenge," the younger of the two said, his voice lowering as he spoke so that the elderly man had to lean in to hear it all.

"Withers? The worthless illusionist we threw out for trying to steal from the restricted area? Seems foolish," the elderly man said, then turning toward Phil he raised his nose in the air and said. "You make it a point to listen to private conversations, do you lad? What are you, one of those newer paladins, lurking about underground and playing with secrets meant for the other orders?"

"I'm a representation of the Eldritch Order, here to get reinstated by the council," Phil said, seeing no reason to lie to them, nor was he good at thinking of lies in a quick fashion.

Plus the truth had the desired effect that he wanted, both of them turned on him and leaned away fearfully.

"T-the eldritch order?" The younger of the two asked. "You were wiped out, your friends won't have a place on the council. You must be lying, I'll get the guards."

"No," the elderly man said, standing and rubbing at his chin. "He has the green flame and it burns with strength beyond my own blue spark. Can't you sense it, Taldor?"

Taldor, the younger of the two, scrunched up his brows and after a few long seconds nodded. "Indeed I can. You've come here to wait out the deliberation then?"

"Something like that," Phil said, smirking. "Who is this Withers character and where can I find him?"

Taldor sniffed his nose at Phil, a strange little action by the smaller and younger of the two. However the elderly man perked up. "Withers is an old fool that allied himself with the gangs in dockside. You've heard of him allying himself with the wandering wraith I assume? I assure you the news is without merit."

"Wandering Wraith, yes I'm after him, anything you can tell me will be helpful in my mission," Phil said, surprising himself with the little white lie. It came out a bit rough, but he'd lied just fine, perhaps he was better at it than he previously thought.

"The idea that an Eldritch Knight could be operating as

the head of one of the dockside gangs is as preposterous as it is dangerous to consider. Go to the dockside slums and find out for yourself. I guarantee you will find nothing but mud and lies," the elderly man said.

"Tasalor, why give this vile creature any such knowledge," Taldor said, shaking his slimy head back and forth. "The idea of another Eldritch Knight just makes me sick. Will you be leeching away our lives before you leave or are you full already?"

"I could eat," Phil joked. Neither looked to find his humor funny though.

The flame inside of Phil urged him to come out as a show of power, but with so many books around, it wouldn't be a good idea. Still he had to suppress the anger that swelled inside of him as his flame touched near the surface of his skin. It was a great and powerful gift, but one that he had to be careful about, especially now that he'd lost his main node on his left hand along with much of it up to the elbow.

He wore a metal prosthetic over which his armor had been attached, it even had the shield affixed to it though he had to do some special rune work with Seph to get it to activate. He had several metal bands with runes on them connecting his upper nodes of the left arm to the lower section of his shield. It wasn't as quick or as powerful as using his main node, but it was a decent work around.

"You boys enjoy your reading," Phil said, standing and heading for the door.

He'd gotten out the door and halfway to the exit when someone grabbed him from behind. He recognized the man as the one that led them to the council meeting in the first place.

"Where is your companion?" He asked, then thinking

better of it, he said, "A decision has been made, you must come to hear it."

"I'm alright," Phil said, knowing full well what they'd decided. Seph told him there was no way they'd go with it, but it was a good reason to get inside of the citadel.

"Oh," the man said, letting Phil go. "I suppose I could just tell you. Your request was declined and furthermore they wish for you to be taken into custody as well as any other Eldritch Knights you've created. So if you could just come with me."

"Fat chance," Phil said, letting his fire flare around him for a brief second. The man, who was clearly not ascended but a servant of them, fell backward in shock. "You tell them they can come collect us at the place they tried to wipe us out. We will be ready for them."

That was the fire talking, Phil knew, but he let it rule over his emotions in that moment. There were decades if not more of tension and grief dealt to Eldritch Knights because of a mistake of their past.

Eldritch Knights had a faction of people that had taken a dark path of consuming others spirits to grow stronger. It was a technique that Seph refused to teach Phil, but one that he had to admit he wished he could learn, if for nothing more than to have an edge over any of his enemies. He knew himself well enough that he wouldn't go about sucking entire villages or cities dry, but temptation took many forms so Seph kept the secret to herself.

"I'm leaving, if you send anyone after me, they will die," Phil said matter-of-factly. "Don't force me to take lives unnec-essarily."

Phil was no longer the scared boy he'd been when he entered Haven. The world that was branded as a program but he now knew the truth. Haven was a true and living place, likely it was a mix of magic and technology that had brought him here along with so many of his people. Though he knew not of his people's motivations or even their whereabouts, other than a sect of Paladins that had tried to kill him months back, he was wary of trusting strangers now, be they earthlings or Kotharians.

CHAPTER 6
JAMES

H e lay back on his bed at the Hungry Hog, this was his third night sleeping there and he had become quite accustomed to the pleasures of the place. The beds, while not much more than cloth wrapped around hay, were comfortable-while also occasionally itchy. The food was consistently appetizing, and the entertainment enriching. Z'Jhack had let him play for nearly an hour tonight, and they drank together while sharing stories of misadventures.

A thought occurred to James as he relaxed. He had noticed a pattern in the cloth belts he'd been collecting from the low-level gangster mobs. The cloth belts he had been collecting from the mobs in different parts of the slums had meaning. Each belt was dyed in a distinct color, some even had crude emblems on them. In all he had identified four unique group-ings, with slight variations, mostly differences in the emblems.

Straining through his memories of the day's activities he put another piece of the puzzle together. Businesses and homes had similar, if not longer, strips of the cloth hanging from doorways. Either these were all gang hideouts or perhaps they were under the protection of the gangs.

There had been less mobs roaming the streets today than the previous, perhaps they didn't respawn as quickly as other games. James began to worry. The AI in Haven were incredibly advanced, he only needed to think of Z'Jhack and his crazy stories of escaping nobles houses after spending nights with princesses and princes to be.

If the AI were that advanced, then surely the cause and effect of James actions were bound to create a ripple effect in the balance of the area. He decided it would be best to move on to a new part of the city tomorrow. He wasn't afraid that he might die and have to respawn, as nearly all of the mobs he had encountered thus far had been malnourished wiry thugs who couldn't fight their way out of a cardboard box, but if the gangs had any elite boss mobs, he would probably be drawing their attention soon.

A sudden clang of metal hitting wood tore James's attention away from his musings and into full action mode. He made it to his feet just as the window facing the street opened all the way and a black clad figure slipped in, daggers out and at the ready. The weapons had a blue tint to them that didn't register as any kind of metal James had encountered before. The newcomer looked like a stereotypical ninja assassin-shorter than most people James had encountered so far in Haven and covered in layers of black cloth, the only exception being a maroon headband with a finely embroidered snake in black thread. An assassin for one of the gangs perhaps.

James had placed a dagger on the window in such a way that if opened it would clatter to the floor and alert him. He was glad that he had, because the window hadn't made a single squeak while opening.

Damn Farstil and his well-maintained tavern, James smiled at the thought and rushed his attacker, club swinging up to meet him. The would-be assassin, ducked James's strike expertly and slashed at his side. White hot pain flared across his ribs, and he turned, the grip of the club connecting to the side of the attacker's head.

What would have been at least a stunning blow for the mobs he'd encountered so far, didn't seem to faze his attacker at all. The maroon cobra assassin, James had decided that the snake most resembled a cobra, had pivoted in such a way that he was about to deliver a killing blow to James's neck with his blue daggers.

James grabbed hold of the attacker's hands and threw himself atop him. He out-weighed the ninja significantly, but the smaller man was squirely and nearly slipped out before James could get him into a proper hold. Despite his small frame the assassin was strong, very strong. He released his weapons and twisted his grip, pressing on James's hands with crushing force, an audible crack sounded.

Despite James's training, the adrenaline, and so many painful injuries, he yelped in surprised pain. With the force that only surprise, brute strength and rage could bring forth, James got his feet under him, lifted the black clad attacker and threw him at his door.

The wood, while looking sturdy enough, gave way with a sudden crash of splints and creaks. James's left hand screamed in pain, something was broken. He wasted no time, swiftly moving forward, pulling a dagger from his boot. The attacker would not live through the night.

However when he got to the mess of wood where the assassin should be, he instead found Mick holding aloft the assassin by one massive arm. If the attacker looked small compared to James, then he was tiny when put against the girth and size of Mick. The black clad figure was still alive, his daggers repeatedly stabbing into Mick's outstretched arm. But Mick didn't even flinch. He just stood there; his grip white as he pressed ever harder around the attackers neck.

James' eyes widened in surprise as he examined Mick's arm. The cuts were healing just as fast as they were delivered.

"What are you?" James asked, his rage beginning to subside already. "You heal as fast as a forest troll." James recalled a popular fantasy epic game he would play with Dave, Phil and the rest of his crew. They'd decided to play the bad guys, so he knew a thing or two about the regenerative powers of some of the monster races. He hadn't expected there would be mobs like that in a human city.

With a final grunt of effort and a satisfying crunch, Mick dropped the dead body of the assassin.

"You totally stole my kill," James complained in mock frustration.

Mick grunted and his gaze leveled at James. "You are under the protection of the Hungry Hog while you rent a room. But tonight is your last night. We won't put ourselves in the middle of their politics."

"Who," James asked, kneeling to loot his stolen kill.

"One of the Tor'I sent their personal enforces to kill you," Mick said as if that explained it all. He must have noticed the blank look James gave him because he continued. "The four factions of the Tor'I? No more than thugs and gangsters really, but they aren't without power. The leaders themselves are said to be ascended, but their enforcers are highly trained and still very effective."

"Aw got it," James said, finding a place for his two new blue daggers. "I made the local gang leaders mad. They must have figured out I was the one killing all their street mobs. Well that just means it's time to move on I suppose. I doubt I'm ready to take on boss mobs just yet."

Mick watched him, a look of confusion on his face now, before turning and making his way down the wooden steps to the main tavern area. James just barely heard him mutter something to the effect, 'crazy Koths', but couldn't be sure.

James walked in silence down a dark dusty road. He had decided that it was time to leave, and did so in the early morning, slipping free from the Hungry Hog before breakfast had been served. He wasn't stupid, if someone had been sent to kill him, they likely had a pair of eyes watching him. Using the darkness of night, James hoped to escape whatever tail might be following him.

This game was more advanced than anything he'd previously played. It probably had to do with the nature of it, James realized. The Haven simulation wasn't built to be a fantasy swashbuckling murder hobo free-for-all. Cause and effect were in full swing here. Kill an NPC, his NPC friends, or gang members in this case, would come looking.

Something about that bothered James. AI had become extremely advanced over the last decade, all you had to do was talk to Eve, Phil and Alice's AI that the entire team had a hand in one way or another to help build, to be convinced that AI might as well be called a living thing.

James had no issues killing mindless NPCs whose only programming included pathing code, minor dialogue, and aggro ranges set by some cubicle jockey. How did he feel about killing off fully built AI with minds that might be considered sentient? He wasn't sure, and he pushed the thoughts down not ready to confront that reality just yet.

The ground was hard beneath his feet, not because he had escaped the perpetual muck and mud of the dockside slums. There was a chill in the air and the coolness of the morning had been enough to frost the sides of the buildings and freeze the mud. He wasn't sure that he was walking the right direction to escape the area, but he trudged onward regardless.

Eventually he would find his way out, he hoped. If he still had someone tailing him, they were damn good at their job. Deciding to take another quick right, James pressed himself against the side of a burnt-out building and peaked around the corner. He waited, but no one appeared.

Letting out a sigh that was more frustration than relief, he did a quick inventory of his weapons. His new favorite daggers, the blue steel ones he'd taken from his would-be assassin, were both tucked away on his waist. He had decided to throw away the gang emblemed belts, hoping that as he moved to other parts of the city he could pass as a normal citizen. Instead, he'd ripped strips of black cloth from the assassin's fine clothing to make himself a new cloth belt.

What he wouldn't give for a sturdy leather belt.

His other weapons, several daggers of a variety of sizes, and his battered club were placed across his form.

After a suitable amount of time, in James's mind at least, he pushed off the wall he'd been leaning on and began his walk towards new killing fields.

He chuckled thinking about the reservations he'd had just minutes before. This was just another advanced game and in games NPCs die. Let the philosophers debate the higher points of the meaning of life, James was here to collect loot and kill mobs.

But maybe this time he could find hideous monsters to kill instead of human mobs. It was much easier killing ugly monsters, no grey lines in that, James nodded to himself, yes that would be much better.

Unfortunately, it seemed Haven had other ideas.

James turned the corner and found the path ahead blocked. Four figures stood amidst a heavy mist that clung to the ground. Not even one of them looked like they belonged in the mud filled, ruined alleys of the dockside slums. A chill ran unbidden up James's spine.

On the left was a man armored in pale white, almost sickly looking, armor. Runes were engraved all over his pale armor, pulsing a soft green light in the darkened alley. His tattered black cloak hung over his shoulders, obscuring his arms. He had his hood up and despite the glow of the armor his face was a pool of thick blackness that James's eyes couldn't penetrate.

Instead of feeling any kind of fear from the slightly terrifying figure James almost cheered aloud.

Magic!

James began to bounce on his feet in excitement.

There was magic inside of Haven, this changed everything!

Continuing his scan of the group he noted the two in the middle, a male and female all clad in black cloth and leathers. The woman was slender, but her tight clothing left nothing about her femininity to the imagination. She had blonde hair with streaks of black running down her shoulders and stopping just below the neck. The man standing next to her was her opposite in almost every way. Where she was slender, he was built as thick as castle walls.

There was nothing feminine about his form, he was all masculinity. He had a thick jaw, square with a hint of a beard showing. His eyes were inset and hard. But his eyes, hers as well

James realized, were pools of gray stirring mist. A dim light that reflected in their eyes and made them stand out.

The final man looked like the illustrations of old timey wizards, and appeared the least threatening compared to the three standing beside him.

He wore blue oversized robes, had a pointy hat of the same color, except for the black tip at the top. He held a large book that he struggled to keep ahold of with his spindly arms. James was ready to write this wizard off as the least threatening, when he caught his eye.

His eyes were hard, and James felt as if he could see the vast ageless power that resided behind them. Out of the three, this older looking man was the one to watch.

"Nice day for a stroll, eh?" As he spoke, he grabbed the edges of his coat and pretended to be warming himself by closing the coat together. The decorative leather handles of his blue steel daggers were soft in his grip as he closed his hands around them.

The motion caught the attention of the black leather clad woman, and she grinned at James, her hand came up and she waggled a finger in his direction.

The warrior clad in armor stepped forward, his hood hung low obscuring his face in a pool of black. "You have done great damage to our ranks." His voice was ethereal and echoed off the walls, making it sound as if he spoke all around at once.

The female rogue with black streaked hair spoke next. "You will die here if you are not careful." Her voice came out as a low whisper, the same ethereal quality to it.

Next the brute stepped forward and said, "Recompense is necessary."

James looked over to the wizard expecting that he would speak next. His forehead was beaded with sweat and pinched in either concentration or constipation. He met James's gaze and his face relaxed, and he spoke.

"Here's the deal, street scum," His voice lacked the ethereal quality of the rest, instead it had a nasal quality to it that made James grin. Whatever he had said next had been lost to James in the moment of distraction.

"I'm sorry," James said, suppressing his grin. "You were saying something?"

Light flickered around the three forms that flanked the odd wizard and his face turned a shade of red before continuing. "I said if you want to live you will prove yourself to the Tor'I. We aren't easily impressed, nor do we care to be wasteful. Your dispatching nearly one hundred of our street enforcers, whether by guile, strength of arm or mind, you are a resource that should not be wasted." The wizard's words started at nearly a shout before tapering off at the end to normal speech.

"And do I 'prove' myself to the Tory?" James said, purposely replacing the 'I' sound at the end of the word with a 'e' sound to keep the hot-tempered man on his toes.

"The *Tor'I* have selected a task for you to complete to prove that you truly are worth *not* disposing of." The wizard obviously enjoyed hearing his own voice and still hadn't gotten to anything close to resembling a point.

James stayed quiet for once, just giving the man a deadpan stare.

"Yes, well," the tall wizard shifted on his feet and pulled a folded piece of paper from his robes. "You will find the details here and we will be watching. If you attempt to leave the path outlined in the documents, you will be swiftly disposed of." The letter fell from the wizard's hands and floated over toward James, who plucked it from the air.

He looked up just in time to see the four depart. The

armored man crouched low and jumped. His leap easily took him over the top of one of the buildings, green and black haze following behind him like the trail of a rocket. The two in the middle, the roguish woman and the brute, both casually turned and in a puff of black smoke disappeared as they walked. Only the wizard left by conventional means, slowly hobbling forward as if one of his legs were injured or perhaps time had taken its toll on him.

James watched until he turned the corner before ripping the papers open and reading. They were detailed instructions about how, when, and where to steal a book from a place referred to as 'The Grand Citadel'.

"Finally," James said as he clutched hard to the documents. "I got my first quest!"

CHAPTER 7
PHIL

Phil had a quest now, find the book by locating this Withers fellow and perhaps a lead on another Eldritch Knight, the Wandering Wraith, but first he had to get back and report to Seph, or she'd have his hide.

Leaving the citadel no one tried to stop him, it wasn't until he was walking through the streets toward the exit he was planning on taking, that he heard a rustle behind him. Several guards were coming right for him at a jog and they wore the armor of the citadel, bright golds with a mix of blue capes. As gaudy as they were weak, Phil mused as his power swept out and around him.

Green flame pushed everyone back and the guards stopped short.

"Stop in the name of the Council of Orders. You are to be taken into custody for crimes committed," said the lead one, he might have been something a bit more than just a guard, since a golden flame began to rise around his left arm.

"You don't want to fight me," Phil said, then suddenly all of the guards were summoning power, from golden lights, to blue sparks, to a mix of white and purple that swirled around them.

"I believe we do," the leader said, and they unleashed their powers at him, causing more than a couple people to dive out of the way.

Phil held up his shield and caught the first blast on his false arm, then summoning forth his fire he lashed back. His flame came with such intensity that it swallowed up the lesser attacks and scorched the ground.

His voice filled with power and practically vibrating as he stepped through the still burning green flames, he spoke as if he were the very reaper himself.

"To stand against the Eldritch Order is to court death, turn aside and forfeit your lives," Phil said, punctuating his words with another flare of green fire that singed armor and capes alike.

The show had worked beautifully, these were all ascended, but they were weak compared to Phil. He had an intensity inside of his power that they couldn't match, this newer generation of Kotharians had this problem, or so Seph had informed him. The more diluted the blood the weaker they were, the fact that these were being used as mere guards meant they were the weakest among the weak.

Only the leader stood his ground, figuratively at least since he was on his ass at that very moment. But he didn't backpaddled while all those around him turned and ran.

"Don't make me kill you," Phil said, his voice barely loud enough to be heard over the roar of the flames.

The man looked ashamed suddenly and he stood, pulling a sword out that instantly became engulfed by flames.

"I need only slow your retreat, our most powerful warriors will come and cut you down, pretender," the leader said, and

Phil respected him in that moment as he stood alone against impossible odds.

It didn't stop him from attacking with enough force to blow him backward, effectively knocking him out and burning his skin away to nothing. But even the weakest of ascended had decent healing abilities, so he'd live.

Phil turned and left the city, no one dared step in front of him and he quickly faded into the tent city outside the city to be sure he lost any approaching guards too foolish for their own good.

It was while he walked through the stench and sea of people living outside of the mighty Kothar city, that he found himself listening in on conversations and in general trying to blend in.

"Gimme whatcha gots and we's only going to hurt you a little," said a slithering voice from ahead.

"I'll break you," came a response from a strong willed youth.

But as Phil rounded the corner he saw that the young man, with dark hair and striking purple eyes was in no position to be issuing threats of breaking anyone. He was already limping from a wound and held what looked to be a piece of a coffee table leg in one hand while half a dozen gangly looking people surrounded him with knives.

The scene triggered a memory in Phil of his past and he couldn't be still, but before he could interject himself, the boy acted. He swung his club at the leader and took him out in a single strike, then turning he caught an attacker from behind under the jaw. If he'd been able to continue to move with that same burst of speed he might have had them all, but as it turned out he was fated to die.

But Phil wasn't one to listen to fate's call any longer. He

lunged forward and put himself between the attack, not attacking himself, just taking the stab to the chest and growling at the attacker. Then with a burst of movement he smacked the weapon free from another thug, giving his new fighting partner time to swing his club around and take each of them down.

By the time the fight finished, Phil had been stabbed several times, but he healed almost immediately to each of them and his new friend had won his battle.

"You have spirit," Phil said.

The young man, no more than twenty, Phil realized now, turned on him, club raised. "I'll bash you in too," he spat the words and Phil wondered if he'd been mistaken about the boy.

Then off to the side, where the boy had been fighting and defending he saw a little strip of a girl, perhaps a sister or something based on the same purple eyes.

"I'm not here to hurt you," Phil said, keeping his words gentle but firm.

"We don't have anything worth taking," the young man said, never lowering his guard.

"But I have something to give," Phil said, pulling his cloak back and showing his ascended armor.

The young man looked unimpressed, so Phil continued speaking.

"I can offer you safe haven among the ranks of the Eldritch Knights. You don't have to live in squalor anymore, you have a fighting spirit that ought to be kindled and built up, not smashed down."

"You offer something for nothing," the young man said, confusion clear to see on his face. "No one does that, what do you want?"

Phil smiled, this boy was turning out to be exactly what they were looking for. "It is true that I want something from you. We need soldiers and you've got the spirit I'm looking for. Come with me and I will give you the power to challenge not three thugs, but three dozen at once."

The young man smiled at that. "Names Steffan, and that there is Mercy. You promise to keep her safe and I'll be your soldier and I'll take your power."

Phil smiled, and held a hand out for the boy. He shook it and Phil got the first sense of his inner power, it was more vast than he expected. He might not have to half ascend this boy after all, somehow these orders had missed a fully ascendable child. Steffan helped his sister up and they followed behind Phil toward the gateway that led him home.

CHAPTER 8
JAMES

J ames sat at a small writing desk, six distinct coins laid out in front of him. He'd found a place to stay for the night just outside the slums in a rather nice place called the 'Roaming Raven'. It was twice the size of the Hungry Hod and served a great deal more meal options, as well as beds that rivaled his pillow top mattress from the physical world.

He had been told what each coin was called and their general value by a talkative female barkeep, Selendra.

She informed him that the largest coin, a square thick grayish-white colored coin with a hole in the center, was worth several month's work for a tradesmen trained in a basic trade. He'd forgotten the names she gave them already, each exotic and not worth remembering. Instead, he assigned his own names based on color and previous games he'd played.

"I will call you," James said, lifting the grayish-white coin from the table. He had only one of these left, having taken them from a small chest that a larger group of thugs had been transporting. "You are a platinum coin."

Next, he picked up a mint green colored coin. She had told

him this was the next in value, worth much the same as the platinum coin but used more commonly in foreign trade.

"You'll be called," James scratched his chin, not really sure what to call a green coin. "Mint coin!"

He spread the remaining four, these would be easier. A gold, silver, copper, and a dull iron colored coin sat before him. She'd informed him that the value and metal were much what he expected. Each of these final four coins, save the iron dull ones, were of the same design. Squares with holes in the middle.

The gold coin was worth two months' work, the silver one month, the copper only a day's labor, and the iron coins-if you could call the square flat pieces that, were worth a day's labor for some of the poorer citizens. She had mentioned that the iron bits weren't official currency, but their value as a material, iron, was used to create the smallest exchange rate of goods.

All together James had one platinum, three mint coins, eight gold, two silver, twenty copper, and thirty-eight irons.

Instead of dropping a pile of coins, he'd paid five coppers for his room for the night, a warm ale, and a hearty stew. He was doing his best to adjust his views. If this were going to be his forever home, he needed to treat certain aspects of his life a little differently.

James had no plans to stop adventuring and looting mobs, the realistic combat, thrill, and excitement of it was just too addicting. He had been much the same back in the 'real world', but here in the Haven simulation, or game world, as he liked to think of it, he often got distracted by the opportunity to experience excitement and adventure nonstop.

The real world.

James had done his best to not think about the reality of what would happen to earth in the coming months. Everyone he knew and loved, that hadn't already died or, in Phil's case, made it to Haven, would be dead.

He wondered what had become of Phil. So far everyone he met had been NPCs, or if they weren't he had no way to tell the difference.

Phil had transferred, according to Doctor Vikar, only hours before James. He pictured Phil, his once strong form slowly withering away as the months passed. It was horrible to lose someone, but poor Phil had to watch Alice, his sister, die over a long drawn-out period of time. James's group of friends thought they would be cursed with a similar fate for their friend Phil.

If it hadn't been for Doctor Vikar James was certain Phil would've died before the end of the world had a chance to kill him.

A knock on the door startled James from his reminiscing. A quick swipe saw all his remaining coins back into their leather pouch. The chair squeaked under his weight as he stood and moved to open the door.

A curly haired blonde woman wearing a white blouse tucked into a blue skirt stood in the doorway. She smiled cutely and leaned forward in a greeting of sorts. James tried, but failed, to keep his eyes from her half-exposed breasts, the V-neck shirt was much to lose to keep things tucked in tight.

"Hello there, my name is Diana. Hobs sent me to see if you required any laundry done." Her voice was sweet and alluring. She fluttered her purple eyes up at me as she spoke. She stood nearly six feet tall, but James was taller still.

"You know," James said, letting his coat fall from his shoulders. "I would love that." James slipped his clothing off, until he was completely naked. Reaching down he picked up his pile of clothing, only his jacket remained out of the bunch and handed it to the red faced maiden.

"I- uh," Diana struggled for words, before pulling herself together. "I'll *personally* have this returned to you by the end of the day. This evening." She blushed again and turned to leave.

"Oh one quick question for you," James said, reaching out a hand to grab lightly on her exposed shoulder. "Is there a place I can draw a bath and perhaps someone who can run out and grab me a new set of simple clothing?"

The young woman shuttered from James's touch, turning to answer him.

"There is a bathing room downstairs," Diana's grin widened, and she continued. "Give me some time to heat water and grab a measuring string. I'll personally see to your requests."

"Diana you are a godsend. Here let me get you something," James said, stepping back into his room he grabbed a golden coin and pressed it into her hand. "Whatever is left you can keep. If it isn't enough, let me know and I'll get more."

Diana's eyes went wide, her grin disappearing. With the swiftness of a seasoned bar maiden, the coin disappeared into a pocket sewn into the dress. "It will be enough," She assured me before hurrying down the steps and into the lower floor.

Diane was true to her word and proved to be a very stimulating host. The bath had been warm, the new set of clothing comfortable, and the company pleasing.

Night had fallen, the temperature with it. James held Diane tighter, the warmth of their naked bodies keeping them both comfortable. All thoughts of, if his sleeping with an NPC was wrong, had vanished after Diane's dress had hit the floor. Besides, he assured himself, only his mind had been uploaded to Haven—if he understood the process right—so he was much the same as they were now. Just a complex stream of zeros and ones.

She woke up then, her head swinging around in momentary confusion.

"It's late," James whispered into her ear, "Go back to sleep."

"I shouldn't," Diane's words were a sleepy mumble and for a moment James thought she might stay, but she pulled the covers off and a sudden chill had James closing them tight around himself. "That was fun. If you stay here again, look me up."

Before James had a chance to formulate a proper response, she left out the door, closing it softly behind her.

The sudden chill and loss of his sleeping companion pushed James fully awake. Slipping out of the covers he dressed and opened the curtains, letting in light from two different moons. Diane had done a good job fitting the clothing.

It was a simple outfit, thick long sleeved white tunic, black loose slacks, an actual leather belt, and the cherry on the top, a pair of black polished boots. They weren't new, but he was sure they were all the better for it. Having been worn in just enough that they felt supple and soft as he walked. She had also found him a few pairs of under garments, socks, and a cloth sack to carry it all in with a tie string at the top.

He imagined he was a proper adventurer now. The amount of coin he'd given her must have prompted her to go above and beyond, because all these items had been much more than his original ask.

Feeling refreshed and ready for the day, James gathered all his items and set out into the night.

It had taken him several hours, and well past breakfast to reach his destination, but he'd made it. He was as close as he needed to be to get a decent look at the massive building his quest called, 'The Grand Citadel'.

His trip through the city so far had made several things abundantly clear. The first being that the city's size was enormous. The map he'd purchased in the early hours of the morning was said to be only one section of the massive three sections that comprised the city-nation.

The map's scale was questionable, but the seller had shown him his location and then pointed to the Citadel. It looked close, less than an inch or two away, with the entire length of the map being a foot and a half square.

That tiny inch or two had taken him hours of walking, jogging, and a short wagon ride—he'd hitched a ride to the back of a wagon being pulled by two massive looking buffalo creatures. That ended when they noticed him and threatened to call the guards if he didn't detach himself.

But for now he was where he needed to be, scoping out his target. The letter had indicated that on the second day of the fourth week of the ninth month when the sun reached the highest point of the sky, James would be able to enter the gate, giving the name 'Emissary of the Je'duun'mar'dee'. It hadn't included any special letter or badge to help my story, but assured him that if he went, while holding this letter close, at the prescribed time and took no longer than an hour, he would be able to accomplish the mission.

It hadn't taken much asking around to find out that the date the letter mentioned was still two days away. But James wanted to get a good feel for the comings and goings of the people entering the citadel. He wasn't planning on failing his first quest.

It didn't take long to see that he would be severely under dressed in his current attire. There were two types of people coming and going. Servants, all of them wearing clothing nicer than his, but walking with heads bowed and out of the way of the second kind. The others were armored, robed, or clad in leathers of glowing magics.

He looked like neither but given enough time he was certain he could pass as a servant. He had to squash the temptation to jump one of the magically armored men and take their armor. This was a mission of stealth and hiding in plain sight would be his best option.

It took over half of the coin that he had left, but by nightfall he had accomplished several important tasks.

He had a nice, but not too nice, set of clothing that he would wear to disguise himself as a fancy servant. The outfit even came with a feathered hat, to James's amusement. And lastly he found an apartment just outside the nicer part of town, paying for three months in advance. That had caused the biggest hit to his wallet, costing the rest of his gold and leaving him with only a few silver, copper, and iron coins.

The accommodations were comfortable and bigger than the studio apartment he lived in before coming to Haven. There was a kitchen, a sitting room, two bedrooms, and a washroom that contained water pumped straight into the bronze-colored bath. His landlord, a plump man of middle age and a thick white mustache, has shown him how to heat the water by lighting a fire under a small furnace where the water was stored.

James sat in the sitting room, the light of the fireplace making shadows dance in the corner of his vision. It was a cold night again, but the fire did its job well, keeping James comfortable and warm.

He'd decided that he would only take a single dagger, in the same fashion as he'd witnessed so many others wear. With a grunt he made it to his feet and found the tall free-standing mirror in one of the bedrooms, pulling it from its place and setting it within range of the fire light.

The clothing he'd picked out matched the styles of the servants, but he looked ridiculous. The colors were a mix of purple and gold throughout the outfit. The hat was a poofy monstrous thing with two long white feathers tucked into the brim. The coat and slacks had the same annoying stuffing that had them bulging out. The coat shoulders looked like two gold and purple pillows, while the thighs of the outfit made sitting awkward.

The only item that he enjoyed of the set were the dark black boots, he now had three sets of boots each of various levels of use. The new black polished ones he wore now had a stiffness that would ease with use, but they looked wonderful. Shiny and reflective across all the surfaces and ending in a strap that tightened them around the calf.

The belt that the storekeeper had insisted was in fashion, was a hideously dyed golden color. The black leather sheath that held one of James's blue bladed daggers, stuck out against the gaudy gold belt. Luckily the finely made daggers had handles that matched the costly attire he now wore. Dark brown supple leather wrapped the handle, and a simple silver pommel adorned the end.

Satisfied that he looked the part, James undressed and readied himself for the night.

Arriving at the Grand Citadel at the time appointed by the old man, James took a deep breath and readied himself for his first quest. He'd taken it a bit on faith that it would be worth doing, since this was basically just a simulation or video game, gave him the confidence that what he was doing would be the right way forward.

The air was chilly and his odd outfit didn't help with how ridiculous he felt. His steps fell heavy on the stone, each footstep making more noise than his other pair of soft and subtle boots. He would do this quest and hopefully get an epic loot reward, before going back on an NPC killing spree in a new area of the city.

Or perhaps he could get another quest and get directions to where he could kill monsters instead of people. There was something to say for killing monsters over people, even NPC people.

His memory slipped into the previous night when he'd held Diane's naked form close to his own. It had felt so real, so warm and lovely. It made him wonder if he should feel bad about taking out so many NPCs after he'd slept with one and all. But that was for someone else to worry about, he had a quest and he needed to stay on mission.

Servants, wearing similar clothing to him, were coming and going now, so he took his chance and with a deep breath, began to walk to the entrance.

All of the other servants seemed to get entrance without any questioning from the guard, but as soon as James got within several feet the guard put his hand on his hilt and narrowed his eyes at him.

The guard wore full plate armor, minus the helmet that only covered the top of his head and a god awfully gold and purple tabard covering most of the polished steel chestplate. He had size on James by a good three to four inches, but James had him beat on width. It was his cold hard stare that had James reaching for his dagger, this guard was all business and he didn't like the look of James by the look of his gaze.

James forced himself to keep his hand away from his dagger, instead clutching the letter close and preparing his words.

"I am the Emissary of the Je'dunn'mar'dee," James said, trying his best to get the pronunciation correct.

The guard tilted his head to the side and didn't say a word. Clutching the letter tighter and feeling like he might have been pranked, he repeated.

"I am the Emissary of the Je'dunn'mar'dee," Jame said. He couldn't help but place a hand on his dagger, ready to take out the guard and make his own way in, but the guard finally seemed to snap out of whatever had him so enthralled.

"Welcome," his voice came out almost robotically, was this a sign of poor programming James wondered and he almost missed the rest of what the man said, "We are glad to receive the Emissary of the Je'dunn'mar'dee. Please enter."

With that the guard stood aside, but something was odd about the way he moved, very rigid and stiff. James looked around, feeling like he had eyes on his back and swore for a second that he saw an elderly man limping away into an alley. Had that wizard done something to the other NPC to gain him entry?

James had a plan to follow so he looked back at the letter and followed the instructions. Go left, then right, then right, then left, up the stairs, through the door and into the library.

The inside of the citadel was huge, with high arched ceilings, paintings lining the walls of battles and people, as well as armor displayed here and there. The floor had a red long carpet that led straight where he saw the first left that he needed to take.

James had never been so tempted to start stealing loot as he was right now. The letter had been specific about him taking only the single book and nothing else. Eyeing the armor around him and wondering if it would be a decent fit, James took the first left, then nodding to a pair of servants, he took a right, then another right, and final left before he came upon a grand staircase.

He walked up it, getting looks from the armored and finely dressed folk around, no other servants were in this area, but James kept his eyes cast down and continued on with his quest. The door he had to go through had guards, something the letter hadn't mentioned.

James clenched his butt cheeks and went for the door as naturally and calmly as he could. One of the guards made to stop him, but the other nodded his head and he stopped.

"Go right in," he said, winking at James.

James, confused but grateful, nodded his head and went into the room. It was a library like no other, filled to the brim with books from ground to ceiling, and the ceiling was a high one for sure. Tables were sprawled out here and there, many people taking seats in them to browse the tomes. James was interested in only one, so he followed the directions to find it.

According to the letter it would be found in the tallest stack in the eastern corner of the library, in a restricted area that would require James break a lock by placing his hand on it and speaking a series of words. He found the location and did as the letter requested, feeling a surging warmth inside himself as he did it. This was the closest thing to magic that he'd experienced thus far and he was practically giddy over the feeling.

His hand felt tingly now and he pushed open the wooden

door to find a dimly lit area filled to the brim with smelly books. It was like someone had a mold problem by the smell of it, but he wasn't going to complain. Instead he dug right in, grabbing tomes and looking for titles. It turned out that almost all of them had titles on the inside but not on the outer leather covers, which increased the time it would take him to find anything.

He heard someone coming and quickly shut the door, before quietly going back to work. Finding several books that seemed promising, he set them aside for another look later.

After some time he found the book that he was supposed to locate as well as one about a runic language that seemed pretty magical, so he took it for himself. He had to learn one way or another so he might as well do one for himself.

Slipping out of the room with both books in tow, he noticed several guards below, searching the library for him no doubt. He ran the length of the upper corridor when shouting started from below.

Hoping for the best he ran up to a stained glass window and kicked the glass aside. There was a rather steep roof, but he needed a way out so he took it.

CHAPTER 9
PHIL

Phil found Seph going through some kind of katra when he arrived, flames dancing around her as she slashed her sword here and there. She was a master of the green flame and it showed by her movements and control.

The keep, they'd moved there after a time and began repairing the broken huts around the main building, was alight with activity from the tree folk that had joined their cause. Ned was a ways off helping repair on some of the buildings and he waved to Phil when he saw him.

Stopping her moves Seph took in the sight of Phil and his two new companions. The look on her face was about what Phil expected from her, she did not care for surprises.

"You've brought outsiders into our sanctum," Seph said, looking like she was about to face palm. "Are you killing them to keep our location a secret or am I?"

"Here me out," Phil said, motioning for Ned to come join them. "Give me the book we found."

"I cannot," Ned said simply.

"Why not?" Phil said, looking around and seeing that their conversation had caught the attention of a few other treefolk.

"I gave it to Seph as you ordered, she was most pleased to receive it," Ned said, his speech was getting better but speaking the common tongue was difficult for them, their own language, something they never spoke around outsiders.

"Oh," Phil said, turning an awkward smile onto Seph. "Then you already understand why I've brought these two here."

"I can guess," Seph said, but the look on her face told him she wouldn't care to guess after all.

"Okay fine," Phil said, letting out a sigh as he prepared to launch into it. "We need more Eldritch Knights, even if they are only these half ascended hybrids. The treefolk are fine additions but they can't wield the green flame without breaking oaths and dying shortly after. I bet that with a bit of work we can half ascend them as well. We could bolster the ranks of the Eldritch Knights once more."

"A foolish idea from a foolish leader," Seph said, her words hard. "But a leader you are and I am no longer here to say which path we should follow. So if this is what you choose to do, listen only to my advice and make your own decisions."

"It gets better," Phil said, smiling wide now, though he knew that even that gesture would likely annoy Seph and bring harder training in the coming hours. "Steffan here, I've been doing what you said and keeping myself open to the power in others. I don't know if I'm wrong, but it seems like he has the potential, like a decent amount of it as well."

"Let me see," Seph said, gesturing for Steffan to step up. He did so without fear, his chin raised in defiance but his eyes betrayed a hint of his true emotions, a touch of fear and apprehension.

Seph pressed her hand onto his chest and listened. Phil knew by her surprised expression that he'd done right, sensing the power that lay within Steffan.

"It would appear you have potential enough to be considered for an order, though the head of our order exaggerated a touch concerning how much power you might have. Are you interested in taking on the curse of mixana?" Seph asked.

Phil had filled in Steffan about the basics of the Eldritch Order and what would be expected of him. He knew he'd have training ahead of him and his only wish had been that his sister remain safe through it all. The girl, a tiny slip of a thing maybe twelve or thirteen years old, stayed quiet the entire time saying not even the whisper of a word.

"I am willing and able," Steffan said, showing that straightforward confidence that was turning out to be his trademark personality quirk. Time would prove whether or not this was a winning trait or something that would hamper him.

"And you feel he is a good candidate?" Seph asked, turning her attention to Phil.

"He fought against many foes without fear to protect the one he loved," Phil said, giving the reason he'd considered the boy right off, he had nothing to hide from Seph. "I think that is a quality that will be beneficial to our cause."

"Very well," Seph said. "Tomorrow at dawn we will do the ritual to unlock his potential, but we will not prime him for the flame until he's received proper training. I will not have any case like yours on my hands, Phil."

"I understand," Phil said, then turning to leave and get out of his armor so that he could attend to some chores, he was surprised when Seph spoke again.

"What of the girl?" Seph asked. "We are not a caretaking

facility. Are you not interested in the fierce fire that burns within her heart as well?"

Phil turned to the girl, her eyes downcast and looking toward her brother. "I didn't think to check her for potential," Phil admitted.

"Come to me girl and look at me when I speak to you," Seph ordered. The girl shied away at first, but with a whispered word from her brother, she stood and looked Seph in the face. "What is your name?"

"I am called Mercy," she said in a quiet squeak of a voice.

"Well Mercy, can I lay my hand on you and sense your potential? Would you too like a chance to protect your brother and wield power beyond your imagination?"

A fire suddenly burned in her eyes as she lifted her chin a bit in imitation of her brother. "I want to protect him, show me how." Her words came out stronger than before and Phil reached out with his sense to get a feel for her power without directly touching her.

He hit upon a flame burning there that, while strong, was not quite as strong as her brothers, though she was young and that power might grow with age, if what Seph told him was true about maturing into power.

Seph stepped forward with a side-long look at Phil, likely feeling the way he'd reached out and sensed her. There was a certain feeling one got when the magic inside of you moved outside your feeling. It took only a hair's width of power to do what Phil had done, but it was an advanced technique regardless that even Seph struggled with.

Such was the power that Phil wielded, though he had only hints and guesses at why he was so powerful. The god of the treefolk, an ancient remnant of their kind, had told him that when transferring over a new race they were given the highest potential of power, that power only weakening with blood as time passed.

Laying her hand on the purple eyed girl with dirty brown hair, Seph breathed in sharply. Her eyes went wide and she took a step back. Perhaps, Phil thought, it worked better to sense power on contact, because Phil hadn't been so astonished at her power.

"You've got power beyond even my own at your age," Seph said and Phil could tell she was saying this in part because of the shy nature of the girl, but Seph wasn't the kind to lie, so she obviously still felt some power from her.

"I do?" Mercy asked, her voice sounding weak again. "I do." She repeated with more strength and not as a question.

"Would you be willing to be my apprentice, allow me to take you under my wing and teach you all that I know. These men need a powerful woman to show them the proper way to wield the green flame after all," Seph said, as she leaned down before the shorter girl and spoke softly.

Phil had never seen this part of Seph before and it made him a bit jealous. She'd been so stern and hard to him, never sweet or kind.

"I'll do it!" Mercy declared loudly.

Steffan stepped forward shaking his head. "No, I won't allow it. I agreed to take this curse on, but not my little sis. You can't have her."

Mercy surprised all present by speaking first and with fire in her voice. "It is my decision, you aren't poppa. They are dead and we have to watch out for each other now. Together we will be unstoppable!"

With that Phil finally fully turned back and regarded Seph, who looked right on back through him.

"Something you'd like to add, Head of the Eldritch Order?" Seph asked, sarcasm dripping from her voice.

It was clear the dynamic between them, mentor and mentee. He inclined his head and spoke words he'd gotten used to saying despite his new title as head of the Eldritch Order. "No Master, nothing to add," Phil said.

Seph shook her head, she'd told him to stop calling her master since he took the seat as head of the Eldritch Order, but he did it to annoy her as she had told him to call her that in the past.

"Then shall we speak of your failure to get the book I require to save Adam?" Seph asked, stepping forward and speaking in a hushed whisper that only Phil heard.

"I've got a plan," Phil answered. The remnants of a plan forming in his head that would require him to go undercover and do things he couldn't believe he was considering.

CHAPTER 10
PHIL

"Don't overthink it," Phil called out to Steffan as they traded blows. "You've got the speed and strength now, just unleash it!"

He'd been training with Steffan for roughly a month now, his plan had required some fake documents and other items that took time so he was left with the task of training up Steffan after he was unlocked.

He had all the increased strength and power of an ascended without the fire waiting to burn him out just yet. Seph said this state could only be maintained for a certain period of time, but it was nothing like the forty-eight hours Zarrick had given Phil.

With all that aside, both Steffan and Mercy were progressing far faster than even Phil had. It was like these two were born to fight, or at least had been fighting their entire lives in a far more real way than Phil ever had. It was inspiring to see them progress, but Steffan was still holding back. He couldn't match Phil for speed or strength, which he was certain he ought to be able to.

"I'm doing my best," Steffan yelled back, his defiance showing its head as it did when he became too tired.

Phil had used Seph's example on training and mentor to mentee relationships, telling Steffan that he ought to call him master and respect him or die. The threats came off half hearted from Phil though, not carrying nearly the weight Seph's had.

But Phil could punish him in other ways. He rushed forward and struck with the flat of his blade in two places before Steffan could parry his third blow, and only just barely.

"Feel the power," Phil said, going in and striking him with another three combo, this time he parried two of the strikes.

Steffan yelled in painful frustration and launched himself at Phil, sword ready to cut him down. Phil causally turned aside each blow, his footwork perfect and his form impeccable. Seph had taught him well and he wouldn't fall to an arrogant child.

"Tell me," Phil said as he weaved through attacks, returning as many blows as he parried, "you want to remain weak so that no one can protect your people, was that your main motivation?"

Steffan's face went red and he moved just a hair faster, but his movements were reckless and erratic. Phil stepped back to give himself some room, slapping away a near miss from his face in the process. If he could just push him a little further he might access his full might, but what to say next?

"I think your sister is progressing faster than you, look at her," Phil said, gesturing with his sword and Steffan actually took the bait and looked. The flat of Phil's sword smacked against Steffans face and he spit blood. "Aw did I get you?"

"I'll kill you!" Screamed Steffan, rushing forward with speed to rival Phil's own.

Good. Pull out everything you have.

Phil still parried and dodged the attacks, his expertise and skill outweighed the anger fueled speed his apprentice was currently showing. Back and forth they went, this part of the fight was meant as conditioning. A way for Phil to pull out all he could from Steffan before he slowed it down and taught him the finer points of sword play.

In that moment, Phil missed having Adam at his side. His faithful companion would have done well to help train this newest generation of Eldritch Knights. Already Phil was talking with Steffan about other potential people he thought might join up. He had extended family that were in such a poor situation that while likely not as ready to ascend as Steffan, might be good candidates for half ascension.

Using the tent city outside the city as a recruitment area wasn't Seph's idea of a good idea, but Phil had convinced her that those that Steffan already knew should be fair game, but he had plans to extend even that in time. If they were going to face off against Zarrick and by extension the council of orders, then they were going to need a small army.

Seph had told Phil that getting into the citadel and announcing themselves would likely bring a force of combined Orders against them, but so far it had been rather quiet. It had been worth the risk at the time, because he thought he'd be getting Adam back, but without the book his and Seph's research and trials were at a stand still.

The actual body that Adam would use was already formed, thanks to the blacksmith of the treefolk, but the runes needed and incantations required were a mystery. They'd studied the golems at the gate, but even those had been alien to Adam, so they weren't much help. What they needed was a book on the subject that could guide them through the process.

Turning his attention back to his fight with Steffan, Phil realized he'd let the boy put him on his back foot and so pushing forward he turned the tide of the battle. Steffan ended the fight panting and out of breath, meanwhile Phil's flame carried him through with enough power that he was barely breathing hard.

The Green Flame was a magnificent thing, something that grew more powerful with time and training, according to Seph. But what interested Phil more was how it interacted with his core of magic as time went on. At first he could easily feel the two as separate entities, but now, it was hard to distinguish them as the fire and the pure power within him mixed and swirled.

Phil was meant to control this adjustment to a certain extent, he was still training with Seph and she said pure power was required to ignite runes, so letting the flame completely consume your inner power wasn't wise. But Phil wasn't convinced that he could ignite runes with his green flame, he'd seemed to do so several times with his arm shield, but Seph spoke of it as if it were different.

She said it had a set of rare runic formations that she'd never seen, but when included worked with the others to purify the flow of power, magnifying it. In the end Phil just accepted that he still had loads to learn, since technically he was barely a tier one Eldritch Knight, though on paper he was also the leader and highest ranked.

Seph spoke of the difference between the branches of Eldritch Knights, how there used to be Pale Riders—Eldritch Knights who focused on the physical strength of being an Eldritch Knight and often paired with great beasts to ride into battle. Then there were Lore Wardens, which Seph had belonged to. They studied and preserved the nature and learning of magic within the order. And finally there were the Flamebound, whose entire focus was around the green flame and mastering it beyond any others.

It was the Flamebound that originally discovered the leaching effects of the fire and how to suck away energy from victims, which led to the downfall of the order. Phil was walking the path of the Pale Riders, despite not having one to lead him. There were several tomes hidden deep within the area of the Eldritch Keep that spoke of how to properly become one, so with Seph's help Phil progressed down the path.

He had plans to take Steffan down the same path, though he had to admit he didn't understand the tier system used within each to denote rank, which had initiated all the way to master, but that wasn't so important right now as their ranks were so small. It was enough to say that Phil was their leader and Seph his second in command, though her voice carried much more weight than merely a second in command.

The tiers were Initiate, Apprentice, Adept, Knight, Master, and though Seph said none existed anymore in any Order that she knew of, Grandmaster. To reach the level of Grandmaster, one had to become one with their inner power, reaching a oneness that made them almost godlike in their power.

Seph was a master, but she claimed that she'd progress no further, as her own studies didn't take her to the path of a grandmaster or furthering her connection with her flame. In fact, she claimed to do so was folly, but Phil still secretly wished to uncover the truth of it and claim that title someday.

"You're doing better," Phil said, throwing a towel to his Initiate. He technically wasn't even that, and Phil had called him an apprentice time or two, but it was more out of want for something better to call him than any indication of his current standing in the order.

"And you drive me toward madness with each fight," Steffan practically spat the words. Then taking a deep breath he softened his tone. "Thank you Master for bringing out my power."

"Better," Phil said, smirking. "Remember, if you are angry now, just wait until you've got a fire burning within you. It will take all you have to control that flame and not let it control you. These lessons matter, but so do your studies, so go meet with Seph while I tend to some business."

"Yes, Master," Steffan said, this time managing to sound serious and genuine. He bowed and left, putting his training sword aside just as Ned came up to talk to Phil.

"He's a wildfire waiting to catch," Ned said, shaking his head slightly as he watched the young one go. "You ignite him a little more each day. What will happen when a true fire burns within him? I think you will have a run for your money, as you say."

"I think," Phil said, slapping his friend on the shoulder in a friendly gesture, "that it's time to test some half ascension marks. Are you still sure you want to go through with it? I know your people stance on mutilating your body, it's a last resort for you."

"None of my brothers have agreed yet, but I hope to show them it is worth a little pain. Our ancient oaths cannot be activated without the sap coverings, and without the elixir that the flamer caller provides we wouldn't even be as able as we are, so it is owed I think," Ned said, speaking with their unique accent that Phil had a hard time placing.

"Ned'turu," Phil said, saying his full name for once and looking him in the eyes. "You owe us nothing, we owe you and your people a great deal. So much so that I fear we won't ever repay you."

"It is my choice, is it not?" Ned asked, and Phil relented, nodding.

"Let me go over the runic formations one more time with Seph and then we can try applying them to you. I'd feel more comfortable with Seph doing the runes as mine aren't perfect just yet, I can't keep a perfectly steady hand like she can," Phil said, making a mock swing of his missing arm that currently had the shield prosthetic attached to make it look as if he'd not lost a hand after all.

"Very well," Ned said and Phil went to interrupt Seph's lessons so that they could do a forbidden ritual on a race of people who were more closely attached to the Eldritch Knights and the green flame than anyone else Phil knew of.

The sky above the keep green orange from the setting of the sun and the snorts and sounds of the mixana beasts in the field grazing caught Phil's ears. They were peaceful most of the time, only reacting when someone carried the flame without the soul of their brethren inside of them. Even so, the mightiest of the beasts locked eyes with Phil and seemed to whisper into his mind.

He wanted what Phil wanted, the Order to grow and become whole once more. This was the first step in that process, the first cornerstone to be placed before the foundation could be built.

CHAPTER 11
STEFFAN/PHIL

S teffan stiffened as his *master* came to interrupt his and Mercy's session with Seph to ask about some important Order business that we weren't privy to being a part of. It was so annoying to be left out of a group that was supposed to be taking you in and making you a part of it, but Steffan could understand to a point. They were new and outsiders, he didn't trust them as much as they didn't trust him.

But that was the way of the world, trust was something to never give and to always seek. He'd trusted his parents to keep them safe, and that had failed miserably. It had been up to him and him alone to ensure the safety of his family, which in this case meant Mercy. Though Phil had joked about Mercy progressing further than him, in some ways it was true. He could see her training with Seph and she was faster than he was by a good measure.

Sure she didn't have the ferocity that Steffan felt and displayed, a trait he was very proud of, but she could move with the grace of a heavenly being.

He watched as Seph left, giving them orders to practice

their runes on the slate boards they'd been given, but Steffan set his aside to speak with his sister, who diligently tried to copy some of the runes they'd been studying from the book.

"You're progressing well," Steffan said, to which Mercy just blushed and nodded. "I'm serious. You might soon be able to give a hit or two."

"I wouldn't hit you," Mercy said, her voice soft and gentle. It was no surprise that her demeanor matched her way of dealing with matters, but it was a weakness that Steffan admired in her.

And there was no doubt it was a weakness in the harsh world they lived in. But it was one he'd fought hard to ensure she kept, a sort of innocents that he wished he'd been able to hold onto for longer himself.

"I know," Steffan eventually said, putting a protective arm around her and pulling her close. "You don't have to do all this you know."

"I want to," Mercy said, suddenly speaking up as if Steffan might forbid her if she didn't show some enthusiasm toward the task. Then settling, she continued. "For as long as I can remember someone has been taking care of me, keeping me safe, or trying to protect me. But Seph says I'll be able to be more than that, she says I'll be able to protect you when she is finished training me."

"And you want that?" Steffan asked, worried that this Seph was taking away her innocence by teaching her the ways of violence.

"I want us to be able to protect each other," Mercy said, her words barely a whisper at this point. "You've done so much for me, I just want to return the favor."

"You owe me nothing," Steffan said, catching her eye as he spoke. "You do this for whatever reason you feel fits, but don't go into it thinking you owe it to me. I'll always protect you, no matter what. This isn't something that is owed or done for reasons to be owed. I love you sis and I'll always keep you safe if I can."

"But you can't always," Mercy said, her voice gaining strength. "That is why it is so important for me to also grow stronger. Seph says that I'll have the power to do whatever I want and this is what I want, to help you."

"I understand, kiddo," Steffan said, messing up her hair in the way she hated. She squirmed out of his arm and shot him an annoyed look, which he just smiled right on back to.

A scream from a distance caught Steffan's attention and he was on his feet within moments. "Stay here and I'll check it out," he said, his sister nodded, going back to her slate board work.

Phil explained to Seph once more, then had Ned explain that he was ready, before she was finally willing to help. It was an untested procedure that even the author of the way to do it spoke of it as if it weren't something to be done. But they needed more Eldritch Knights, which meant experimenting with what they had access to.

The treefolk warriors who'd joined wanted to help, Ned most of all, though still it felt as if Phil might be taking advantage of their willingness and for the last time he tried to convince Ned to wait till they'd tried it on others, but he insisted.

With that out of the way they began their work. Seph went over the runes once more, tracing them out on a slate board she'd brought, erasing them and doing them once more. Each time they looked perfect, but she insisted on getting it right before starting.

After a time she began her work, placing a hand on Ned's chest she began to sear the runes into his very soul. The pain was evident on his face, but he didn't cry out, not yet at least. It wasn't until the last part of the process, in which the half opening on their soul to the power beyond happened, that he screamed out in agony.

The book spoke of this process being the most difficult and painful, saying most wouldn't have the fortitude to mentally survive this part, but Ned had been training with Seph and already he had a mental fortitude above that of a normal person. So only moments after screaming, he cut it off, and clenched his teeth hard.

Steffan came running up to them, pulling aside the cloth door that hung giving them the little privacy they had and backpedaling immediately when he saw Seph at work.

"Get out," Phil growled, but Steffan was transfixed as lights and a green aura seemed to pulse and shine around Ned. Something was happening and Phil instantly forgot about Steffan and focused on Ned instead. Reaching out with his power he felt for the man's core and potential.

What he found was different from what he expected, like a half-formed core that radiated with the heat of the green flame, despite the fact that Seph hadn't lent him any flame.

"Seph, what is happening?" Phil asked as she disengaged and fell to a knee.

"The process is so much more complicated and power consuming than it outlines," Seph said, getting back to her feet and placing a hand back on his chest, this time likely to sense what she'd done instead of burning runes into his soul.

"Can you see what I see?" Phil asked.

"I can," Seph said, a hint of amazement in her voice. "This must be unique to their people, so ingrained into the green flame for ages that they seem to have a spark of it even without it being gifted, as if they are born into the power."

"It is as you say, we are born with it," Ned said. "The Flame is always burning, if quietly, inside of us."

"This flies in the face of all I know about the passing of the Green Flame," Seph said, sounding more than a little perturbed over the situation. "But I admit there is precious little we know about your kind and their long history with the flame."

"Is he stable, will the flame burn him up now or what?" Phil asked, concern for his friend overriding his sense of accomplishment in achieving what they'd planned.

"His flame is weak, I imagine he won't even be able to manifest a living flame or not without difficulty, but as far as I can sense, it does not eat away at him as a borrowed flame would," Seph said, her eyes shut in concentration as she tried to fully understand and view what had happened to Ted.

"Then it is a success. I am Shleppo now," Ted said. "I feel different, but I am myself still. This is good news, I will tell my brethren and they too will want this new power."

Ned left, passing a stunned looking Steffan who'd still said nothing but listened intently. "What effects might this have on their race's transformation into Dea'tren?"

"Leave us," Seph commanded Steffan, who stiffened and left without a word. "Speak of secrets in secret, not to all the ears that might hear it. Though you wear the heart of Mixana on your chest, you act as if you are only an Initiate."

"Oh," Phil said, looking to where Steffan had been. "I honestly didn't think."

"You didn't think," Seph said, interrupting him. "But I am

tired, my tonic will be enough to stop their transformation for a time, but it is an inevitability of their race that they will eventually become the very beasts that hunt those woods. How much more powerful we've made the next wave of dea'tren by doing this, I cannot say."

The thought of Dea'Tren that could spit fire and heal faster than they already could, wasn't something Phil really wanted to consider, but Seph was hard at work on more tonics to stop the evolution of their species into what they were becoming. Surely with her help, and a more abundance of sap, they would be fine for some time.

Perilill's voice sounded in Phils mind when he thought of her refusal to take the flame caller's tonic, despite the trust she had with them. Phil had worked with her to get more sap and collect seedlings from Dea'tren infested areas, but still he worried for her. The Ah'tehetah were especially strong and needed for such hunts, and with most of them coming to live with Phil, he'd felt like it was his duty to help as much as possible.

Making a mental note, as Seph left, to go check on Perilill, he remembered his other plans and wished he had more time then he did. So much to do and so little time to accomplish it all. He felt a pulse of warmth come from the orb he kept close at all times, Adam's way of reassuring him that it would be alright.

Pulling out the orb he inspected it. Zarrick had prepared it to be used as a soul stone for a golem, so there were almost visible scratches on an otherwise perfect surface. Seph didn't know the process that was involved with it, saying only that the runic work was far beyond her. Which is why they needed that book, it all depended on a book that Phil had to get from a man named Wither.

CHAPTER 12
PHIL

Everything was coming together. He had his disguise, a promise from Seph to watch over Adam's soul, and all the paperwork he needed to get into the city without any worry. Another several weeks had passed and Steffan was nearly to the point where he was going to take the flame and begin his training to slay a mixana beast, but Phil might very well miss all that as his plans involved him spending some time in the slums of the Kothar city.

It was amazing to him the scope of the Kothar city, easily several times the size of some of Earth's biggest cities, though the buildings weren't as tall so population density wasn't as bad. But from what Seph had told him, the Kothar city was made up of three major cities that bled together over the ages to become the massive affair it is now. Properly known as a City Nation, as the borders of Kothar weren't much further outside of the actual city.

Meaning they relied heavily on trade with other smaller nations that were more agriculturally focused, which also explained to Phil why they sent out so many troops to aid in this peasant war that was slower coming closer and closer to the city. Led by a man known as the Peasant King, literally peasants of a neighboring kingdom overthrew their monarchy and were marching to unite all peasants under a single banner.

Phil liked the idea behind it, but he didn't intend on mixing himself up in any conflicts that didn't directly aid the build up of the Eldritch Knights. This organization had become his new family, his purpose, his life. It was no longer about being safe and finding a place to live out the rest of his years.

No. He was in this for life and meant to make the most of it. His sister, Phil thought, would be proud of him finding people that he could truly connect with, even if it were only a handful so far.

But Phil would grow his family, already they'd taken in half a dozen new recruits that were said to be family to Steffan, if distant. They all agreed to be half ascended, one or two being able to be fully ascended. They all accepted what it meant to be an Eldritch Knight, because it meant a change for the better for them.

The life outside the city, in the literally tent city surrounding most of the Kothar nation, was harsh and people died by the dozens each day, either by starvation, gang related violence, or tribal feuds—this being one thing each had to swear they'd not perpetuate as they planned to recruit from as many as would and could be trusted, tribal, gang, or otherwise.

So it was that Phil found himself bidding farewell to his friends and new family to go venture into the city to do his secret mission. He'd cut his hair down to the scalp and left a months worth of growth on his face, making him unrecognizable at first glance. It pained him to leave so much behind, but he refused to be parted from the heart of

Mixana, so he took it with him, wrapping it in a leather star to disguise it.

When finally he left, he made his way through the forest to the tree city of the Ah'ehra and found Perilill waiting for him at their gate. They always had eyes on people coming and going from the main road.

"You come to see me?" She asked, eyeing him with a curious look. Phil returned the look, before breaking into a smile and bowing slightly to her.

"It is my duty to stand ready for when you call," Phil said, reciting part of an oath he'd made to her following her people's darkest day when the mother tree nearly burnt down. They'd lost a solid quarter of their population, small as it already was, that day. Then another quarter had joined with Phil, saying they would not wait to become Dea'trene, when the flame caller promised a way to slow the transformation.

It went against their oaths to their people and their culture, but they'd made the choice as hard as it was, that they felt would benefit their people the most. It meant more sap for those that were left, meaning they'd last longer in hopes that a new generation could be born and souls distributed.

"You come to use the gate?" She asked, seeing right through Phil.

"If it pleases you," Phil said, bowing his head ever so slightly once more. Perilill was beautiful, Phil knew this despite the sap shell that made her look more alien than human. Which made some sense considering she wasn't human, but a species all their own that was only humanoid in form, but ever changing as their DNA mutated.

She smiled, a gesture that was hard to catch under the sap shell, but Phil knew what to look for. Holding out a hand, Phil took it and they walked toward the city. He knew by experience that she'd release his hand, a gesture of affection, before they reached the gate, but Phil appreciated the small time they had. He'd grown close to her over the months, savoring each small visit he got to have with her.

A part of him wondered why he even bothered, though she showed affection back to him, it was unlikely that they'd be able to have any real relationship, but it didn't stop him from caressing her hand with his thumb as they held each other's hands.

Phil had learned by hard experience to take the love of others without qualms or hesitation, lest you lose what precious time you have with them to begin with. Though it had been a different kind of love, his sister and Adam had taught him that precious lesson. He'd both loved and lost each of them, but with Adam, he hoped for a glorious resurrection and perhaps a window into what lay beneath the exterior.

He thought back to when he'd first found Adam's Soul Stone and how it had appeared next to him when he'd entered Haven. It couldn't have been a mistake, he was almost positive now that Adam was a version, however different, of Eve the AI he'd built with his sister and crew. Those thoughts led him to his crew and he wondered if any had been able to make it in after all, or had he been the last?

A heaviness washed over him as he realized that he ought not to hold on to any hope that they made it, so terrible was the backlash from that dark AI and the company it worked for. How they'd come up with such a being of fierce evil and determination was another thing altogether that Phil worried about more than he needed to, being inside of Haven as he was now.

"You carry much weight on your shoulders," Perilill said, stopping him before they reached the gate and grabbing hold of his other hand. "I understand this look, for I have it often."

Phil said nothing, instead he pulled her into a hug and they shared their warmth. It was a solid minute or two before they broke it up and Phil stared down at her with a feeling that he couldn't chase away.

"I'm going to kiss you now," Phil said, then thinking better of it added, "If that's okay."

Perilill merely smiled, and nodded, before stepping up on her tiptoes as Phil leaned in and kissed the sap around her lips. It wasn't as sticky as you'd think, almost like a second layer of skin than anything else, but he yearned to feel the true warmth of her skin against his. The kiss lasted mere moments, but Phil felt as light as a feather afterward.

"Thank you," Phil said, feeling stupid after saying it. Why did he need to thank her for a kiss, that was just silly.

"Thank you," Perilill said, emphasizing the words.

Phil made it to the city and his plan was simple. He'd get in with the gangs in dockside by offering his services, surely anyone wanting to be a thug could get into the work easily enough. Seph had some contacts in the city from older times, one such contact had set up Phil a place to stay at a tavern called the Hungry Hog.

Apparently the bouncer owed her a favor or two and she'd called them in to get Phil a place to stay and an introduction with a few local thugs looking to hire muscle for an upcoming job. Beyond that he was on his own, but he figured once he got into the swing of it, he'd be able to hunt down information on this Wither fellow on his own.

Seph had tried to call in favors for information on him, but not even the bouncer was willing to say a word about Withers, be it good or bad.

The guards that day let him in with no issue, he wore simple but worn clothing, all pack of the act, one so he didn't get a shake down from guards and the like and another because he wanted to fit in the poorer section of town. He'd even left his armor and weapons behind, relying entirely on his ascended abilities to get him through.

So imagine his surprise when he made it to the Hungry Hog, a place at the edge of the Dockside slums, and the door had a slit revealing a pair of eyes looking right through him. What interested Phil more was the immediate measure of the man, he was ascended, yet weaker than most, but Phil had been letting his feelers out already, hoping he might come upon Withers all by accident.

Seph hadn't mentioned anything about the bouncer, who she said was named Mick, being ascended, so she might not have known or didn't think it was worth mentioning. Knowing Seph it could go either way.

Entering the establishment when the door swung wide, Phil took in the room. It was dimly lit yet filled nearly to capacity this evening. He took a measure of Mick, who stared him down with equal measure.

"No fights or I'll throw you out on your arse," Mick said by way of introductions.

"The sparrow calls and the fox hears," Phil said, repeating the phrase he was meant to say to the Mick fellow so he could get the info he was promised along with the room and board.

Mick's demeanor shifted immediately to one of fear as he took Phil in once more. Leaning down he whispered, "You the one she's sending? Head of the Eldritch Knights?"

"And I'd like it kept quiet if you please," Phil said back,

clearing his throat and putting a hand on the man's shoulder to back him off. He moved, stiffening under Phil's grasp, as if he was afraid he might be lit on fire.

"Course, course," Mick muttered. "Follow me and I'll get you set up. Farstil, I need that room and a hot meal."

A heavy set man with a large mustache and darting eyes grunted, throwing a key to Mick who snatched it out of the air with surprising agility for one his size. Soon Phil was getting settled into a fairly nice room with a sitting room and a bedroom. It appeared furnished and when he checked found clothes in the dressers.

"Someone lives here already?" Phil asked, curious why he hadn't been given one of the smaller rooms he'd seen on his way up. The doors had been open on two of them, showing them empty.

"This is my room," Mick said, gesturing to the room at large. "I'll be staying elsewhere so you can be comfortable."

"That's alright, I'll take one of the smaller rooms," Phil said, walking back out into the hallway. "I don't want to draw extra attention."

"Suit yourself," Mick said. He seemed to be getting more comfortable as time went on. Something about him knowing who exactly he was, head of the Eldritch Order, had rubbed Phil the wrong way and had definitely put a fear into Mick.

"Let me ask you a question," Phil said, leaning forward. The large man had to duck down a little to be close enough for a private exchange. "Why wont you tell me about Withers?"

It could have been a trick of the light, but Phil could swear that his eyes went black for a second and he stepped back as if struck.

"Can't," was all he said, before turning away. Then thinking better of it, he turned back and leaned in. "Best you don't use that name if you want to stay under it all. The contact I've got for you is willing to hire you as muscle, but don't show your full strength either. His name is Nathan, bald fellow with a green shirt sitting alone at the table below. Can't miss him, tell him Mick sent you."

"Got it," Phil said, dropping his bag.

Mick went downstairs and grabbed a new key for the room Phil was going to occupy before Phil locked the door behind himself. Going back down into the bustle of the room, a man played some sort of music on a modified looking guitar, singing alone as he played. Phil barely glanced in his direction, his mind on his quest.

Finding the green shirted man was easy enough, though he wasn't the only one with green on he was the only bald man with green. He sat across from him and the bald man looked up from his drink to scowl at Phil.

"Mick sent me," Phil said quickly. "I'm here to be the muscle for the job."

"I'll be deciding what youse be," the man said. "Names Nathan Gaffer, you look more like a lookout than a muscle. I saw how you took this room in with a glance, don't think I didn't."

"I'm the muscle," Phil insisted, already he was sure he didn't like this Nathan fellow.

"Okay muscle, youse going to have to bust a few heads for me, as a way to show you've got the chops," Nathan said, grinning ear to ear.

He had dark brown eyes and yellowing teeth. His face was several days in need of a shave, and his head was bald but for some patchy hair on the side. In all he looked like he belonged in a place like dockside, down to his clothes with holes in them and his shoddy looking dagger at his side.

Phil noticed most people, especially Koths, had blades at their side. He'd need to acquire one to better fit in, but that could be handled later, first he had to convince this thug he was worth hiring.

"What's the job pay?" Phil asked, deciding to act as if he'd already got it to throw the man off.

"Pays in coin, standard rates and all, but youse ain't got the job yet," Nathan said. Then standing he motioned after Phil to follow. "Come on."

Phil followed Nathan out into the dark night, Mick throwing him a look of confusion, but Phil just ignored it.

"Cause you came recommended by Mick, I won't guts you right here," Nathan said over his shoulder as they walked. "But I expected a big fellow, like the one they caught clearing the streets some months back. You look spry, but strength likely ain't youse best feature."

"You've got dirt in your ears?" Phil asked, letting his anger wash over him a bit as he worked out a new plan. "I'm the muscle, give me your stupid test and let's be done with it."

Nathan whistled then and two burly looking men, both bald as well, came out from the far end of the street.

"See those thugs, thas Tim and Todd, they call them the double Ts. I tooks ya over to their territory, you make it back to the Hungry Hog in one piece and I'll give you the gig. If nots, then oh well."

With that Nathan showed speed that surprised Phil, by sprinting off the way they came. It was only like eight streets down, but Phil was certain he'd find his way back.

Two more thugs appeared behind him and he was boxed in.

"This is hardly a fair fight," Phil said, looking over to the thugs named Tim and Todd, not even bothering to recognize the two smaller thugs coming up from behind him.

"Thas how we like it," the one on the left said, Tim perhaps? If that made him Tim then Todd spoke next.

"I'm going to eat you alive, tiny man," Todd said through gritted teeth.

They reminded Phil of old wrestling videos he'd watched back in the day of costumed wrestlers going at it and using punchy one liners.

"You misunderstood," Phil said, turning and punching one of the thugs in the chest, throwing him back harder than he meant into a building where he hit with a bone crunching thud. "This isn't a fair fight for you guys."

The fight started with haste after that, the second thug from behind slashed at Phil with a dagger and Phil leaned into the strike, dodging it and smashing the man's hand between his own. He let out a scream and Phil smiled.

Next came the two men that would put Doctor Vikar to shame with their size, standing nearly seven foot something and easily being four hundred pounds a pop.

A kick to Tim's knee caps brought him down and a follow up punch to his face knocked him out cold. Next Todd tried to grapple with him and he let him get his handhold, lifting Phil straight off the ground. When he threw him, Phil twisted midair and landed in a crouch, unharmed by the throw.

This was enough to make Todd's eyes turn into saucers and he turned to run. But Phil wasn't finished with the fight yet, he grabbed hold of Tim and with a quick twirl, threw him into Todd from ten feet away.

Thus ended the quick fight and left Phil barely breathing hard. It wasn't fair to pit an ascended up against none ascended, his strength was something of legend now and they never stood a chance. Phil made his way through the bodies and picked out their coin purses, gaining him some much needed coin. Next he took the best looking dagger and put it around his waist. Finished with his looting of the thugs, he kicked a groaning Tim in the face, putting him further under, before heading back to the Hungry Hog.

Nathan was all too surprised to see him, demanding how he escaped in hushed whispers. Phil just smiled and flexed his hands until his knuckles popped.

"I'm the muscle," he repeated and this time Nathan just nodded that he was indeed going to be the muscle.

CHAPTER 13
JAMES

Many things occurred to James as he rocketed down the side of a steep inclined roof toward the ground. One, this video game world had turned out to be very much realistic and he'd just made a very bad mistake when it came to the laws of gravity. Two, he had zero plan for how he was going to survive said mistake, but he was frantically looking for a way out of his several hundred foot free fall death.

It just so happened that as he fell and hit the edge of said roof with a high incline, his grip proved to be much better than he expected it to be. Grabbing hold of the side of the roof, he held on for dear life. Fragments of glass and shouts from above followed his abrupt stop, but James wasn't one to stay idle for long.

Already he began to move sideways toward an adjacent corner that might be his saving grace. It had what looked like a pipe or something similar snaking down the length of the building and he would be the first to take advantage of such an opportunity.

His hands met metal and stone, sliding from where he'd

been dangling to a pipe set affixed to the outside of the massive citadel. It must have been a recent construction, James decided, for it was awfully clean and well set into place for something of its nature. Moving down the pipe as swiftly as he could while maintaining a 'don't look down' mentality, James moved ever closer to the ground.

This was some quest, James decided, he'd have to get more of these before the day was out. The thrill of the adventure wore off as blisters began to form on his hands and he saw a small crowd peering up at him, some armored to the teeth.

"Well shit," James said, trying to think what he could do to get out of this situation, but before he could make any rash decisions, a cry of alarm came up and James looked just in time to see what it was.

Several hundred peasants in rags and covered in dirt had appeared out of nowhere and were rushing the citadel. Suddenly James wasn't the center of attention any longer, so he sped up his descent and hid the ground running.

Right past the armored folk who cried out in alarm as figures rushed all around them, none of them seemed to fall beneath the practiced blows of the experienced swordsmen. James found out why a moment later when he literally ran through one of the peasants.

It was all some kind of illusion, which meant he better hurry because he wasn't as safe as he'd first thought. He stopped trying to avoid anyone and just bolted right for the nearest alleyway. A cry of alarm went up behind him but he didn't turn to see if he was being chased. Instead he ran his ass off, not ready to fight men in full armor when he had so little himself.

He continued to run, alley to alley, until finally he made it back to the room he'd rented, and slipped inside. He waited out the entire day, as his instructions said, before heading to the dockside slums. Then as he turned a corner he was met by a familiar sight, the old man who'd given him the quest.

"You've done wonderfully," the man said, this time he was alone, no others around him, but still he gave off an air of power that James was sure meant he had power or magic of some kind.

"Quest complete," James said excitedly, handing over the book he'd tucked away. "Now about my rewards."

"You've proven yourself useful to us, don't worry about rewards for you've got one coming," the old man said, then he disappeared as suddenly as he had appeared before him.

"What in the freaking lame ass shit was that," James said, more than a little frustrated at the lack of tangible rewards or additional quests. "Maybe I need to go back to killing thugs for loot, because that quest was wack."

"You'll be killing and stealing no more," came a voice from behind him and he turned to see three armored figures walking right for him. The voice had echoed with power and James immediately knew he was outmatched, but that wouldn't stop him from trying.

He pulled free his only weapon, the nicest dagger he owned and bared his teeth. "Come and get me," James taunted as he backed into an alleyway that was narrow enough to force only one attacker at a time.

Unfortunately for him, the alley was occupied by another armored figure who wrapped his arms around James in an attempt to subdue him. But James was no one's fool and he plowed his elbow into the man's gut, then threw him over his shoulder before turning to run. He almost went for the man's sword, but he knew less how to use that weapon than he did a dagger or club.

Sure games he'd played had provided some experience, but they always had assistant programs to aid you, Haven seemed to have none of that mess, so utterly gritty and real in all ways.

James made it to the end of the alley where three more guards waited for him, backing up he saw them closing in on both sides and he needed a way out. There were no windows this low, but if he could just climb up enough to reach one of the higher windows. He began to climb as swiftly as he could between the narrow buildings, pushing against each side to leverage himself up, but he'd only made it up six feet when a sharp pain filled his back.

He dropped in a painful heap as a spear was pulled out of his back. Holding his dagger out he swung it wildly.

"Fuck this shit!" He screamed, getting up and slamming himself into the spearmen, taking him off his feet. He managed to find an opening in the armor as he swung wildly, drawing blood on the soldier.

But strong hands, much stronger than he'd ever experienced, grabbed hold of him and threw him like a ragdoll. A man in noticeably golden armor had appeared and his eyes glowed with a fierce fire. Flames began to burn up his arm but they glistened golden in the darkness of the alley.

This son of a bitch had magic, James realized with a grimace. Might as well go out in a blaze of glory, was his next thought as he rolled to his feet and faced off against the golden armored magic man.

The battle was short, but James did all he could to defeat his foe. He started off by grabbing a fist full of mud and slinging it at the golden fireman, before charging forward right into his grasp.

This wasn't what the fellow must have expected because James took him down and the flames around his hands went out as he grunted from the impact. Stabbing over and over again into his neck James was sure he'd won, but the man acted as if the wounds were nothing, grabbing James and throwing him with such casual force.

It was enough to knock the wind out of James and have him reeling. This guy was some kind of freaking overpowered cleric or something, because he had already clearly healed from a multitude of stab wounds to the neck.

Before James could make it to his feet the golden man was on him, kicking and punching with reckless abandon. James took as many hits as he could, before he knew death was next. Blood filled his vision and he tasted it in his mouth.

The dagger had been lost in the melee and throws, but James punched and fought with all he had against the overwhelming strength of this newcomer. It wasn't entirely in vain either, the golden armored man grunted several times from James's hits, but he never slowed or seemed to tire from the beating.

It was too much and eventually James let his guard down enough that a blow struck him in the head just right and he was out cold.

CHAPTER 14
PHIL

The job was a simple one. They had plans to knock off a warehouse in a rival gang's territory. It was said to be lightly guarded but Phil didn't exactly trust Nathan's leadership abilities, though it seemed like he got orders from on high, so perhaps the intel was good after all.

He'd spent the last week running little errands, shaking down people for debts owed, breaking things at eating establishments that were behind on payments and the like. None of it was what he'd thought he'd be doing with his life, but he needed information on this Wither character and he'd found someone willing to talk about it.

A chatty man named Leon, with bright red hair and pale skin, he was as big as any Koth, but skinnier than most of the brutish race.

"They say old Withers is a wizard," Leon said, it was just the two of them in a hideout they were meant to be guarding, Leon was, funnily enough, the lookout as he was said to be one of the fastest runners around. Phil acted as the muscle in this odd job, the big job not happening until that weekend.

"Where is he, why is he so secretive?" Phil asked, trying to play the part of a curious new recruit.

"Dangerous questions," Leon said, tsking Phil several times before continuing. "But I had them as well when I first signed on. He's the head of the organization, one of the four major crime bosses that runs the dockside slums. Only the high ups know his location, he's a very secretive guy."

"How does one become one of these higher ups?" Phil asked, he needed to move up in this gang's hierarchy and fast.

"Looking to make the big coin halls eh? I can't say about moving up, but they notice people who stand out. Since I'm the fastest legs in the gang, I get the most important lookout gigs. You are lucky you got to be assigned to me, word of how you handled the twins got you this far, keep doing shit like that and you'll be doing great."

Phil wasn't sure that Leon was as great as he was acclaimed to be, and he was wary of showing off his power too much. He'd have to do something to get higher in this organization though and strength of arms was something they respected from what he could tell.

"I'm looking to make a splash," Phil said, smirking at the cross eyes Leon. Despite his crossed eyes, red hair, and pale skin, Leon was a pretty likeable guy.

"You ever talk to that girl you've been going on about?" Phil asked, deciding he needed to sprinkle in some less pointed conversation to keep Leon talking.

"Oh Mary? You know I wanted to but I think ole Freddy is sweet on her and he's a tough son of a bitch," Leon said, then considering something he added. "Perhaps you can break in his teeth for me and tell him you're sweet on Mary so I can swoop after?"

"Not likely," Phil said, chuckling at his harebrained idea.

He had lots of such ideas, part of what made him such a good conversationalist, he always kept the words flowing.

"Oh common, you break him and I'll take the goods," Leon said, laughing a fair bit himself now. "What if I could get you a chance to move up? Perhaps we go knock off some rival gang hideouts and steal their loot all ourselves. We'd be damn heroes."

"We'd be dead men," Phil said, his laughter ending. "Don't do something like that, extra risks aren't worth the reward if you're dead."

"Yeah yeah," Leon said. "I bet with your help we'd be fine. Hell we could even hit the corner that the twins work at and you can show me how you put them out of commission for so long."

"Isn't happening," Phil said, not liking the new direction of this conversation. Leon was a gossip and if he learned something about Phil's incredible strength despite his size, he'd be in a spot of trouble.

But there were other rumors that he'd wanted to learn about, and Leon and he were stuck together for at least another few hours before their relief came.

"What do you know about the Wandering Wraith?" Phil asked and this stopped Leon dead in his tracks.

"Only that you shouldn't even say his name," Leon said, much more afraid of speaking of him than Withers. "The man is a freaking specter and an ascendant. They say he is a freaking Eldritch Knight! You don't fuck around with an Eldritch Knight, they'll suck your soul right away."

"I hear he isn't the only Eldritch Knight lately," Phil said, testing the bounds of Leon's knowledge.

"You heard about that too?" Leon said, eyeing Phil with a critical eye. "Bout the whole Council declining some upstart who pretended to be an Eldritch Knight. To think they'd try to join the council again, after what they did, as if."

"You know a good bit about Order Council business," Phil said, lifting a curious eyebrow.

"I like to stay informed," Leon said simply.

He truly was an oddity among the gangs, his speech more normal than most, lacking the poor speech patterns that Nathan and the lot had. It might be that Leon was a bit of a spy himself, though Phil wasn't sure yet. He'd keep that in mind when sharing information though, you could never be too careful.

"You know where to find this so-called Eldritch Knight?" Phil asked, flirting dangerously close to the line he didn't want to cross information wise. "I bet if we took him out we'd get some attention."

"Can't get attention if you're dead, right mate?" Leon asked, echoing Phil's words back to him.

"Risk versus reward," Phil shot back. "I think I can take him." He cracked his knuckles and they shared a light hearted laugh.

The conversation devolved from there and Phil kept it away from more serious topics, even if he had come at it in a more joking manner at first. Time went by and finally they were relieved, each of them going their own way.

The night of the big heist came faster than Phil was expecting, his days being filled with odd jobs and shake downs that sped the passage of time. He sat in his small room, though tonight would be the last night he stayed here, as he'd been invited to one of the hideouts as a permanent resident. Leon said this was something that usually meant you were going somewhere and joked that Phil should remember him on his way to the top.

Phil was sure it had to do with his success rate with shake-downs and territorial disputes he'd been involved with. Most of the shakedowns for restaurants like pubs and taverns, had been easy enough. He'd put down their bouncer, every place in the dockside had a strong man at the door, then he'd nicely request whatever was due. He found that treating people like people and not breaking their stuff was a more successful tactic.

He'd been getting a reputation as a strong man that no one could match, a little worrying for Phil as he wasn't half the size of most of the men, but he'd used more tactical takedowns and pressure points as much as brute strength, so he hoped that figured into his reputation. If perhaps they thought he was just a smart fighter, then it would attract as much attention as him having several times the strength of a normal Koth.

Beyond that Leon had started a rumor—with Phil's drop-ping helpful little hints—that he was actually from an island nation where the people weren't as large as Koths, but they were just as strong and focused on more tactical combat, where Kotharians tended to be very direct and forceful in their combat approaches, it suited their normal size and strength.

Of course not everyone in Kothar were Kotharians, it was a diverse nation city that held many races from the corners of the massive continent. Several of the races, whatever their names were, Phil hadn't remembered, were very human-like in their size and strength. For instance, whatever race Seph was, one of the islanders, smaller and tended towards red hair, were common enough that many Koths had crossed between them and given the red hair trait to people like Leon.

Though the oddest of the people were the orange skinned folks who Phil still remembered calling themselves Shohuth's.

Thea having been one such Shohuth, the odd lady that had brought him back to health and also killed a random stranger out on the road merely because he wished for death.

Phil splashed water on his face and drank deeply of a cold cup of ale he'd been provided. It wasn't great, but the coolness of it helped keep the heat of the day from his mind. Despite his new resistances to heat and temperature changes, his body still sweat a good deal in the summer heat. With two suns you had to deal with a lot of heat.

Collecting his final bit of things he'd collected over the month he'd been around, he bid a silent farewell to the room and went down to thank Farstil and Mick for their accommodations rent free as they'd been. Both gave him a quiet farewell, nodding their heads and letting him go on his way in peace. They'd be glad to be rid of him, he'd been getting a reputation and people were finding out where he lived. He wouldn't be surprised if an assassin were to come knocking through the windows soon if he stayed any longer.

When one didn't immediately appear at the thought, Phil counted himself lucky and went on his way. He reached the designated area some ten minutes later, as it wasn't terribly far from the Hog's Head.

He gave the required password at the door, getting him inside where he was the last to arrive. Leon and Nathan, along with half a dozen others had gathered together around some stacks crates and were talking in low voices. Leon, upon seeing Phil, waved him over. Phil dropped his items by a side wall, confident that he had nothing worth stealing and joined Leon.

"Now that we're all here," Leon said, talking over the group. "Let's get moving."

Nathan glared at Leon, as it was meant to be his show, but Leon just kept on smiling, oblivious to it.

They moved out into the streets as a single unit, converging on a distant warehouse where they had plans to sabotage and steal. This was the big job he'd been hired for and Phil felt a certain measure of excitement as they neared the area.

The night was cool and the moons were bright in the sky. It was because of this that they saw the two massive thugs, Tim and Todd, standing barring their path some mile still from the warehouse.

"We wants payback," Tim said, then turning to his equally huge brother Todd said, "Ya, we's know you cheated before."

"I'll handle this," Phil said, sighing.

Stepping forward both Tim and Todd took a step back as Phil approached, alerting him to a trap. He dove to the side just as several bolts were loosed at him, missing them all by mere inches.

His first instinct was to throw fire and consume those who dared to attack him from a distance, but he withheld the flames in favor of pulling free his dagger. The glint of steel against moonlight informed him there was a second volley ready to go, so he threw himself to the ground once more, barely avoiding that strike as well. It was so close in fact, he felt a tiny line of pain on his arm as one such bolt tore through his clothing.

His own small force of thugs were already on the move, pulling clubs, daggers, and in Leon's case, a thin sword out, ready to fight. They forced open a nearby door to gain access to the roof just as Phil made it back to his feet. He threw his dagger end over end with such force that even though it hit on the flat side, it knocked out the man he struck.

That was one rooftop bandit taken care of, only three more at least to go. Using his increased strength and agility, Phil practically ran up the side of the building, each hand hold and step launching him a great distance. It was like a full grown man fighting against a couple of toddlers armed with spoons, they stood no chance.

He made the top of the roof and a bolt smashed into his chest, causing him to stop for only as long as it took him to rip it free in a spray of blood. He'd heal, but now he was worried about anyone finding out he had been hit in the first place, these men would need to die and fast.

With deadly intent he ran forward, slashing out with his forearm as he reached the closest thug. His head went flying from his body as if Phil had used a blade and his shirt was covered in more gore. Next he rushed to the final rooftop attacker on this side of the narrow alley only to find him knocked out cold and his dagger laying beside him.

With a flick of his wrist he cut the man's throat and thought no more about his death than he did cleaning his teeth, so hot was the fire burning within him wishing to be free.

His companions appeared on the roof, just as Phil turned and jumped across to the other side with ease. He landed just as two bolts thunder past him, missing him by mere inches. Looking up he knew his eyes were burning with green fire, it couldn't be helped so he kept his gaze on those that wouldn't live long enough to tell the tale of what he truly was.

However they knew as they looked at him, throwing their weapons aside they began to run. But Phil wasn't only stronger than his opponents by many times, he was faster. He moved with the insane speed of an ascended and slammed into the first victims back, slashing up with his dagger and further covering himself with blood and gore.

The final man screamed something at him incoherently and Phil just smiled. They'd made it into the darkness of the lower room and fire burned all around Phil despite his attempts to hold it back.

"Burn," Phil whispered and all of his flame funneled around the other, burning only what he wanted, the man and leaving the rest of the building intact. Such precision and control was something Phil had been learning, but he felt power leech from his amulet, guiding him to be more careful than he could have been without it.

The man died in seconds and Phil withdrew the flame and let it rest within him, duty fulfilled. He left the house and stopped anyone from going in to check on the dead with a simple shake of the head.

"They are dead and need not our assistance," Phil said to Leon as he tried once more to get past him.

"Right, but we can still loot them before we go," Leon said, a hungry look in his eyes. "And you look like quite a mess there lad, you're going to need a new shirt."

"Leave it," Phil said, his tone more dangerous than he'd meant, but it did the trick, stopping Leon dead in his tracks.

"Tim and Todd?" Nathan asked, looking over the street that was now empty of anyone, including corpses of the twins.

"Didn't have time," Phil said. "Although they've on my shit list now, so don't expect them to live out the week."

Phil surprised himself by meaning the words he'd spoken. He'd never thought of himself as a murderer, but ever since merging with his flame, he couldn't bring himself to leave threats undealt with. Even Zarrick and Golder remained on his mind frequently, what they would be doing to move against him and if they needed to be dealt with.

Then there was the casual show of wealth and power Zarrick had shown, perhaps Phil wouldn't be a match for the aged tiny man, but he had a feeling that before his days were done, he'd find out.

Phil removed his shirt, showing his muscled form that was without injury, much to Leon and the other's surprise, discarding it in the filth of the alley. He didn't like being half naked, but his shirt was ruined and they didn't have the time to back track as they'd already be later than planned on the warehouse hit now.

They made it to the warehouse and Phil was surprised to find nearly a dozen men with clubs, knives, hatchets, and a two crossbows lined up outside the building as if expecting them. Then he saw two shadowy figures, taller than the rest, behind them and he knew. Tim and Todd had joined forces with this gang, or perhaps they'd already been on their side he didn't pay attention to the gang politics as much as he should.

A smile kept on his face while the others looked disheartened by the turn of events.

"Lights here and there," Phil said from the shadowy alley they hid in. "Take them out and I'll lay waste to their lines. It will take you time to circle around, but go in two large groups just in case they have more patrols."

"I'll stay with you," Leon said, giving Phil a look that said he wouldn't be swayed, but Phil tried anyways.

"No you wont," Phil said. "I need to hit them fast and hard or not at all. You will only slow me down."

Leon looked at Phil for a long moment, the rest of the team seemed ready to follow Phil's lead, as crazy as the plan seemed, but not Leon, not yet at least. Phil let a glint of green fill his eyes for only a moment, but Leon saw it and his eyes went wide.

Suddenly he was taking a step back and nodding. "Right, yeah I'll go with them," Leon said, gathering himself he added.

"Be safe and nimble. Don't burn us by failing." Then he winked.

Phil let out a breath, hoping his trust in Leon wasn't misguided. But it worked, they left to circle around, it would take them a solid ten minutes at least to get around and show up in the right places, but then Phil planned on having the situation fully under his control.

After he was sure they were gone, he stepped out into the light and Tim and Todd, from within the shadows, gave an audible curse.

"I'm back, did you miss me?" Phil asked, chuckling as two bolts slammed into his chest. His powers, coursing within him and healing him as fast as he could breath, took care of the injuries within moments of Phil pulling them out. He held them for only a second before throwing one like a mini spear at the closest thug.

It worked surprisingly well, stabbing him through the throat, however the second bolt went sideways, just smashing into some random thug's face. They charged all at once after that and Phil summoned fire from deep within himself.

The entire battle took less than a minute, he used the flames to position his attackers, but was careful not to burn them less he leave evidence of what he was behind. Instead he crushed faces within his hands, broke bones and then necks as thugs fell.

In the end it was only Tim and Todd cowering and begging for their lives pressed against the loading gate.

"What did we do to bring the wrath of the Wondering Wraith down on us?" Tim asked, terror evident in his tone.

Interesting, Phil thought, they think he is the Wondering Wraith. This presented him with a plan that, unfortunately, meant that one of these two would have to remain alive. Using a club he casually found on the ground, he killed Todd and turned to Tim.

"Tell all that will listen, this is what happens when you try to mess with the Wondering Wraith, if I see you again, you're dead. Tell anyone what I look like, and you're dead. Understand me?" Phil asked, putting his face as close as he could to the towering giants face.

The man must have wet himself he was so scared, but he nodded and rushed off and out of the area.

CHAPTER 15
JAMES

C hains kept James in place, though they weren't needed, he knew when he was beat. In his current state of being beaten half to death, he had no doubt that he was the loser in this particular contest of strength. He'd lost plenty before, so it wasn't that it really hurt him, it was knowing he didn't have any way to overcome such a powerful opponent.

He had no magic, he had only his strength and wits. This video game world or whatever it was, really went out of its way to show him that he wasn't much when compared against truly powerful opponents. But that would change, James decided. He would find a way to get access to that magic and he'd come back to destroy this golden boy and his weak ass magic.

They walked for some time before he was placed into a wagon and taken some place else. James didn't even try to track where he was going, so down were his spirits. But he had a hope and he held to it. If this were truly a simulation and the humans were meant to be the heroes, he could only assume as much, then he'd get his chance.

That made James wonder about humans in general,

millions had been sent to Haven, yet he'd only seen these half giant people mixed with a few other odd races, but no one that could pass as an average human. Perhaps he'd gotten his starting location messed up and that was why he was suffering through this shit experience.

"Load out," Came a call from outside the wagon. It had stopped and James hadn't noticed.

The door opened and he was pulled out by a pair of armored folk, wearing leather armor by the looks of it, worn and tattered they'd used it plenty of times. Both men had helmets on their heads but their faces were open to James. He memorized those faces, adding them to his 'to kill' list as they kicked his feet from under him, making him fall into a pile of mud.

They laughed and took out short wooden shafts, like batons but bulkier on one end that was wrapped in leather. The first strike barely phased James, so much pain from a variety of cracked bones and bruised muscles. But the next strike hit a particularly tender spot and James found himself again.

He got to his feet, catching the next blow and putting his head into the attacker's face. Blood poured freely as James smiled down at the man, then a blow to his head sent him reeling. More grunting, yelling, and eventually pulling as they dragged his mostly limp body into a darker place, throwing him down and releasing his chains.

James lay there for several minutes before regaining any sense of self, then looking around he found he was one of many in a large holding area, dimly lit and plenty dirty. The front wall he'd come through was barred and the back wall had a single window with bars stuck into it, spaced a fist length away from each other.

James did a quick tactical count and assessment of his surroundings. Twelve people, two looked at him with a hunger he didn't like, while the ten others carried on casual conversations amongst themselves.

The two hungry looking individuals began a slow walk toward him and James stood, ready to fight once more, though it pained him to do so.

"Fresh meat," One of them said, the uglier of the two. He had fresh bruises all over the right part of his face and a nasty slashing wound down his right arm. He wore nothing but rags and despite his bravado, he walked with a slight limp on his right leg.

"Borris thinks you look tasty," the other said, whether his name was Borris or his partners, it wasn't clear and James wasn't in a conversation mood at the moment.

Cracking his neck to one side, James raised his fists, ready to fight.

"Oh," the first of the pair, maybe Borris, said. "He has fight left in him. You'll do good in the arena, should you survive the night."

The other sneered as he neared, producing a shank of some kind—it looked like a sharpened piece of rock with cloth wrapped around as a handle.

He'd deal with him first. As the knife wielder drew near, James let his mouth fill with blood, it was easy as he had several cuts and seemed to be coughing it up as well. He spit the blood at the man and went for the offending arm, but he was too slow in his injured state and he missed as the man reared back in alarm.

Instead he caught a blow from the second man in the head that sent him reeling backward. These two, despite their looks, had some fighting experience and seemed to work well together. As one laid into James the other cleared his eyes and came at him with the shank.

Before James could stop him the blow landed hard in his side, pain lanced through him and all he could think about is this wasn't the way he wanted to die. He didn't even know how or if respawning worked yet, so he had to keep himself alive.

He bit and clawed at the closest of the two, positioning him in such a way to block the repeated stab attempts from the shank. It worked, the first man cried out as the second stabbed him in the back.

"Oh," the second one stopped to say. "Didn't mean to hitcha Borris."

Borris, the slightly larger of the two, drew back and punched for James, but adrenaline had filled him enough to give him back some of his reflexes, so he turned just in time to miss the attack and see another man joining the brawl.

As if two opponents weren't enough when he was terribly injured, they had to add more into the fray.

This frustration in the change of events lasted all but two seconds, as the newcomer punched the knife wielder in the back, likely hitting a kidney because the man cried out and dropped the blade. With a swiftness that didn't line up with the size of the man, he scooped up the blade and ran it across the man's neck, dropping him where he stood.

Next he turned his attention on the one atop of James, but during the distraction of the man being cut down, he'd already gotten the upper hand. James held the man in a tight neck hold as Borris kicked and tried to scream out. His body went limp, but James held it for several seconds afterward to ensure the deed was done.

A noise from outside their cell caught his attention and he stood just as the new fighter tossed James the shank and he caught it deftly. Guards opened the gates with batons ready and James knew it hadn't been a kindness the man had just done, giving him the shank. All of the prisoners hit down to their knees and James followed suit, dropping the shank and landing atop it with his knees.

It dug into the muddy floor and he was sure they wouldn't see it, but the closest guard grunted and stars filled the room as James took another hit to the head, bowling over in pain.

They found the shank and beat James some more, pain being a near constant presence in his mind now, it almost like he could shut it out as some foreign thing separate from his own experiences. Then a sharp kick to the face brought him back to reality, his eye would be swollen for sure.

James took a nap after that, the pain so much that he wasn't really sure if he fell asleep or just passed out, but the end game was the same, he rested. When he next came to, it was with a man standing over him, bright purple eyes, dirty blonde hair, and a smirk on his face.

"You look like hell," he said. "Names Pete, what's yours?"

"James," James said, or at least he tried to say. It took him three attempts before a passable phrase of his name came out but he managed it all the same.

"Well James," Pete said. "You've got two choices. Live or Die. Make it quick, because if the guards think you aren't going to be worth a showing on the arena floor, they'll just hasten your death. Its time to sit up and start healing."

James groaned, but he managed to get his ass underneath him, sitting up. He took in the room, two bodies less than before and everyone but Pete minding their own business. As he looked Pete over, he was a large man, like most James had come across, but he had a narrow face and a jaw you could cut glass with.

This was the very man that had ended the fight for him, keeping him alive before betraying him with the shank.

"Thanks for that," James said. "I guess."

"No hard feelings," Pete said, putting a gentle hand on his shoulder James felt a warmth from him that was hard to explain as it spread from his touch to the rest of his body. "Sit still while I heal you as best I can." He said this part in a low whisper, glancing over his shoulder as he spoke.

"You can heal?" James asked, matching the low hushed whisper.

"I'm ascended, yes, but I'm as weak as one can be and still be ascended," Pete said in answer. "Our little secret though."

James had so many questions, but he respected the man's privacy, mostly because much of the pain of the past day was beginning to fade and his mind started to turn again.

"How do I get ascended?" James asked, again in a hushed whisper.

Pete laughed and cut off the healing as the sound of guards came to their cell. Looking over, James saw them pointing at him and talking in low voices.

"You able to fight?" One of them called out.

James stood, though he was still stiff, the healing Pete had done hastened his healing by at least a few weeks if he had to guess.

"I'm able," James said, though he wasn't sure he wanted to fight for the first time in his life. He wanted nothing more than to curl up and fall asleep for a week or two.

"Time to fight," the same guard said.

"Good luck," Pete said. "Try not to die."

CHAPTER 16
PHIL

B y the time everyone else arrived back from knocking out the lights, going the long way to be undetected, Phil stood amidst the chaos of his battle, dead bodies everywhere.

"What? How? Yous a monster of a brute!" Nathan said, struggling to get his words out with any level of coherency.

Leon just shook his head, winking at Phil again when he made eye contact with him. He would be in trouble if Leon let slip what he thought he knew, but it was worth it so far. They were good to steal the goods and burn down the warehouse as planned.

"Get the loot and let's split," Nathan declared and the rest of the men went to work.

It took maybe two hours for them to load several hand carts and push them out of the area. No one bothered them, they'd won the day and it was well known by now. Phil just hoped this got him what he was hoping, a meeting with this Wondering Wraith.

He was sure the man would be just as interested in someone claiming to be him while also showing all signs of being an Eldritch Knight. Or perhaps it would spook him and he'd go underground, either way Phil would work out what to do next.

Several days passed and Leon caught him as he was going out to find a bite to eat. In truth he had the next few days off and was planning on escaping the city for a two day trip back to the Eldritch Keep, but destiny had other plans.

"He wants to meet with you," Leon said in a low whisper.

"Who does?" Phil asked, unsure who Leon meant at this point.

"My boss, the Wandering Wraith," Leon said, smiling wide. "You knew I was undercover from another gang didn't you? That's why you showed me what you truly were. Well he is very interested in meeting another Eldritch Knight, so no more sneaking around, let's go meet him."

This wasn't quite the turn of events Phil had been hoping for but it would do just fine. "After you," Phil said, gesturing that Leon should lead the way.

He did so and into the dockside slums they went, traveling backway alleys and side streets for a solid hour or perhaps even two with little conversation along the way. Finally they got to a semi-better part of the dockside slums, the streets were pathed in cobblestone and only one in three were missing. But overall it was a step up from the harsh muddy streets of the dockside slums.

"Red house with the black and gold gate, two streets down, knock twice and wait to be received," Leon said, then turning he left Phil before he could ask any follow up questions, slipping in a nearby alley.

Sure enough as he traveled down the streets he realized he was in a residential area with nicer houses with gates and well kept grassy gardens in front, one even had a fountain, but not the red house. The red house was two stories tall with shuttered windows of white with red brick siding. The front area was well maintained, but simple. The gate creaked slightly as Phil pushed it open and headed for the door.

The door was black, standing out against the red brick and he knocked as instructed, once then twice, before awaiting to see what would happen.

A slit in the door like a mail slot but much higher, opened up and a pair of grey eyes looked out, before grunting something Phil couldn't catch and swinging the door open.

"Follow me, my master wishes to meet you in the study," said a well dressed elderly man who was wearing clothes fit for a special occasion—all white and black with shiny shoes and all —or perhaps he was just a fancy butler.

With a quick glance behind himself and checking that his fire was strong and ready to lash out if things turned deadly, Phil followed along. The entryway was dimly lit but a hanging lamp and a large staircase led to the second floor, but they didn't take that way. Instead he led Phil to the left hallway leading back to a series of closed doors.

Pushing the furthest down on the left, it opened up to a decently sized library filled with books. There was a fireplace burning and set into the far wall providing most of the light. Four different lamps hung on the walls, providing additional, if dim, light to see by. The room had the smell of books that had weathered with time and Phil couldn't help but take one off the wall and examine it.

The book turned out to be one on a history of the Koth nation. Phil skimmed it but right now he wasn't interested in history, he wanted books on runes. So going from book to book he searched for any that might fit that bill, but found nothing but more histories and even a few stories that must have been works of fiction, telling of great black dragons that could travel between the stars.

"Enjoying my collection?" Came a smooth voice from behind him and Phil turned to see a younger man, one who couldn't have been more than twenty years of age by the looks of it yet his eyes burned with a soft green glow.

Phil stoked the embers of his own green flame until they burned with a bright intensity. "I found nothing useful," Phil assured him, turning and truly taking the man in.

He had black hair, eyes that glowed green, sharp features and ears a touch too big for even his massive form. He was a Koth, that much was plain to see, but he wore no armor or other signs that would set him apart as an Eldritch Knight, other than the eyes. Even his clothing was barely a step up from what rags Phil wore.

"Not a fan of history?" the man asked, sitting in a lavishly plush red chair next to the fireplace and gesturing that Phil should sit on the one across from it. He did so.

"I'm looking for a specific book," Phil said, letting the fire die down a touch and his eyes return to normal.

The stranger did the same and Phil was surprised to find his eyes remained green, just not glowing.

"The tome that Wither took from the Citadel, according to my little spy Leon," the man said, not stating it as a question but more of a statement of fact.

"Yes actually, but right now I'm much more interested in you," Phil said. "Tell me, what's your name and why would an Eldritch Knight be operating inside of Kothar all this time?"

"Names are temporary, but you can refer to me as the Wandering Wraith as everyone else seems to, until we become friends, then I will share with you the name I had when I first joined on with the Eldritch Knights so many years ago," the Wandering Wraith said.

"And how is it you came to rule over a sect of thugs inside the poorest part of the city?" Phil asked, curious.

"That is a long and unimportant story," he said. His man servant appeared and offered him a drink of red wine in a fancy glass. He took it and offered one to Phil as well, he did not partake of it.

"Suffice to say that I found an opportunity to hide within plain sight and I took it. This isn't the most glamorous life, but I get to enjoy the simple pleasures in life. Care to tell me how a young strapping fellow such as yourself became an Eldritch Knight?"

"Truth for truth, you've told me nothing of consequence, why would I share my secrets with you?" Phil asked, adjusting himself in the seat and growing frustrated with the exchange.

"It calls you to action doesn't it, to burn me away for not giving you what you've come for? The green flame is a marvelously destructive tool, but it has perks that I believe you don't know of. Have you consumed any souls yet?" He asked, looking at Phil with a hunger in his eyes.

"That is not the way the new Eldritch Order is going to operate," Phil said, anger seeping into his response.

"Ah, so you are one of those," he said, disappointment clear in his tone. "Very well. I can give you the location to Withers, but you must do a favor for me first."

"Let's hear it," Phil answered.

"Allow me to return to the Eldritch Order and give me a position of power among the new recruits. I've heard tales of dozens now being swept away from the tent city, I believe you've found a golden hair amongst the weeds and I want to be a part of it once more," The Wandering Wraith seemed hungry for an answer as he squirmed in his seat awaiting Phil's response.

This was not something that Phil expected to hear today, so he just looked at the man and wondered at what he could be up to.

"What part of the Eldritch Order were you a part of?" Phil asked, wondering if he was a Lore Warden as Seph was or perhaps something else.

"I was and still am a Flamebound Knight," Wandering Wraith answered with a touch of arrogance in his voice. "I never made it to the rank of master, but I wouldn't bet against me in a fight."

"Give me Wither's location and I will speak with the Eldritch Council about reinstating you," Phil said. "But first I need a name, a real one."

"Darius Shadowbane is what I was called during my time with the Eldritch Knights. Who is it that gave you the embers to start our order once more? I know of only a few living Eldritch Knights, all of them are in hiding, sworn to never again use their powers," Darius said.

"You might know her as the Crimson Death, but I know her simply as Seph," Phil said, watching Darius's reaction for any sign of recognition.

"She yet lives?" Darius said, standing from his place and nearly dropping his drink. "I fear she won't want to see me but give her this message. 'I've changed and I can prove it.' Tell her this and mean it. She has taken up the Amulet of Mixana then?"

"No," Phil said, his hand going to his amulet around his neck covered in a leather star. "I am the leader of the Eldritch Knights and I walk the Path of the Pale Riders. I must speak with Seph first, but it would do well to have a Flamebound returned to the order."

Darius's eyes went hungrily toward the amulet around Phil's neck and his glass broke in his hands.

"You must be strong of mind and body for the amulet to have chosen you. I once had the opportunity to take it, but I feared death more than I ought to, so I didn't take it up. I will stand beside you, Leader of the Eldritch Order, should you want me," Darius said, tossing his glass to the side as if it were nothing.

The meeting ended with Darius providing several safe-house locations as well as a promise for support against Wither, who he told Phil was a powerful member of the Mage's Order. His specialty was illusions and he'd tricked some poor unfortunate soul into stealing the book for him before having him thrown into the arena games, a death sentence.

Phil took all the information and stored it away, saying he'd be gone for several days, but when he returned he had plans to take down Wither and retrieve the book.

CHAPTER 17
STEFFAN/PHIL

P hil had been gone for some time now, but Steffan was finding he didn't mind so much. He got to do lessons with his sister and the one called Seph more often than not, but he'd also started making recruitment trips back to the tent city per Seph's instructions. They'd grown the people staying at the Eldritch Keep to a surprising number of fifty individuals from the tent city, Seph interviewed and instructed all of them in different ways.

She sent back nearly half of all the ones Steffan found, which he found frustrating, but he was also learning what it was she was looking for, so this last batch she only sent back two annoying boys he was sure wouldn't be accepted anyways. He'd added them in as a test to see if he was getting it right or not.

"That last batch is exactly what I am looking for, good job Steffan," Seph said, walking up to him and giving him some of the precious few praises she handed out.

"Thank you," Steffan said, lowering his gaze in her direction. She was a stickler for that kind of stuff and he had to be sure he followed protocol, because he wasn't certain she was his biggest fan yet.

What he did know was that his time to slay one of those crazy looking beasts was upon him, he'd had the flame a while now and felt like he mastered the basics. She told him that if he waited much longer he'd be burnt up inside, he didn't feel that way but he trusted her words.

Regardless he was to make his attempt tonight, while the others watched on. She wanted to use him as an example of how proper training and preparation would be enough for all those willing to take on the green flame, becoming Eldritch Knights.

He'd been training in both the spear and the sword, but he preferred the spear as did Phil, from what Seph said. He'd even mastered covering his weapons in green flame to slow the healing of the beast. Seph had been giving him helpful hints and tips on how to take one down, and Steffan would heed each of them because he didn't want to die.

He faced off against his sister, she'd be doing her own challenge in the coming months, but Seph had been taking her much slower than Steffan, though he didn't know why. However, she'd been ascended and could fight as well as any of the new recruits, so he enjoyed sparring with her most.

Facing off, he took up his sword and let her go spear, for the greater reach. He wouldn't use his flame, instead covering his blade with it, doing a few test swings to make sure he could still do it as effectively as possible, then switching it off so as to not hurt her. Seph gave him a look as he worked, obviously wanting them to start the sparring match already and telling him with her eyes that he'd be in for it if he didn't hurry.

So without any further interruptions he launched forward with his new speed, slashing out for her with his sword. He almost withdrew the strike when it looked like she wouldn't parry in time, but his feet went out from under him and he realized his mistake.

She'd ignored his shortened strike that he'd opened with to let her get a chance to gain an easy upper hand, and instead swept his feet. He landed hard and had to roll fast to avoid the spear going right for his chest. His sister grinned then, as Steffan rolled far enough away to make it to his feet without being attacked.

Seph was truly doing a number on her, making her a powerful fighter and he realized he'd need to stop fooling around if he was going to win this sparring contest.

"Stop holding back, brother," Mercy called out, twirling her spear in a showy fashion.

Returning her grin, Steffan called out to her. "Make ready then, for I'm coming at you with all I have."

Green flames erupted along the length of his blade and he let the fire fuel his attack. Rushing forward he struck a death-blow for her chest, but the attack was turned away and he took a hit on the arm from the longer weapons reach. But he didn't stop there, no, he turned and scored a glancing blow on her arm, drawing blood.

The green flame would ensure that the wound took much longer to heal, but even so she showed no sign of pain, spinning her spear in a downward arc that Steffan was forced to block and give her space or end up on the pointy end.

The battle continued with back and forth strikes, Steffan barely having the upper hand and Mercy showing the skill she'd acquired under Seph's tutelage. Finally after several long minutes of back and forth, Steffan saw his opening and took it. His sword came down on her neck and stopped only a hairs distance away.

"I've got you now sister," Steffan said, panting.

"And I you," Mercy said, thrusting her spear forward just a touch and Steffan felt its bite.

"You are getting better," Steffan said, shooting a look toward a grinning Seph. "Why can't she also challenge the mixana beast, she is my equal when she wields a spear."

The same wasn't true sword to sword or spear to spear, but that wasn't something Steffan wanted to mention at the moment. He just wanted her to progress with him and not have her flag behind.

"I'll be the one that decides when she will take the challenge and receive the flame, I suggest you remember your place, initiate," Seph said, speaking loud enough for all to hear.

The assembled warriors paused long enough to hear, but then they too continued their sparring matches, each of them wanting to impress Seph in one way or another.

The time eventually came that he was to challenge the Mixana beast and Steffan wished he felt anything but anxiety over the moment.

Phil arrived through the portal and took a moment to look at the constructs or golems that stood guard there. They had black metal and a design not that dissimilar from Adams original design. The longer he looked and tried to feel at the magic behind them, the more he hoped he'd be able to bring Adam back. It would be nice to be in contact with his soul once more, Seph having held onto it for him during his undercover quest.

He walked through the purple light of the mother tree and encountered no one as he made his way to the exit. They were avoiding him, he knew, but after so much time he wished to be greeted by a friendly face. None came and he made his way into the woods and past Seph's old cabin before going into the woods on the fairly long journey to the keep.

He made it before nightfall and was greeted by a sight that surprised him. Nearly five dozen people, tree folk and Koths were gathered around green flame bonfires while Steffan did battle with a mixana beast.

"He's doing well?" Phil asked, thinking he'd snuck up on Seph. She didn't flinch or show any sign of reaction, just nodding.

"He is," she said, indicating the battle that didn't look to be going well at all.

Steffan was covered in blood and stabbed over and over again into the Mixana beast with various levels of success. Phil knew the pain and horror of such a fight, the beast always turning out to be more powerful than you imagined, but he could do nothing but watch. He did note that this particular beast was several times smaller than the one he faced, but it was to be expected.

The mixana beast that stepped forward was meant to be the one you'd most equally match spirit wise, so it could come in all sorts of shapes and sizes. Turning his attention back to the fight, Phil watched it unfold.

Steffan fought brilliantly, Seph had been teaching him well in Phil's absence. He got himself free of the beast and twirled his sword in his hand, eyeing a spear that had fallen not far off. Wreathing his sword in flames he shot forward and cut deep into the beast's face, before turning to grab the spear, letting his sword fall to the ground.

Green flames ignited the spear and Steffan pointed it at the beast, throwing powerful flames from the tip in an expert showing of using the green flames. The beast of course was barely phased by it, unlike any other opponent, it was practically immune to the fire. The flames only helping in slowing the wounds' healing and nothing more.

Steffan realized this too late as the beast jumped from within the flames and landed atop him. Perhaps he was smarter than Phil gave him credit, because he let the spear impale the beast as it came down, funneling more flames into it. Phil could feel the beast weaken under the internal onslaught, unable to heal damage done to its heart fast enough.

Just when Phil was sure the battle was done, the beast bit hard into Steffans next, ripping a large part of his throat out. It would be a battle between healing factors and who would die first now.

Steffan tried to scream, but Phil could tell he couldn't any longer. To the side, Mercy, his younger sister, stepped forward, spear in hand, but Seph raised a hand, stopping her. She wouldn't allow anyone to interrupt the ritual, this Phil knew for sure. So instead they all watched as the light faded from both the beast and the young man's eyes.

In the end, Steffan won out, the beast going still before he did and suddenly a wash of power could be felt as their two spirits merged. Suddenly fire sprung up from his wounds and Steffan went stiff as he was healed from death's door.

He'd done it, Steffan had completed the ritual and was now a true Eldritch Knight.

CHAPTER 18
JAMES

The moment they left the stank filled holding cell they put some kind of bracelets around his arms, they didn't restrict his movements but they must have some point, or why put them on in the first place? They led James down a dark corridor and into a small room filled with armor and weapons. They didn't seem afraid that he'd take one and strike them down, but that is exactly what James planned on doing. However the moment he tried to do just that, picking up a weapon and swinging for a neck, his entire body gave out in a wash of pain.

"Stupid man," said one of his guards. "You fight who we want and no one else. Got it?"

"Got it," James said almost robotically as he stood. He did not want to feel that pain again so he was suddenly feeling very agreeable.

"Pick out whatever you want and you fight in five minutes," the other guard said, turning and leaning on a nearby wall.

James took it all in, all of it was made for someone around

his size or bigger, so he quickly found a metal chest piece that wouldn't restrict his movements too much and then looked for a weapon. If he was about to be in some kind of arena fight, which seemed the most likely outcome, then he wanted something for both close quarters combat and distance fighting.

He found a dagger that had a sheath, and affixed it to his leg, it was a smaller belt look and the only place that made sense. Next he found a decently sized mace, with many deadly points to it. And lastly, he took a trident and felt very aquatic as he swirled the odd spear like instrument around a few times. Hell if there'd been a net he'd have grabbed it too, but he had no such luck this match.

"Times up," One guard said while James continued to peruse the items. He straightened, looking at the guards for any sign that they were going to activate the pain bracelets again, but he saw nothing for them to do it with, so he relaxed.

He allowed himself to be led to the next room, which ended up being a narrow staircase that led up into sunlight. The shafts of light caught his skin as he rose and it felt amazing. He could almost make out some cheers and jeers from above, but suddenly a loud announcer voice cut over all of them and he heard only them as he ascended the staircase.

"Today we have a new challenger, a man named James. This one is serving for the crime of murder and theft, he has been sentenced to fifty bouts within the arena, but can he survive even one? Just watch and together we will find out!"

The cheers of the crowd redoubled.

"Also joining him are the Slayer of the Bay and Codwick the Merciless. They are both on their fifteenth bout and neither has been even close to defeat, so this ought to be a good bout indeed!"

More cheers with some jeers mixed in just as James reached

the peak of the staircase and out onto the arena floor. Instead of the movies where the floor would be covered in dust and dirt, this one was cobblestoned and clear of any debris. There were flaming pilons spaced every ten feet or so in a wide circle, and glowing words that James couldn't understand traced onto the ground in random spaces.

Straight across from him emerged a heavily armored man wielding a massive two handed sword nearly the length of James trident that he held tightly in his grasp. The armor was rather ordinary, save for the fact that he seemed to be wearing full plate, making him a hard to pierce target. Good thing he'd chosen a bludgeoning weapon.

To his left he heard a shout and turned to see about the same distance as the first competitor, a new one wearing almost no armor and wielding two shorter blades.

He looked like a wild man and had more scars and fresh wounds than James had ever seen on someone still standing. Even from a distance, James knew that each movement would be slower for the scars and painful due to the open wounds. However, as if to prove James wrong, the man did a backflip and transitioned into a kick and slash, showing his crazy agility.

"The fight will last ten minutes, anyone alive at the end, wins a round, if all perish then no one wins. Finish your bets, because it is time to fight!"

Came the voice once more booming over the cheering and James finally saw where it was coming from. A raised tower set into the arena stands, which were packed filled with people of all kinds. The tower held a box for very fancy looking people and a man in blue robes spoke into his hat, somehow amplifying his voice that way.

Movement ahead caught James eye's, the agile one was coming right for him, so he readied his trident for a deadly throw. But before he could let it off, he felt something behind him and going on instinct alone, threw himself to the floor. A jet of flame washed over him, heating him up but not burning him.

He rolled to see a giant wingless lizard finishing a jet of flame and looking around hungrily. The agile one was now fighting against a scaled cheetah of some kind, with multiple tails and yet somehow it seemed to be nearly invisible in the bright light of the sun.

This was not what James expected, he thought as he stood and readied himself against the wingless dragon, for what else could he imagine would spit fire and have scales? There was a certain amount of thrill to fighting his first monster, but James had to be careful because he wasn't alone in the arena and he was fairly certain that his arena friends would kill him just as much as help him if the opportunity arose.

Rolling out of the way of another burst of flame, James straightened and struck out.

"Critical hit!" James yelled, as his trident hit the side of the scaly creature's neck and a liquid that began to burn as it touched the air around it appeared.

"I'm going to level up any time now," James said, speaking to calm himself more than anything. "Then perhaps," he paused to dodge a strike from the giant lizard, "I'll get some damn magic."

Something from behind him caught his attention, a whistling of the wind, and he threw himself to the side and missed losing his head as the agile one swung with his swords, having defeated his own monster.

"Why so agro?" James shouted as he thrust forward with his trident, keeping the swift attacker back.

144

"Shut up and fight!" Screamed the other, but he was forced back by a spurt of fire, just as James made it to his feet.

"How bout we kill the monster then fight?" James asked in a rush.

The agile one, brushed off some flames from his shorts, adding more holes to an already holy garment, before looking at James with hard dark eyes.

"Deal, but only if you team up with me against Codwick," Slayer of the Bay said, James decided to just call him Slayer from that point on.

Considering his predicament and the way this arena was meant to work, James hesitated but in the end he would use whatever advantage he could get.

"Deal," James said, purposely putting his back to the man to see if he'd take the easy shot.

Nothing came and despite James better sense screaming at him not to trust the man, he felt him come up beside him, blades ready. The announcing continued to give a blow by blow of the fight and people jeered when he announced that there 'looks to have been a team up!' But the armored Codwick wasn't doing any better on his side, fighting some kind of mutant gorilla, so Slayer and James had time.

James kept his strikes coming, while the Slayer danced around getting the dragons attention with sharp cuts to its face if it looked away. The wingless dragon, perhaps there was a name for such a creature, but James didn't know it, wasn't doing good. It cried out in pain as another strike to its neck drew forth more of that burning fluid.

Back and forth the melee continued until finally the beast just collapsed under the cheers of the crowd. They were chanting a new name and James stopped to listen for a moment as the announcer acknowledge it.

"It appears the newcomer has made a name for himself already, as he slew a drake in his first match the crowd is chanting his name, James Flameborne! Born of the flames, will he survive long enough to earn the name or will he flame out on his first match? Keep watching for only time will tell!"

Codwick managed to slay the mighty gorilla lizard mutant just as Slayer and James turned to regard him.

"I'll go in fast, you smash his head with that mace," Slayer said, rushing forward. James nodded, if only to himself, and tossed the trident aside. It had done its job and now he needed to focus on opening a can of whoopass.

Cadwick's armor made him a deadly target and Slayer nearly went down to a strike from the massive sword before James even made it over to the battle between giants. Ducking a wide blow, James came in and smashed hard against Codwick's side, denting his armor.

But in an odd turn of events, he had to dodge back as a blade from Slayer came a bit too close and would have hamstrung him.

"Watch it!" James screamed, but the Slayer only smiled and kept on his attack against Codwick. It became clear that if he gave him an opening he'd take it.

A roar filled the arena as more monsters appeared and the three had to cut off their attacks or be taken out.

"Half way there boys," Came an echoing voice from Codwick's helmet. "Let's give them a good show and we all might make it out alive!"

Then he cut a swath with his sword, nearly killing an unexpecting James, meanwhile Slayer dodged it with ease. Keeping his eyes on both of them as they ran toward the new threats, James was careful not to open himself up to an easy attack.

What James had assumed had been three new monsters

turned out to be a three headed hydra standing nearly ten feet tall. It was large but not so big as to make it unkillable, or so James felt.

"Time's nearly up," Slayer said, James barely heard him.

"Kill the beast and we all get a win," Codwick echoed from his helmet.

"Then stop trying to kill me," James said, dodging a casual strike by Slayer.

"Extra points if someone dies, you know how it is, or at least you will," Slayer said, rushing forward to meet the monster.

Together they fought hard, but even after the announcing announced the end of the time limit, the beast fought on. It spit fire, lighting, and a breath so cold that it iced the floor. Each head stayed focused on one of the fighters trying to do it in and James thought for sure they'd entered into a losing fight, when Codwick managed to take one of the heads off with a mighty cut.

Meanwhile, all James had was his mace and though he was getting plenty of hits in, the fiery breath of the hydra made it hard to approach. Meanwhile, Slayer had covered his icy head with several slashes and it was slowing considerably.

It wasn't until Codwick appeared to help James that he realized how ineffective his weapon was against such a foe. Dodging a strike meant for him, it continued on and struck the hydra, drawing blood. Within minutes, where James continued to try and slow it by smashing hard against it with his mace, the beast slowed enough for Codwick to get the killing blow.

That was a sword right through the chest of the beast, not cutting off another of its heads. James was just glad it wasn't like the hydra of mythos that grew more heads when one was cut free. Praise Odin for that luck.

The beast went down hard and right before his eyes it separated into a spray of lights. James kept his guard up, so he saw the strike coming before it was too late.

"Codwick watch out!" James yelled as Slayer stabbed him right through a small opening under the neck. Blood sprayed out and covered the Slayer, just as the announcements started once more.

"Time is up and all monsters have been defeated. Oh looks like Codwick let his guard down a little too soon, if he survives that strike he'll be looking for blood in the next match up. We have two, potentially, three survivors, so if you bet on the house losing, today you win!"

James stood beside Codwick, not offering any help but keeping the Slayer back with his mace raised. The man had proved to be a killer in all aspects of the word and James needed to be careful.

"Drop weapons," came a call from two guards entering the arena. Their voices didn't carry all that well over the cheers and jeers of the crowds, but James threw his weapon aside when they repeated themselves a few seconds later. Slayer did the same, and he smiled all the wider as he turned his back on James and walked for the opening he'd come out of.

"Follow me," One guard said, while the other checked on Codwick. Pulling off his helmet, James wasn't surprised to see lifeless eyes staring out and confirming what he'd feared, the man had died from his wounds.

CHAPTER 19
PHIL

Phil greeted Steffan with a wave and a head nod. He was truly one of them now and Phil had missed most of his training because of the dockside slums quest. It made him feel a bit disconnected from the group, something he didn't want as he was the head of the Order now.

"I've nearly completed my quest," Phil said, lending Steffan a hand up. "Do you still want to follow the path of the Pale Rider?"

"I do," Steffan said without missing a beat.

They'd discussed the paths you could take as an Eldritch Knight, his sister already leaning toward taking the same path as Seph, Phil had hoped to add Steffan to the path of the Pale Riders, but much was lost on how to do such, only a few books giving Phil directions on the best way to walk the path.

One part involved them going into a distant mountain range where they'd encounter a lesser breed of mixana beasts that could be tamed via the green flame within them, giving them a calvary of types that the other orders didn't possess. Or at least Phil knew of no other Orders with such abilities.

"Good," Phil said, taking Steffan under his arm. "We have much to talk about and study and very little time. Tell me, how has your lessons in combat with Seph been? She is a master teacher, that much I know."

"It's been alright," Steffan said, offering very little insight and casting his eyes down.

"Let me guess, she favors teaching your sister or you and it annoys you?" Phil asked, bringing his voice down into a whisper.

Steffan stole a glance toward Seph and Mercy, then shook his head. "I feel like she is ready to challenge a mixana beast, yet Seph holds her back."

"I understand it might be frustrating," Phil said. "But she knows better than even I when someone is ready to face off against the mixana beast. It takes more than strength of arm to fully embrace the green flame, you should know that better than most now, so give her time."

Steffan nodded, but Phil wasn't sure he'd gotten his message through to him or not. But they walked in silence together as a celebration started around them. According to Seph it was tradition to prepare and search the remnants of the mixana beast among the Order, something they'd not had the chance to do when Phil had slain his.

So they partied along side a bigger host of people than Phil thought Seph would have allowed to join the Order. It was something else and Phil made a note to speak to her about it. Even he hadn't guessed that they'd increase their ranks so fast or why she was in such a hurry to train out so many Eldritch Knights.

With the night growing colder and most of the people having slipped off to bed in the many rebuilt buildings around the outside of the Eldritch Keep, Phil sought out Seph to have a much needed conversation with her.

"I'm tired," Seph warned as Phil approached. He'd not gotten a chance to speak with her alone and he had dire news that needed to be passed on.

"I'll try to be quick, but I have news of an Eldritch Knight working in Kothar," Phil said, this caught Seph's attention enough to have her sitting back down and gesturing to a seat beside her in front of the fire.

They were alone and free to speak of heavier matters now, so Phil launched into it. Telling her of his entire adventure and his meeting of the Eldritch Knight who called himself, the Wandering Wraith. Then when she didn't seem to recognize the name he gave her the name that he'd gone by as a member of the Order, Darius Shadowbane.

"Darius yet lives?" Seph said through clenched teeth. "Why is that not surprising."

"What do you know of him?" Phil asked, it was clear that Seph wasn't a fan, but why?

"He stood by my side along with my husband, until the day he ran from the Order all together, the coward. When it appeared that there would be no clear winner, he chose to take his own path," Seph explained. "It wouldn't have mattered, one Flameborne wasn't going to be enough to turn the tide, nor was how I survived any more honorable, but I don't want to get into it."

"Then you think we shouldn't offer him a place amongst us?" Phil asked, he truly wanted to know her mind on the situation before deciding his own, harsh as her opinion might be.

"I would only say that you should not trust him and expect that when events turn dire, he will flee before he will fight to the end at your side," Seph said. "Although," her tone softened as she spoke, "he is likely the last of the Flameborne and he could teach as well as any, though he never achieved the rank of master."

"My mind was going across the same line of thinking," Phil said, smirking a little. "Even if we can't trust him completely, we can learn from him and he can raise up a newer, more loyal generation."

"There are many among us that would be good candidates for Flameborne training," Seph said, nodding her head. "The choice is yours, do you take the risk and trust him or do we leave him out of it entirely?"

Phil thought it over and weighed the cons versus pros before deciding that they couldn't afford not to have him. "I'll reach out to him with an invitation to join us. He seemed eager enough, whether that was a mask like the one he wears now, I can't say, but I'm willing to risk it for the growth of the Order. Speaking of the growth of the Order, we've grown in size considerably. I thought I was going to have to twist your arm to allow Steffan to recruit more people?"

Seph met Phil's gaze and held it for a long moment, before shaking her head as if she was considering telling him something but couldn't decide. "It is enough to say that I know now more than ever that we need to grow and adjust to the times. No longer am I the sole Eldritch Knight, we've a healthy breeding herd of mixana beast that will provide enough flame for dozens to be converted every few weeks, so we might as well take advantage of it. Besides," Seph said, turning her gaze into the flames, "I won't be here forever and we need to start forming a ruling council to advise you. Soon I fear we will see the reaction from the council and we will have to prove ourselves strong if they are ever to accept us back."

"You really think they'll attack?" Phil said, surprised that they hadn't already with how certain Seph had been.

"I'm surprised they didn't attack that very day, it would appear that your old friend Zarrick hasn't shared with them the runes to activate the gate, so distance is our friend right now. It will take them several months to reach us with any kind of force, and I've been ranging our scouts far and wide to keep an eye out for them," Seph said.

"So you truly think they'll take the long way to attack us?" Phil asked himself more than Seph as he considered the size of the force they might send and realized he might have some contacts that could gather information now. "I might have contacts, thanks to the Wandering Wraith, that could look into it."

"I've had my own contacts try and pry information, but so far nothing has been reported," Seph said. "So please do what you can for we will need as much warning as possible if we are to face a true force of combined Orders."

"How many would they send, do you think?" Phil asked, recalling the numbers he'd seen in the council of orders and how many more must be attending to things around the city. Ascended were rare but not so rare that you never saw one, in fact even in the Dockside slums Phil came across one or two, Mick being one of them.

"Much of the ascended are sent to fight in the Peasant Wars, but I imagine they'd be able to field enough to overwhelm our current strength rather easily," Seph said, her gaze still not leaving the fire. "When the time comes, you must fight to the end and do not give in to the temptation to feed off of their power. We must prove we are different."

"It might help me to know how, so I don't stumble upon it in battle," Phil said, but Seph shook her head.

"No," she said. "The secret dies with me if I can help it. Now tell me, how has your fake hand been treating you? I've been working on a prototype to allow you full movement and node access, but without the book on golems, I don't know that I'll ever finish it."

"It works well enough for beating up thugs," Phil said. "But I can feel that I am not as strong as I should be with it missing. Left arm or not, I can't imagine how much more power I could bring to bear if I had both nodes working."

"Then bring me that book, do not stay here long, Adam and perhaps even the fate of the Order rests on retrieving that tome," Seph said.

"I'll leave at first light tomorrow, I'm needed to get Steffan on the right track for being a Pale Rider, then I will go," Phil said, Seph nodded and together they stared into the fire for another several minutes before Seph departed.

CHAPTER 20
JAMES

"A rough fight eh?" Pete asked as James was let into the holding cell with the remaining prisoners in his cell block.

"I made it back didn't I?" James shot back, finding a corner he sat down, wanting to be alone with his thoughts for once.

Pete wasn't having it though, he came on over and sat beside him.

"How many did you kill?" Pete asked, his bright purple eyes seeming to shine in the darkness of the room, whether a trick of the light or not, James noticed it.

"I killed a monster, couldn't do much else, but one man died," James said, his entire body burned from exhaustion and he didn't know how much longer he'd be able to stay awake.

Pete must have noticed, because he sat up and put a hand on his arm. "Rest, friend, I'll watch over you until they call me out for a fight. We get a day or two between fights, rest while you can."

James didn't trust Pete, though he couldn't say why, but Slayers actions had put him on edge and he didn't want to trust anyone, much less someone while he slept. But he had little choice. His body was shutting down, so he looked up to the dirty blonde haired man and peered into his eyes.

Something there comforted him, it was impossible to tell a man's character by a look, but James was sure now that this was a good man, he didn't know how, but it allowed him to slip off into a deep sleep moments later.

Time slipped away as he went into the blackness of his dreams. He dreamt of a black dragon consuming him with flames as black as night, all consuming and powerful. Just as it seemed like the darkness was going to be too much and over-take his very being, a green light pierced the darkness and he saw the face of an old friend. Why Phil was visiting him in his dreams, he did not know, but he felt at peace thinking of his friend and wondering where he'd gotten off to.

So much so that by the time he awoke all he could do was think about his friend and how he needed to escape and find him. Pete sat where he'd been the entire time like a marble statue, unmoving and stiff.

"How do we get out of here?" James asked, his voice hoarse. He cleared his throat and tried again, but Pete held up a hand to forestall him.

"You have to win," Pete said. "Win enough and you'll be set free, crimes paid for."

"How close are you?" James asked, Pete grinned down at him.

"I've got a few more fights left in me, they won't take me down so easily," Pete said. "In fact I think I can make you stronger too, if you are open to it."

Pete was whispering by this point and James leaned in to continue the conversation. "How?"

"You've strength enough to be ascended, and I just so

happen to be someone in a position to do that for you," Pete said, his smirk returning.

James had no idea what that meant and his face must have given it away because Pete looked shocked, leaning in closer when he next spoke.

"Where are you from to not know of Ascension?" Pete asked. "Never mind, it doesn't matter. We are short on time and you'll need rest afterwards. This will only take a moment, but it is dangerous, far more so in our current condition, but it will make you far more stronger than you could imagine. I won't be able to share the duality inside of me with you, lest it kill you before you can kill the right beast, but ascension alone will bring you to a level of power unmatched in this arena."

"Do it," James said, meeting Pete's eyes. This sounded a hell of a lot like magic and if this would unlock his ability to do magic, then this quest just became worth it.

Perhaps this was just the game's logical system way of getting him access to magic and abilities, through a side arena quest. A bit of his spirits returned as he thought about it that way, but Pete's next words gave him pause.

"You mustn't scream out, or the guards will come, but the pain will be great," he said, raising his hands as they started to glow.

Pain unlike anything he'd felt before, deep and visceral hit him, but he kept his mouth clenched shut. His body was lifted off the ground just a tiny bit, but he couldn't really notice it over the pain. Several of his teeth crumbled under the force of his clenched jaw, but the pain was nothing compared to what was happening within his chest.

He blacked out before screaming, thanking the gods above that he'd been able to withstand the pain without letting out a cry.

He woke an undetermined time later with Pete over him, pressing a rag against his forehead. He felt different, stronger, his lungs filled with air easier than before, his sight felt enhanced in a way unlike anything he'd ever experienced before. He felt like he could pluck a strand of hair from the air and tie it in a knot, before it realized it was disturbed.

"Level up complete," James muttered, sitting up and having to stand a moment later because he was practically bursting with power.

"You survived!" Pete said, his voice a bit louder than he meant and his hand went to his face. "You are the first one that has survived the process, I was beginning to wonder if I was doing it wrong." His voice returning to the whispered tone as he spoke.

"Risk and reward," James said, cracking his neck to the side and feeling more powerful than he could ever recall.

What was more he could feel something inside of himself and he closed his eyes to focus on it. There was a core of power thrumming inside of him, feeding his new strength.

"I've got a ton to teach you and very little time," Pete said, but just then two guards entered and pointed at Pete and James.

"You two are up for a duos match," the guard said.

When they didn't immediately stand, pain lanced through them both from the bracelets. It was a familiar pain, but nothing compared to what he'd just experienced. Beside, even that it didn't seem to hit with the same gusto as before.

Still he groaned and showed mock pain, similar to how Pete did beside him. Then standing, they walked over to the cell door to be led to yet another fight.

"Duos mean we don't have to kill each other, so I'll watch

your back and you watch mine," Pete said, whispering and getting a look from one of the guards for his trouble.

James nodded, wondering what it was that Pete had wanted to teach him and hadn't gotten a chance to do.

The fight was much the same as before, except that there were three teams of two. Slayer made it back out into the field and James set his sights on taking the killer out if opportunity showed itself. A real dragon, with wings this time, appeared before Pete and James, but something was different from before.

This time James could sense something about it, something immaterial.

"You can sense that it's just an advanced illusion, can't you?" Pete said, speaking loud and clear, but even so he was barely audible over the roar of the crowd.

"It sure hurts for an illusion," James said, readying his spear that he'd brought with him, sword at his waist along with a mace hanging on the other side. He'd opted for the same chest plate as before, seeing as it had served him well.

"The most advanced illusions are barely indistinguishable over the real thing," Pete said. "They employ some high level mages to do such tricks, but do not assume they are harmless. They will kill you the same as the real thing. Try to hold back and not kill it in a single strike, lest they figure out what we truly are and pair us against harder foes."

"What?" James asked, but Pete was already off, wielding a long spear and leather armor over as much of his body as he could fit. He'd spent so much time on the armor and picked the weakest of the materials, that James wondered what the deal with it was, but he'd learn that secret soon enough.

Running after Pete, James found himself almost too fast for his feet, and he stumbled and fell. He'd expected a certain amount of higher speed, but that was ridiculous. He'd need to limit himself to a jog or find more time to train his new body.

Jogging forward, he had to slow even more when he caught up with a grinning Pete.

"Easy now, just half speed," Pete warned and James finally took the hint, slowing even more.

With everything moving at what seemed like half speed to him already, it was easy for him to take things at half speed, slowly pulling out his weapon and swinging it for the dragon.

Still it moved with incredible speed and sliced easily into the dragon's hide. Such was the power of his blow that he had trouble pulling back in time to avoid a blast of fire. It took his arm in full and he rolled out of the fire a moment later. The damage had been done, or rather it should have been done, looking down he saw no blisters or damage from the intense heat. Just red flesh that was slowly healing to normal color.

That is when he realized why Pete would cover himself so fully with armor, to hide the healing. No normal person would heal like this, this was freaking magic!

"I'm healing!" James shouted toward Pete, but Pete just lunged forward, slicing at the dragon while moving incredibly slow. It was all an act, James knew that now. He could play alongside Pete and they'd come out ahead no problem!

Sure enough, minutes later, they felled the dragon only to be attacked by Slayer and his partner, whose name James hadn't recalled when it had been announced. The fight lasted mere seconds before a new beast appeared and the duos broke off to face it.

At no point during the fight did James feel threatened by the weaker Slayer anymore. He just moved with a slow pace that James could easily match now. The fight ended with one team being eliminated and all the monsters cleared. It was incredible and James couldn't believe his new power.

The moment they returned to the cells, he turned to Pete and asked the question he'd been wanting to ask since the fight started.

"What was it you wanted to teach me?" James asked.

"We need to talk about preparing your pathways so we can make you even stronger," Pete said nonchalantly.

"I'm ready," James answered.

CHAPTER 21
PHIL

Phil left the Eldritch Keep early two days later, though he wished with all his heart he could stay and continue his training with Steffan. The boy had a bright future ahead of him as a wielder of the green flame. But there was work to be done and he had to do it. So he left in the early warmth of the morning, making his way through the forest toward the tree folk's city and the gate to take him back to Kothar city.

Again he didn't see any treefolk, not even Perilill came out to see him, something that left him feeling strangely sad. He'd grown close to her and he almost went to the great tree to see if she would speak with him, but thought better of it. They had their duties and he had his, it would be best to not let those wires cross.

The journey back to the dockside slums took most of the day, but he made it back to the hideout and went to his room only to find someone snoozing on his bed in a sitting position, clearly they'd been waiting for him and dozed off. Phil realized who it was only moments later and cleared his throat.

Leon startled awake and looked about frantically for just a

second before regaining his composure. "Boss needs to see you immediately," Leon said between a yawn. "I've been waiting for the better part of two days for you to return, boring as hell."

"What does he want?" Phil asked, he obviously meant the Wandering Wraith and not whoever their boss was meant to be in this particular gang. Leon was just as much a spy to this gang as was Phil, but neither of them had much need to worry. Whoever the leader of this gang truly was, whether it was Withers or not, Phil would stand before him and tear him down.

"Has news for you that can't, well couldn't wait, it has waited a good bit now and it's probably going to be my ass on the line for it," Leon said, sounding more bored than worried.

"I'll go meet him now," Phil said, turning to leave when suddenly Nathan appeared in the doorway.

"Where yous been?" Nathan asked, a hostile look on his face. "No matters," he said before Phil could even come up with something to say, "my boss wants to meet with yous about a job. Mighty impressed from the last one."

"Can't right now, I gotta run an errand," Phil said, sure that he'd get closer to his goal of contacting the Wandering Wraith, then he would keep this ruse up.

"We insist," came a voice from behind Nathan as two burly men appeared behind him.

Phil could take them out, he knew it, but then his cover would be blown and any hope of finding information would be blown with it.

"Fine," Phil said after a long pause. "But if I don't like what I hear, I'm punching my way out."

This got both of the strongmen to shift their weight around as if getting ready for a fight, but Phil kept his posture relaxed, ready to lash out death at a moments notice.

"He's just kidding, les go," Nathan said, gesturing over his shoulder as he turned and walked through the middle of the two thugs. Leon stayed in Phil's quarters giving Phil a look that said, 'hurry it up', before Phil left after them.

Phil followed him, not at all caring that he was putting his back to the two weaklings. Nathan led him out of the complex they were in and down a few streets to a run down building that looked like it was about to fall apart. Phil had seen it before but assumed it was abandoned. They didn't go to the front, instead going into a narrow side alley and knocking on a side door.

Nathan leaned in and whispered words that Phil didn't catch, and the sound of several latches being thrown filled the alley before the door swung open. A man with a crossbow stepped out, looked at all present and waved them inside.

The moment they stepped inside Phil knew that the outside was just a front. The inside smelled better than anything he'd encountered by the dockside. It was clean and despite muddy prints left by them in the main room, it was spotless.

"Clean your boots," the crossbow man said, holding it ready and pointing in Phil's direction.

There was a basin low to the ground and some kind of real life plumbing attached to a hose. Phil watched in amazement as they sprayed their boots clean, then taking a turn himself he realized the water was even warm. This new world never ceased to amaze him in the luxuries they had randomly when the rest of their technology seemed so archaic.

Having them all cleaned and dried, the crossbow man led them into a waiting room where only Phil was invited to sit and the others left. Phil didn't like waiting, but he waited for a solid five minutes before getting up and looking around the room, his curiosity getting the better of him.

It was a study of sorts, with a desk, bookshelves, and random items strewn about on pedestals. He thumbed through several books, but none of them were what he was looking for. A few had to do with runic formations though and he left them out a bit, trying to decide if they'd be worth stealing later.

An elderly man wearing flowing blue robes entered while Phil was putting a book down and he stared at him. This man looked exactly like what you'd think a wizard in old earth lore would look like, minus the pointing hat. Except, then he pulled out a pointy hat and put it on his head, finishing the look. He held a massive tome in his left hand, barely able to hold it up in his spindly arms.

There was a blazing blue light in his eyes that Phil knew immediately meant he was ascended and likely of the Mage Order.

"You've caught the attention of several members of the Tor'I," the elderly man said. "I'm Wither, the leader of the faction you are seeking to infiltrate. Tell me, Eldritch Knight, why do you meddle in my affairs?"

Green flames leapt up around Phil and he almost called on his amulet for the armor it contained within it, but hesitated as Wither showed no offensive moves just yet.

When Phil spoke it was with the power and authority of the green flame feeding his words. "You've taken something that I require. Give it to me and you might yet live."

"Bold words," Wither said, heaving up the large book with both hands and opening it. "What tome have I that you require? Perhaps a deal can be struck?"

"I've struck a deal with your kind before, I'm not interested in doing so again," Phil shot back, flames forming around his right arm into a concentrated ball.

Suddenly there were dozens of Withers and brutes appearing all around, Phil tensed but didn't attack yet. One of the Withers spoke next, but it was hard to tell which one was doing it.

"I am a master of my Order, do you dare threaten me? Put away your flames and let us speak like civilized beings," Wither said.

Phil let the flames burn bright around him. His heart was racing and he knew that if he let his guard down now he might not be fast enough to deal with whatever tricks his foe might have up his sleeve. But then again, he had the amulet and that gave him an edge that this Withers couldn't count on. He let the flames die out and looked at Withers directly as his illusions began to disappear as well, one by one.

"Who are the Tor'I?" Phil asked, this was the first he'd heard of the term and his curiosity got the better of him.

"You can be," Withers said, smirking. "The Tor'I is the name of the group of Ascended that have been cast out by the official Council of Orders. We work in shadows to accumulate power and build our own smaller Orders of non-ascended. You call them gangs I'm sure, but they are ours, some see them as family, pawns, or tools to be used, but they are ours none-theless."

"But you fight amongst yourselves, the gangs do at least," Phil said, not understanding Wither's explanation.

"Oh sure," Wither said. "We squabble over land and goods, but the Tor'I never fight each other. To do so would be foolish, as each holds vast power that could destroy all we've worked to build."

"I don't want to be a Tor'I," Phil said flatly. "I'm here to get a single book and then leave you in peace."

"Tell me," Withers said. "Is this book about the creations of golems? Written by that weasel Zarrick?"

This was a surprise to Phil, he hadn't known Zarrick had been the author, but it made sense. Though why he'd let the book out of his personal care was another thing entirely. What was Zarrick up to, Phil wondered.

"It is," Phil said, biting the inside of his mouth as he let out a breath of frustrated air.

"Then a simple task I have for you and the tome is yours," Withers said. "You can avoid bloodshed and further unstabilizing the balance the Tor'I have over the dockside. Just do us one tiny favor."

For a long moment Phil didn't answer, so tempted to just cut this man down and search out the rest of the library for the book he needed. But he knew that there was no telling where it could be hidden or what protective measures might be employed around it. No. He would have to play the games of these damned Tor'I.

"What task did you have in mind?" Phil asked.

"I need you to steal a soul stone from Zarrick's Tower," Wither said, rubbing his hands together as he spoke.

CHAPTER 22
JAMES

Several weeks had passed and James had won countless fights. Both he and Pete had grown to be fast friends, his gift to him meaning more than he could express. He'd learned to control his new powers, letting it ebb and flow to increase his strength and decrease it at will. Most of the time he kept it low, not wanting to accidentally show off too much power, but he was becoming adept at funneling power into just his strikes when needed.

"I'm pretty sure we've both only have one fight remaining," Pete said. "Probably why they haven't put us out for the last few days."

"You think they're trying to figure out a way to kill us?" James asked, they talked casually now, not worried of being overheard by the rooms of only three other residents. All who'd been there but Pete had died now, but James and Pete hadn't even come close to death with their hidden powers.

"After the last duels they put us through, six combatants all coming for us along with those monsters? I'd say so," Pete said, shaking his head.

"Why don't we just overpower the guards and leave?" James asked for the dozenth time.

"No way to get these bracelets off, even if we knock them clean out, someone will trigger it and the distance is immense," Pete said. "Best to play their game and just finish out the sentence."

"Tell me more about your Order and how cool the magic is going to be once I get it?" James said, lowering his voice a measure.

Pete matched his volume and smiled as he spoke. "I'm technically a priest, but it isn't what it sounds like. We serve the duality, most of us lean toward one side or another, but I'm pretty balanced. I imagine with you, you'll take on the more destructive side of it but it'll be epic to watch."

Magic, true magic, Pete had told him all about it. There were several Orders and he could technically be a candidate for any of them if he wanted, but he'd decided he'd like to stick around Pete. It wasn't everyday that James felt so close to someone, and there was a lot to like about Pete.

He was an amazing fighter for one, priest or not, the man knew his way around weapons. Then there was his willingness to do just about anything for his friends, James had been saved more than once by his quick reactions and he couldn't ignore that.

"Guards are coming," James said, he heard their footsteps now from a ways off, his hearing having been improved several fold.

"Time for your final fights," the guard said, sneering out the words. "You and you, let's go."

James and Pete stood, neither able to hold back their excitement from what would obviously be an attempt to bring them down before the end. They were shown to the same room as always and James got his weapons and armor on, the same chest plate that had done so well for him, leaving his arms bare. While Pete went ahead and covered himself in leather, James helped where he could, before they both picked out their weapons.

James went with a dagger, sword, and spear. He'd found that with his new strength even a sword would do decent damage to armored foes, hitting with all the force of a mace and cutting on top of that. Pete picked out a spear, leaving all the other weapons alone, much as he did most fights.

"Let's make it a good show," Pete said, smiling wide. "Whatever they send at us, promise me you'll survive."

"I promise," James said, then smiling back at his friend he added, "You too, alright."

Pete just grinned wider but said nothing, a look in his eyes caught James off guard, but he didn't dwell on it, instead rolling his shoulders and getting ready to fight.

The announcer could be heard over the crowds cheering as the two entered the arena side by side.

"We have an exciting match up in the likes we haven't seen in years. Two contestants, you know their names well, are participating in their final bout. But let's not waste words! Let the fight begin!"

James and Pete looked out over the field and no other contestants appeared. While they waited and looked around, the crowd went absolutely nuts, monsters began to appear.

"Round One begins!"

"Round one?" James asked, sparring a quick glance at Pete. "How many rounds are they adding into our final fight?"

"Hold back until you need to use your full power, they'll try to kill us but we will show them we won't go down!" Pete shouted over the sound of the crowd.

Together they ran into battle, weapons ready to take on any foe.

James focused in on a group of thin white skinned elven dudes, each of them looking more wraith than humanoid with how they went invisible randomly in different spots on their bodies. Slashing out with his spear, his attack passed right through the first one but hit the second, sending it screaming backwards into two more.

He dodged a ball of white fire as Pete entered combat with two massive cats, each one moving fast enough that he'd have to dip into his speed for sure. None of these foes were ones that a normal duo would have a chance at defeating, yet James and Pete fought with the strength of several men.

It was a funny feeling, pushing himself to his limits and surpassing them so easily by redirecting the flow of his power within. Never before could he have reacted so fast, or struck so hard, but they were going down, wraiths or not, from his blows, so he fought onward. The crowd was cheering so loudly that it hurt James' enhanced ears, never had the crowd been so large.

Dodging more white flame, the remaining wraiths pushed their advantage, seeming to shift and grow slightly larger as they did. Up ahead James stole a glance at the announcer as he went on and on, then he saw the mages that Pete said were likely in charge of summoning the illusions, there were a few extra today. His vision, as sharp as it was, saw them clenching their foreheads in concentration even from a distance.

They wanted to kill them so bad, but James wouldn't go down without a good fight. More monsters began to appear, just as the final wraith was struck down. Winged nude females with clawed hands and feet, harpies, if James had to guess, flew down to attack.

Using his spear he struck at the nearest feet, blocking its blow, but the others came in too quick and scored cutting blows on his arms. He cut off the flow of magic that would instantly heal it, wanting to keep up appearances by bleeding enough that it could hide the wounds. It was a trick he'd picked up after several bouts where he'd get cut and need to be careful he didn't heal in plain view of everyone.

His arms healed seconds later, but the concentration cost him and he took several more strikes to his face and one blow glanced off his chest armor. He struck out and ran back to give himself some distance as the next wave of harpies came. Then jumping with his increased strength, he took to the air and speared one through the chest.

It wasn't a move that would hide what he was, but he was getting tired and the damn harpies were hard to hit. As he fell to the ground the harpy beneath him blunting his fall, he swung just in time with his sword to cut the feet off another. That still left nearly a dozen others, swooping in and giving him cut after cut.

Pete wasn't doing much better, his armor was in tatters as he fought four giant spiders off at once. Deciding that they'd fight better together, James ran for him.

"Mind if I join you?" James asked in a shout as he slashed through a spider's leg and followed up with a swirling strike to keep a nearby harpy at bay.

"Bringing your own trouble, eh?" Pete said, he was hardly breaking a sweat still, but James could tell he was nearing his own limit of strength he could employ.

"Seems like they really want us dead," James said, slashing out and bringing another pair of harpy feet down to the ground.

"Looks that way," Pete said back, laughing as he did. "Let's disappoint them."

James laughed back, letting his full power finally surge through him, he saw clearly that he was indeed a match for these harpies. He jumped and cut the head off one, while arching downward he caught another in the chest. The crowd went nuts and the announcers said words that ran James blood cold.

"There is no way I'm seeing what I'm seeing! These two are fighting with the power of an Ascended, never before in the judgement arena have we had Ascended fighting for their lives!"

"Secrets out?" James panted the question as he ran back up to Pete.

"Seems that way," Pete said, cracking his neck to the side he did something James had never seen him do before, he used magic. "Might as well show them my true strength."

"Tendrils of black and white snaked around him and shot out at all the spiders at once. Then his body went a translucent purple and he shot out black tendrils at each of the flying harpies, destroying them in sprays of light within moments.

"Holy hell," James said. "I want that power so bad!"

"You shall have it," Pete said, his voice seeming to echo ethereally as he spoke now. "Let's win our freedom and together we will make our mark on this world."

James thought back to his long conversations with Pete, how he was only an initiate of his Order and had been caught with a noble's daughter. He hadn't revealed his true self because he didn't want to shame his Order or lose his position, so he'd allowed them to take him in as a common prisoner. He had so many plans and wanted so much out of life, it was just what James was looking for, a direction to take his life.

With Pete at his side they'd conquer the world if they wanted.

"Round Two Begins!"

More monsters, then waves of illusory prisoners, it was clear the mages were trying to hit them with foes as strong as they could make, but Pete and James ripped through them with ease. The first round seemed to be the strongest they could make them, now they focused on overwhelming odds. Until finally when that failed a final announcement went up.

"The Third and Final round will begin shortly! This will be a one on one fight to the death. Whoever is left standing below will be released, becoming the first one to earn their freedom in several years. Good luck and fight hard!"

James barely heard the words at first, their meaning not sinking in. Pete looked at him, a look of surprise on his face as James kept laughing. Then like a bolt of lightning it hit him and he heard what the announcer had said.

"Pete, what do we do now?" James asked, turning to his friend, unsure what to do.

"We do what we've been doing this entire time," Pete said, his voice hollow sounding. "We fight."

James jumped back from his friend, confused at his sudden tensing muscles as threads of darkness swept out for James, much slower than he'd seen him capable of before. Knocking one of them aside that came too close, he nearly lost his spear in the process.

Pete was just a non-player character, an NPC, so why did James feel so horrible inside at the thought of killing him. It went back to the problem he'd been having as he got to know any of the people here, they felt so damned real. James had been ready to start a life with this man, two best buds against the world, NPC or not. How could Pete turn on him so easily, striking out as if without a care?

"Pete," James called out, but Pete remained quiet as strand after strand closed in and attacked.

James flooded his body with power, focusing on speed as he lashed away each of them, Pete attacking faster and faster. When he finally saw an opening, he failed to take it, instead he rushed forward, taking hit after hit to get closer to his friend.

"There has to be another way!" He shouted, and cut down another tendril of darkness. "Together we can get out of here."

The tendrils stopped and Pete hung his head. "You heard them, only one of us escaped alive. Strike me down, but make it look good or they'll find a way to screw you too! Live the life you've always wanted, find the adventure you talked about so much!"

Tears poured down Pete's face as it went dark again and tendrils came for James faster than before, cutting and stabbing him. James ignored the pain, blocking one in three strikes, but moving ever closer.

He was real, James told himself, he was real, this is not some stupid game anymore. There had to be another way, he had to find another way.

His thoughts blurred as he was forced to go fully into combat to protect himself. He let his thoughts blur to nothing and he just fought to live, the same as Pete. So when his blade pierced his friend's heart, he was almost as surprised as Pete seemed to be. Blood pouring out his mouth, Pete smiled and locked eyes with James.

"Thank you," Pete managed to say between coughs.

James pulled free his spear and grabbed hold of his friend's body as the light left his eyes, never looking away, making sure the last thing he saw was his friend. Because in death sometimes all you can ask for is going out with a friend nearby.

"I'll live for you and I'll pull these bastards down if it is the last thing I do," James said, his words barely above a whisper.

Kneeling over the corpse of his dead friend, he closed the man's eyes and said a prayer to Odin that he be received into the halls of Valhalla. Pete had been real to him and his new found conviction was real. James had a purpose now and he'd see it done, he was going to pull down the government that allowed such brutality to exist. He would become the strongest there ever was and with the pain of his loss he'd tear it all down.

As he stood and took note of each of the Wizards' faces and that of everyone in the box, he marked his first victims for death.

"We have a victor! James Flameborne has earned his freedom!"

The crowd went wild, but all James could hear was the last words of his friend. He would kill them all, everyone in that box would die, then the government would burn.

Guards came out and escorted him away from the arena, his bracelets were taken off and he was left in another cell, alone. With his strength he knew he could shatter the bars and be done with this place now, but he waited. Someone was approaching and trying to be sneaky about it.

"I can hear you," James said, then suddenly a short man appeared before him, looking surprised.

"By the nine hells, you are impressive," he said. "Names Golder and I've got a proposition for you."

"I'm listening," James said.

"How'd you like the power to crush your enemies?" Golder asked, a sly smile on his stout face.

"I'd like that very much, what Order are you from?" James

asked, realizing that this must be a recruitment offer of some kind. Pete had said that others would be interested in him, seeing as he was expectational even for an Ascended. He hadn't really believed it, but looking back he was sure Pete was fighting at his full strength and still James had taken him down.

"No matter what Order I be a part of, what matters is the power I'm offering you will be unique. You will be the first in millennia to hold this power, if you want it bad enough," Golder said, pausing as James finally looked back up at the stout man in leathers.

"A unique magic stronger than the rest?" James asked, it looked like Haven was finally going to start paying off for him. When he stopped thinking of it as a game, then all of this appeared for him, how nice...

"It could be argued that is the case, are you interested or not?" Golder said.

"I'm interested," James said. "What is the Order called?"

"The Order of the Black Dragon," Golder said, his face gone stoic suddenly. "A power to rival even the gods."

CHAPTER 23
PHIL/STEFFAN

Phil reeled back as he heard the words Wither spoke. Infiltrate Zarrick's tower? That had to be impossible, if nothing else it was most certainly a way to find death. He'd have to just give his best to kill this mage and hope he could find the book somehow. Perhaps with the Wandering Wraiths help it would be possible.

Just as Phil turned inward to call his green flame out to aid him, Wither spoke once more.

"He'll be gone along with his mercenary Golder for some time, my intel is good and I've a plan to get us in and out undetected," Wither said.

"Us?" Phil asked.

"Well, you and that traitor Darius, the pair of you are well equipped enough to get in and out on my instructions," Wither said, looking around Phil at his bookshelf. "I've got some notes around here that will help you, just let me find them."

If Zarrick was truly away from his tower and it would be a simple matter of smash and grab while he was away, then maybe Phil could pull it off after all. He didn't like the idea of going toe to toe with Golder and something told him that Zarrick would be even worse.

"Alright," Phil said, relaxing his grip on his green flame. "I'm in. Tell me how we are going to do it."

Wither spent the next hour going over the location and the security measures of the tower, saying he'd have to come to the threshold but once they were in the security shouldn't be so bad. Zarrick was said to be paranoid, but he also rarely left his tower, so he had decent protections outside of it, but not within. This was all conjecture of course, a fact Wither made sure Phil understood. But it was what it was and Phil was willing to give it a try on his word that Zarrick wouldn't be there.

They made a bargain that one soul stone would be exchanged for one copy of the book that Withers had in his possession. Contracts meant little to Phil at this point, but he signed and agreed as he'd done before with Zarrick. Wither explained that they were magically binding up to a point, where breaking one would give the bearer of the contract the ability to siphon a great deal of power if they wished in repayment.

This was power that would come back, but if used correctly it could be leveraged to take down a weakened foe, something he hadn't realized when signing with Zarrick. That meant Zarrick had a power over him if he ever wanted to call on it, the ability to weaken him back to his normal human state for a period of time.

There was so much about Haven and its magic that Phil didn't understand, but he was learning. Getting this book would be the first step to getting his friend back and he could not fail. For failure meant losing Adam for good and he couldn't bear the thought of leaving Adam to the true death that he feared so much. Seph better keep his soul safe while Phil was away, or there would be hell to pay no matter who caused his loss.

Phil left after a time, with written instructions of what he was to do and with a copy of the contract that should give him leverage to make sure Withers stayed to the contract they'd agreed upon. It was odd, Withers kept looking at a space on the shelf and Phil wondered if the book was located there. He'd almost even asked, but decided that now that he'd already signed the contract it wouldn't be wise to show his hand.

The streets were as muddy and smelly as always as Phil took to the street, heading for the nicer part of town, near the edge where Darius lived. Upon reaching the house, he knocked as Leon had shown him and was let in by the well dressed elderly man.

"Withers is aware of my spy and you," Darius said the moment Phil walked into the study.

"I know," Phil said, pulling out the plans to rob Zarrick and tossing them over.

Before opening them Darius just looked at Phil for a long moment. "And you killed him?" He asked, raising an eyebrow.

"Not yet," Phil said, smiling and sitting down. "I could use a cold drink, what do you have?"

Darius didn't answer as he'd opened the plans and realized what they meant, his eyes going as wide as saucers. "He can't be serious," he said flatly.

"As the plague," Phil said. "About that drink?"

"Oh yes," Darius said, snapping his fingers. His servant arrived with a tall glass and Phil took it, drinking it in without a thought.

"Thank you," Phil said. "So you willing to help me rip off one of the most powerful Ascended there is?"

"You don't do things in half measures, that is for damn sure," Darius said. Then waiting for a moment as he scratched at his chin, he added. "But I was serious about my commitment. If this is the path you wish to lead me as an Eldritch Knight, and you are willing to accept me back, then I am in."

"Do this for me," Phil said. "And you're in."

Steffan heard the screams first, but he felt the heat of fire next. All around him blazed fire and smoke. He held out his hands and connected with the flames, turning them green and squelching them out. His hut was only two away from his sisters and he thought he recognized that scream.

The moment he got out of his half burn hut, he was met with a flash of golden flames, which he blocked expertly with green flame, then a tendril of black slashed at his face, drawing blood and giving him a wound that didn't immediately close.

The Orders had arrived with their forces much earlier than Seph had anticipated; what was more, they'd gotten through her web of scouts.

Steffan counted at least four others, two in golden armor, two in robes of white and black, and two wearing black leathers slipping into and out of shadows as they cut people down. So many of the half ascended had fallen, he saw the bodies of at least a dozen, some moving, most not.

"Mercy!" Steffan screamed his flames billowing around him and striking at the closest that dared get close to him.

Then suddenly he was their main focus, two of the rogue-like ones came in from nowhere and slashed at him, but he brought up his sword infusing it with flame and blocked their strikes expertly. Then with a grunt he burst flame all around him, forcing them to get back or be burnt up.

"Brother!" Came a scream from behind him and Steffan turned to see Seph and Mercy appear from a burning building, completely whole and safe.

"You've made a grave mistake," Seph's words somehow echoed above the din of battle. "To challenge us on our own lands. To bring so few and to kill those who are no more than initiates!"

Each word grew in power as green flame swirled around her. But just when Steffan thought she was going to attack, the herd of Mixana beast came out of nowhere, slamming into the force of eight, taking one unlucky paladin down and trampling him.

"Mixana will see us safe!" Seph screamed, throwing her flames into the mess of beasts and striking one intruder after another. One of the rogue types screamed and went down in a flaming heap, but the others defended, dodging and calling out with their power despite the impossibility of it all.

Steffan stood in horror watching the scene unfold, ready to strike down any that survived, but Seph wasn't looking to take any prisoners and her power was a terrible force that he'd not yet seen in its fullest form. She struck out here and there, flames taking forms of beasts themselves and ripping into unsuspecting armored figures.

One of the figures, covered in green flame burst from the crowd and Steffan stepped up ready to do his part. Several more of the half ascended, and more of the fully ascended that had yet to get their green flame began to circle, ready to fight back the invaders.

The green flames fizzled out as the robed figure burst into

black and white lights, tendrils of power shooting out from him.

"You will not defeat me so easily!" He shouted, but he was surrounded, what could he do now?

It turns out, quite a bit. Seph stayed focused on her task of taking down each of the others, while Mercy watched her back, spear in hand and her focus never wavering. Steffan knew what he needed to do, his flame would be enough and he'd show this intruder his power.

"Face me!" Steffan yelled as another half ascended went down from a tendril of power. "You will face me!"

A spurt of green flame caught the man's attention, obviously a priest with his dual natures, bringing him up short as he tried to kill another of Steffan's family and friends.

No longer was Steffan alone and only needing to care for his sister, no! He would stand with all the other Eldritch Knights and he would protect them!

"You will die, child," the man's voice said, and his entire form turned a dark translucent purple as the light seemed to fade around him. "I am a master of the shadow form, you can't hope to best me."

"I will extinguish your darkness with my light!" Steffan yelled, throwing all he had into a double handed fire attack. Shadowy tendrils raised before the man and protected his face. But Steffan didn't relent, allowing his power to flow as he'd been taught, calling upon all the power he could.

Before he was completely exhausted he cut the flames off and readied his weapon, a sword sheathed in green flames. He was already moving forward with blinding speed as the smoke cleared, cutting through several tendrils as they attempted to lash out at him. But as he reached the priest, a burst of dark power hit him and sent him off his feet.

His brethren took that chance to attack, using normal weapons untouched by the green flame. They cut and hacked as Steffan struggled to rise, the blow had left a bloody gash on his chest that wasn't healing. His vision blurred and his mouth went dry, but he forced himself to his feet. He wouldn't allow anyone more to die because of his weakness, no one would stand against him.

With renewed vigor he ran forward, flames wreathing his entire body as he cut and punched his way through the tendrils of black and purple light.

The others made room when he approached, another one having gone down but the others dragged him away still breathing. This was the end, Steffan felt it, he'd reached his limit and he had to put an end to this fight now or risk dying.

Slashing in the patterns taught to him by Phil and reinforced by Seph, he saw a way forward, a small opening and took it! His blade sunk into the chest of the priest, a look of utter surprise on his face as his tendrils went limp before disappearing all around him. Green flame flared in the wound and Steffan was certain he'd hit his heart, so he pushed green flame in and burnt it to a crisp.

Fire flared out of the priest's eyes, still a look of confused frustration on his face as he died.

"Well done," Seph said, running up to him, having finished her work on the remaining attackers. "One got away, but you did well, Knight."

Steffan looked at her with surprise. Had she truly just raised him from Apprentice all the way to Knight? That skipped the apprentice rank altogether, surely she didn't mean to say he had the strength of a true Eldritch Knight?

"You've earned it," Seph said, when Steffan didn't immediately respond. "To be a Knight you must do as you've done.

Stand before impossible odds and come out on top. It is remarkable that you have such potential and none of the other Orders picked you up. That goes for all of you." Seph said, raising her voice. "You've proved today that each of you have what it takes to be Knights of the Eldritch Order if you so wish. It is not an easy role to play, but we will carve out a life for ourselves."

Steffan bowed his head to Seph, she was so much more of a leader than Phil was right now, being as absent as he'd been. He wanted nothing more than to kneel before Seph and swear his allegiance to her alone, but he knew from his learnings that wasn't the way of the Eldritch Knights.

He was proud of his people, glad to have found someone that could see their true potential and use them in a way that made him feel grateful. He knew that the others felt likewise just by looking at their faces. They would fight, as some had, to the death to keep this new life that they'd found. No more starving and fighting for each scrap of food. No, instead they'd fight for a place in this world, and that was a fight they could all get behind.

"We are proud to serve you," Steffan finally said, unable to restrain himself.

"You serve the Order, not me," Seph said, her words sharper than Steffan would have expected, but he bowed his head in acknowledgement. "But you are young, Knight, you will learn in time. I think it is time to bring a few more into the fold, Mercy included. If she is as talented with the spear as she is with the flame, then you will have a new rival."

Mercy perked up at Seph side at that point, looking hopeful but also scared. "Are you sure I'm ready?" She asked.

"I'm more than sure, child," Seph said, her voice softening.

"Now let's clear out these bodies and prepare our fallen for cremation by the Green Flame."

CHAPTER 24
PHIL

Phil made it out in one piece, and Withers didn't try to break the contract. He immediately left to visit Darius and see what the urgent news was that Leon had called him for. He was let into the nice home moments after arriving and sat in the study, waiting for Darius to appear.

"Withers knows about you or us I should say," Darius said the moment he arrived, wearing a formal suit and looking haggard. "I wish I had a better way of contacting you, leaving Leon to fetch you wasn't ideal."

"I know," Phil said simply.

"You know? So you have a better method of contacting you then? Because if you do, I'd really love to hear it."

"No, I know that Withers knows about me because I've just finished meeting with him," Phil corrected.

"Oh shit, did you kill him?" Daruis asked, looking utterly surprised in the moment.

"Worse," Phil said, making a deadpan face. "I signed a contract with him."

"You didn't," Darius said, letting out an exaggerated sigh as he spoke. "It would've been better if you had killed him off and we dealt with the fall out of that, than you signing a contract with one of those weasel mages."

"It'll be fine, I think we can handle the job, if you're still interested in being an Eldritch Knight under my leadership," Phil said, watching Darius for any sign that he was not ready to make that leap.

"Great," Darius said, laughing. "Of course I'm ready, let's go do whatever impossible feat he's requested of you. I hope you are getting something equally amazing from the deal. What are we doing anyways?"

"We are going to knock off Zarrick's tower and steal something," Phil said with a straight face.

Darius' facepalmed and scoffed at the same time. "You what, you can't be serious?"

"Oh it gets better," Phil said. "I've actually been inside Zarrick's tower before, the place is a maze, which means it is going to take time to find what we need. Time enough perhaps for Zarrick to return from wherever he's gone. So we need to go now, we are meeting Withers as soon as possible."

"Back in my day, we didn't bother with sneaking about and such, the Eldritch Order was something to be proud of, they cheered us in the streets," Darius said, looking forlorn.

"Seriously?" Phil asked, intrigued by mention of what the Eldritch Order used to be like.

"Well they did before most of the Order went dark side," Darius said, averting his gaze. "Once the destruction of entire villages got out, we were pretty evenly hated among the people and other Orders."

"We need to go," Phil repeated, as much as he'd love to talk about the old days with Darius, they were on a tight deadline.

"Sure, sure, let me change into my armor and I'll be ready,"

Darius said, leaving in a hurry and disappearing out of the study.

Darius was armored up, making Phil feel out of place, but he shrugged the feeling off, confident in the amulets ability to armor him if he needed. Together they traveled through the streets, speaking in low voices as they went deeper and deeper into the muck filled streets. Darius had a cloak that hid much of his armor but still no one dared bother them.

"You know how to do it don't you?" Phil asked, breaking the silence that fell between them.

"Do what?" Darius asked.

"Drain power from others to get stronger," Phil said, sharing a look with the armored figure.

"I do," Darius admitted. "But I didn't walk that path, will you?"

"I just think I ought to know how to do it, so I don't stumble upon it by accident," Phil said, using the same argument he'd shared with Seph over the topic.

"I won't be the one to show you," Darius said. "Trust me when I say it won't be something you stumble upon. It was born of a lust of power and the technique requires deliberate action to work."

Phil was surprised that Darius was withholding the information as well, but it was probably for the best. He didn't need to risk infecting his new Order with the exact thing that brought down the last generation. They arrived at Withers hideout and the old man came out before they could go to the side door.

"Change of plans," he said, swishing his robes. "I've got news about something and I need to check in on it before we assault the tower. It is on the way so we shouldn't waste too much time."

"Zarrick could return any moment," Phil said. "Are you sure it can't wait?"

"If what my informants told me turns out to be true, we might have more time than I originally thought. It would appear some of my own plans intersected with the great Zarrick's, whatever he might be doing," Withers said, then without another word, he began to walk, swiftly considering the aged appearance of the man.

Phil exchanged a look with Darius, but in the end they had no choice but to follow him, so they did, keeping step with him and making their way into the nicer part of town.

Getting lost in the sights and sounds, Phil enjoyed the stroll into the nicer parts of town, but then Withers did something that surprised him. He called out for a carriage, and the rest of the way Phil had to watch out the small round window inset into the closed carriage as they moved through the city for a solid two hours.

A part of him missed the self-driving cars and features of the old world, but at the same time Phil was so immersed into this new world that he rarely caught himself thinking about what he'd left behind. Never before would he have considered that he'd be in the middle of a fantasy adventure, complete with magic and swords. But knowing his people, times were in for a change, soon there would be guns and modernization. Humans were good for that, no matter the world they found themselves in.

Before too long they stopped outside a massive arena. Withers mumbled something about them staying behind, but Phil ignored him, following after the man. He glanced over his shoulder but said nothing when he saw Phil following.

After a time they stopped in front of a man inside the

arena, a series of stairs had led them to an upper section, not a single soul had tried to stop them.

The man saw Withers and went a little paler, but stayed where he was.

"Tell me and be quick about it," Withers said. "How is it you couldn't do this one favor for me, after what I've done for you."

"You didn't tell us he was Ascended, he teamed up with another and the mages just couldn't conjure anything big enough to deal with them. It wasn't our fault, we should have been told his true status," the man said, he wore fine clothing and had a large gut matched with a heavy mustache.

"I didn't know he was Ascended, but no matter, you tell me you saw him leave with Golder, you are certain?" Withers asked, and suddenly Phil was paying close attention.

Golder was someone he was familiar with, Zarrick's partner and a man that Phil didn't want to cross if he could help it. He'd shown several times his power and he wasn't sure if he'd be a match for the man yet.

"He did, but the messenger I sent after them lost them soon after they left. I'm terribly sorry, but I promise this won't happen again," the man said, sweat dripping down his face.

"No," Withers said, "it wont." And with a wave of his hand a spark of blue appeared and struck the man in the chest. He went down in a heap, his chest smoking and leaving Phil standing there stunned at the action. It was like he'd shot a lightning bolt of blue power at the man, was that how mages manifested their raw power?

"Let's be off," Withers said. "Whatever Zarrick is up to, I think he plans on using that young man for some purpose I can't yet understand. It will take him time, I hope, but we should hurry regardless."

No one tried to stop them on the way out and no alarm came up from one of their men falling dead, likely because he hadn't been found yet, but still the casual way in which Withers struck him down made Phil wary of him. He'd need to be careful around this man when their deed was done.

The carriage was where they'd left it and soon they were on their way to the tower. It was in a very nice part of town, but the direct area around it was abandoned, not a soul to be found. The tower itself was all black and rose up into the air some hundred or two feet. For such a small man, Zarrick sure enjoyed large buildings.

"Give me time to work and do not disturb me," Withers said, raising his hand and chanting a few incantations at the gate. It swung open on its own and Withers looked a bit perplexed.

"Was it meant to do that?" Phil asked, but Withers just waved them forward.

Next he stopped before a ring of stone on the ground inscribed with runes. He sat and began to chant, this time it took nearly twenty minutes before light flared on them and he was standing, hobbling forward.

This continued for several hours until they reached the actual tower and a large wooden door set into it. Withers did his magic, chanting and waiting. After some time, Phil and Darius had been discussing random topics, from how the old Order used to do tasks and how Darius wasn't a fan of chanting, but saying that mages weren't the only ones that could do such magics. He didn't offer to help though, instead he leaned against a tree close to Phil.

A low creak of a door swinging open caught Phil's ears and he was surprised to find a golem, one of Zarrick's creations, standing behind the door looking around.

"Uh oh," Withers said, looking alarmed. "Hurry, kill that thing!"

"Master Phil," the Golem said. "You are most welcome to enter, however your guests must wait outside."

Darius and Withers turned to Phil with eyes as wide as saucer plates, but before he answered any of their half formed questions, he stood and walked to the door.

"Very well," Phil said to the golem. "Take me to where Zarrick stores his Soul Stones."

"At once," the golem said in its usual monotone voice.

"I'll be back soon," Phil said, turning and shooting them both a look.

CHAPTER 25
JAMES

James followed the man named Golder and was brought to a massive black tower. A few muttered words made rings on the ground flash white and they walked forward until they reached a massive wooden door with black metal bands running across it.

"Remember, be respectful, because Zarrick can and will peel your skin from your bones if you anger him," Golder said, then glancing up at James he grunted.

"Of course," James said, barely listening. He imagined what this powerful force of a man must be like, this Zarrick character, but nothing solid would form in his mind, so he just followed behind Golder as he walked into a maze of hallways and staircases.

"What in the hell is that?" James asked as a robot of some kind, looking like a skeleton made of metal, walked past them and down another corridor.

"Don't mind the golems, Zarrick has many doing his tasks for him, they are harmless," Golder said, waving his question away.

"Cool," James said, nodding his head. So this man had an army of metal skeletons, that might come in useful when James overthrew the government here. He'd make himself kind of this city and then he could be certain that it was run correctly and fairly.

They reached a plain wooden door and Golden knocked before a voice called for them to "Enter".

James saw the man, or rather, the child sized man, sitting on a high chair of sorts, smoking a large stogie in the back of the room. He had to suppress a smile, for this man looked nothing like he'd been trying to imagine.

"Does my sight amuse you?" Came the same odd voice. "Laugh if you must, I'll wait to kill you until after."

The little man leaned forward in his chair, the light was so dim in the room that his face was the most lit section of the room as he took a drag on his massive stogie. James no longer felt like laughing when he felt a pressure hit him and he recognized it for what it was. This man, little or not, had a massive well of power and the force of it alone might be enough to crush him.

James bowed his head and spoke in a low voice, being as respectful as he could manage. "I mean no disrespect, I'm here because I was told I could find power. Do you have power to offer me to rival even your own?"

Zarrick was quiet at first, taking another long pull on his stogie. "I do," he finally said and then he snapped his fingers.

Golden appeared in a flash, taking a roll of paper from him and handing it over to James.

"This is a contract for your services. It is magically binding, so please read over every line. If you accept and choose to sign, then I will grant you a power unrivaled by any others and in turn you will help collect certain items for me. Is this agreeable?" Zarrick asked.

"It is," James said without hesitation, taking the scroll and not looking at it. "I will sign right away."

"Read it and return it to me, signed. Golder find him a room and prepare my carriage for a trip," Zarrick said.

Golder nodded and gestured for James to follow.

"Where he keeps finding you lot I'll never know," Golder mumbled as he walked and James looked ahead at him.

"What do you mean?" James asked, they were a ways down the hall now and not at risk of being overheard.

"You've been ascended, but not chosen an Order. Yet you have as strong a core as the first street rat he found some months back. It's most confusing, but it's not my place to comment on it," Golder said, brushing James off as he tried to ask a follow up question.

Making it to the room that Golder found for him, he barely noticed how nice it was, just slumping down on a chair in the sitting room and opening the scroll to begin reading. When he finished, he grunted and looked to Golder, who hovered nearby.

"Gotta a pen?" James asked, ready to sign away his life for power.

They left the next day, leaving the massive city by carriage and walking past a depressing sight of people living in makeshift tents, begging on the side of the road. It didn't take long before they were approaching a massive black ring set into the ground. James didn't even ask what in the stargate was going on, as Zarrick muttered some words and spoke phrases.

A deep blackness settled over the space between and Golder nudged James forward and he walked on through. They arrived on the other side a moment later, and it took James a second to catch his breath. They were up in the mountains someplace high, the air was thin, but his lungs adjusted after mere moments.

The sun was lowered in the sky here, meaning they'd traveled a great distance, James shook his head. Portals, there are freaking portals in this world, crazy.

"The cave isn't far now," Zarrick said. "Just two hours travel."

That two hours turned to three then four before they arrived outside a massive cave, where Zarrick finally declared their trip complete. The armor James wore was oddly comfortable, keeping most of the cold off him and seeming to adjust the temperature for him as he walked.

James followed the slow Zarrick and Golder into the dark cave and saw that it wasn't so dark after all. Inside were some thousand or so weird symbols that glowed with a deep purple light, giving just enough light to see by.

"The keyhole," Zarrick muttered under his breath, but James heard him. Then he noticed Golder, looking pale at his words and drawing his hands closer to the weapons James had noticed he kept hidden around his sides. The small man seemed like he'd be handy in a fight, it almost made James want to try and fight him for the hell of it. But no, he had to stay focused on his goals, he needed more power and then he'd get his fights that he so much desired.

There was a certain feeling inside of the room, James couldn't put his finger on it but every instinct he had screamed at him to run and flee this place. The longer he spent within its walls the more he almost wanted to give in to it. But he held back, focusing on his goal and wishes. He'd avenge Pete and in the process have some amazing fights.

"Time to level up," James said, cracking his neck to the side and pushing against the instincts to flee.

"Make yourselves comfortable," Zarrick said. He didn't seem disturbed by the cave at all, in fact he seemed relaxed in a way that James had never noticed before.

Golder and James shared a look, but Golder spoke first.

"I'll watch the entrance, you watch his back while he works," Golder said, smirking at James.

"Very well," Zarrick said, eyeing James for a moment before sitting down and beginning to chant strange words.

James thought the 'watching Zarrick's back' would be more of a figurative role, but when a weird symbol on the roof of the cave suddenly flashed and a monstrous four armed beast, all hair and muscle appeared, James sword was drawn and ready.

It slammed down, but Zarrick never stopped chanting or moved to defend himself. The beast struck for Zarrick, but James was faster, cutting off a limb just as it swung its meaty fist. However two more fists hit Zarrick, or at least they hit a bubble of translucent blue around him and he opened a single eye in annoyance before going back to his chanting.

The battle raged, more monsters appearing steadily as James took them down, none so hard yet that he was having much of a challenge. Swinging his sword like the madman he was becoming, James let his rage and instincts guide his actions. It wasn't until a large section of his armor was ripped clean off by a spider monster that James realized he was beginning to be outmatched by the stream of opponents.

That was when Golder arrived in a puff of black smoke.

He cut down the spider with a dagger of all things, ending

its life like it was nothing. He whirled and laughed as he cut down dozens of foes in seconds. James helped where he could, but Golder was a machine of death, and he was working at full speed.

The bodies, James realized, weren't sticking around, instead they turned to glittering dust and got sucked back up into the glowing runes on the walls. It meant that this must be working similar to the mages and their illusions. This redoubled James' desire to destroy them, and he cut and slashed with all his might.

Then as quickly as they came, the monsters stopped.

"I've bypassed that part of the security. Both of you go rest outside for a bit while I start the hard part," Zarrick commanded, James and Golder were happy to oblige him, leaving the cave in a hurry.

"So you want Power, do you boy?" Golder asked, sitting on a rock and giving James a perplexed look.

James ignored him at first, his mind still spinning from the battle and the rush of it all. But after a time, while still thinking hard on how powerful Golder had been, James acknowledged him.

"I do," he said.

"And you think this is the only way?" Golder asked.

James wasn't sure how to answer that, sure there were other paths, he'd at first wanted to walk the path that Pete had done, but he wanted more than even that, he needed to be more.

"I need to be the strongest," James said.

He wasn't sure why he even cared so much about these

NPCs or bothered to speak with this Golder man, but he was as invested in this world as he'd ever been and there was no going back now. He was emotionally invested in this world, so he ought to stop thinking about it like it was just that, some game world. No this was his world now, his new reality. He was just as much ones and zeros as the rest of them after all.

"The thing about power, especially the power you are about to partake in," Golder said, his voice a low rumble.

"You were the one that put me on this path," James said, interrupting him. "I needed power and you came to me, what are you trying to get at now?"

"It's just," Golder said, rubbing at the back of his neck and struggling to find his next words. "You have a choice and you need to know more about these powers that we take in. They change you, you don't just remain yourself, it's a merger of spirits."

"And?" James said, unsure if there'd be some quirk to the magic, Pete had said as much, but what did that matter when weighed against what he needed to accomplish? His heart sped up as he considered the awesome power he might get and the powers that a dragon could imbue into someone. It had to be epic, didn't it?

"And you are about to take a poison into yourself and hope it's a cure, I'm just telling you it's not. Zarrick will tie you in so many knots that you'll never get out, this is the only warning you get," Golder said, his voice going lower as he spoke, as if he didn't want to be overheard.

"You're his man, why would you be telling me this?" James asked, wondering why Zarrick's goon was suddenly growing a conscience.

"I'm no one's man," Golder said, growling the words. "I serve myself and my interests first, everyone else is secondary, even Zarrick. And I'm no one's damn errant boy, if that is what you are thinking. I've my own reasons that I must stick by Zarrick, doing his bidding for now, but those reasons are my own. You need to think of your own and make sure you are damned sure you want to walk this path."

"A test then?" James said, figuring it all out. This Golder was just testing his resolve and James wouldn't falter now.

"Aye, a test, but not in the way you might think," Golder said, sighing and seeming resigned. "These changes you're about to get will make you unstable, I'm sure of it, so hold true to your convictions and remember what you want, for you'll be battling yourself to get them done."

"I'm ready," James assured him, with a solid nod of his head and a smirk. Golder didn't seem convinced but he let the conversation lull back into a quiet understanding. James wouldn't be swayed and he needed this power, or at least he told himself he did.

It was already something that he was faster, stronger, and could heal himself rapidly, but getting access to the power of a dragon, it was more than he could have dreamt about receiving.

"What powers will I get when I merge with this dragon spirit?" James asked, pulling together little bits of information to come up with what Golder had meant by merging with this new power.

"Control of the black flame for one," Golder said. "Other than that it is hard to say. My Order gives me control over shadows and the like, but the raw power we can wield appears like arcing slashes of energy, but that is in its most basic form. As you learn to control it, mold it, there will be no limit to what you might accomplish, but since you'll be the first I've ever heard of in a Dragon Order, I can't really say, truth be told."

"I hope I don't grow wings," James said, letting a bit of light hearted humor fill his voice. "I mean I'd love to fly and all, but fighting would be much harder with massive wings on my back."

"You won't grow wings," Golder said, chuckling a bit himself. "The changes are spirit deep, they will change you but not physically. At least I've never heard of such changes happening before. Zarrick will guide you, he knows more about this lost Order than anyone else. Just remember what I told you, be true to yourself."

"I will," James assured him, nodding his head. He would, he told himself. He would stay true to his quest and seek vengeance on those who wronged him and killed his friend.

After a pause of silence between them James broke it with a question he'd been wondering.

"What can you tell me about the duality of the priest Order?" James asked. He wanted to know more about the Order that his friend had been involved with, before he was forced to put him down. The weight of that didn't hurt as much as it ought to, instead he transferred all the pain toward his hate of the people who forced him into that situation. James wasn't the type to blame himself when the blame was better suited to be pinned on someone more deserving.

"I know little of the other Orders, truth be told," Golder said.

"Why do you follow Zarrick?" James asked, transitioning to another thought he'd had, but he doubted Golder would give him much. NPC or not he was pretty tight lipped about some stuff. So he was surprised when Golder opened up to him a moment later.

"I'm here to get vengeance on a betrayal, and take my rightful spot at the head of my House, but I'm not nearly as powerful as I need to be yet," Golder said, practically growling the last few words.

Surprised by actually learning some part of what motivated Golder, James tried to dig deeper to see what he could learn. It was fascinating to him how deep they seemed to make the backstories of the various characters. It really lent a realistic view of them, like they truly cared about their past and did things according to those motivations.

"I can understand that," James said. "Who betrayed you?"

"My brother," Golder growled. "Damn him and his endless ego."

"I never had any siblings, but I can imagine-," James began to say but Golder cut him off.

"You can't imagine, and I'm done with this idle chit chat, steel yourself for what is to come and keep your yap shut," Golder said, suddenly hostile.

James sighed, he'd hit a raw topic and that was the end of any information he was likely to get from the man. It was frustrating, as he wanted to know more of the backstory, it was helping him distract himself from the pain that wouldn't truly go away. He'd cared for Pete and those feelings had been growing into something bigger, a love like he'd not felt, but he imagined was close to what one man felt for a brother, blood or not.

He'd had friends before, but never as close as the bonds he felt with Pete. Even his buddies the 'Green Hats' hadn't been the same. Suddenly the image of Dave dead at his side hit him and he felt a sting of regret. He'd cared about Dave most of all, but he hadn't allowed himself to feel that pain either. It all threatened to overwhelm him if he lingered on it too long, so he didn't. Instead he focused on the anger and rage, he'd stoke those flames and bring them down on the heads of those responsible.

———

A sudden cry of alarm went up and Golder was moving into the cave so fast that James barely tracked him with his vision. James stood and ran in to find Zarrick a smoking mess, but alive. Golder held him up and Zarrick soon regained consciousness.

"The things I do for them," Zarrick muttered under his breath, but James heard it, not understanding but tucking the information away for later. Zarrick had his reasons and James would figure them out as well, he would work out all their motivations eventually.

"You alright?" James asked, but Zarrick was already on his feet again and walking toward him.

"Yes, yes, I'm fine," Zarrick said, seeming more flustered than James had ever seen him before, though he'd only known him for a short period of time so he might always be like this. "You need to stand over here."

Zarrick grabbed his hand and slowly took him to where he'd been sprawled out only a few moments before. James hesitated and Zarick gave him a look.

"Am I about to be hit by something too?" James asked, raising an eyebrow at the diminutive man.

"You are," Zarrick confirmed.

"I thought so," James said, stepping forward into the spot regardless.

"A black flame will attempt to enter you, but first drink this," Zarrick said, handing him a small vial. James took it without question and popped the top.

"The entire thing?" James asked, right as he was about to do just that.

"The entire contents, yes," Zarrick said, exchanging a look with Golder.

James took it down like a shot of whiskey, it had a minty taste to it and he almost belched afterward but held it in, trying to have some manners in what was about to be a life changing event for him. He felt something within him blossom but it was hard to pinpoint what was happening exactly. An odd sort of comfort washed over him and his body began to feel warm. It was noticeable since the cave was rather chilly.

"Stand here and prepare yourself," Zarrick said, and he started chanting again. Cracks began to open up in the floor all around James, small things barely noticeable if not for his enhanced vision he might have missed them. Then the black smoke came, swirling around him and the heat hit a new level of extreme.

James grunted in pain, but it was well within his pain threshold still, so he just clenched his teeth and took it. Then it got real and before he knew what he was doing, he was screaming in pain as black flames rose up from the cracks and began to consume him. It hurt more than any pain he'd ever felt and he could have sworn he cracked several teeth as he went from screaming to clenching his jaw in fast repetition.

Then it was gone, just as fast as it came and James hit the ground hard, his knees buckling as he tried to fall onto them. He lay on the ground for only seconds, before he felt something inside of him, a fire burning away at him, but it wasn't painful anymore. He could feel it fueling him or he was fueling it, it was hard to tell really.

He felt angry, he felt wronged, how dare they imprison him! He was one of them, they would pay for such injustice with their blood. He wouldn't rest until their corpses fed the ground and their blood watered the crops.

Black fire appeared all around him as his anger boiled over into new heights. He screamed again, but this time in unbridled rage. Raising a hand he shot at the runes set into the wall, trying to burn them away, though he knew not why he desired their destruction. However powerful he was, he wasn't powerful enough, not yet. The runes remained where they were, flaring in response to his show of power but otherwise remaining the same.

A pain in his chest took him suddenly and he fell to a knee as his fire flared and funneled into a form around his neck. The next thing he knew there was a wicked looking dragon's head amulet, black as obsidian, sitting around his neck. He touched it and a voice spoke into his mind. The worlds were ancient and foreign to him, but they spoke of vengeance and injustice, two feelings he could get behind.

He embraced the voice and feelings that came with it, then suddenly the world around him went black as he lost consciousness.

"You will be my emissary to the world," Came a voice that shook James to his core. If there ever was a voice that sounded evil, this one hit it on the head. There was no doubt in James mind that he'd just aligned himself with a power that was not inherently good. But a part of him, deep down, didn't seem to care so he just took the words as what they were.

"I am ready to serve," James spoke into the blackness around him. As he did so the world seemed to zoom all the way out and he saw the great blackness was actually a massive world sized black dragon, with several rows of wicked horns and several rows of black teeth, all matched up with four sets of blood red eyes.

"My kin will rue the day they betrayed me, you are the start, the first step to my release, go forth and spread chaos and destruction!"

"I will," James promised, the flame burning within him pushing him to speak the words and his entire body wanting nothing else than to act on the impulses.

Then as quick as he was pulled into the dream surrounding him, he was pulled back out. Finding himself on the ground, he sat up and spit out a mouth slick with blood.

He turned just in time to see Zarrick perk up and mutter something under his breath. "Someone is in my house," he said. Then turning he left the grave, shouting behind himself that he'd "Be back in a day or two. Train him up and prepare him to face the dragon, we've little time to dally."

CHAPTER 26
PHIL

It was truly a maze inside of the Tower and Phil was glad to have a golem showing him the way. The tower was much as he remembered and feelings of inadequacy and foolishness followed. But he squashed them down with the help of the green flame burning within him. He knew he was enough, he was strong and able now, he didn't need the help that had been offered and though he was grateful for the path it put him on, he wouldn't be repeating that particular mistake again.

Which in turn brought his mind back to Withers and how the man had weaseled him into signing another contract. But this was one he could fulfil and finish without a problem. He'd be done with Withers within hours and have the book. Then blessedly and finally he'd be able to begin the work of bringing back Adam, his dear friend.

His heart ached when he thought about him too much, but the friendship he'd given him and the trust he'd shown, warmed him in place of that ache. They were feelings he'd gotten used to feeling, but to finally be on the way to getting the book, it filled him with a joy he couldn't yet describe, washing away the pain.

"Will you report to Zarrick that I've entered his tower?" Phil asked, figuring he knew the answer but he ought to ask.

"He is already aware," the golem said. "Although if he asks me for specifics of your entry, I will be obliged to tell him all. Do remember that you are a welcomed guest here, his offer of friendship has not yet been rescinded."

This caught Phil off guard, why wouldn't have Zarrick updated his golems with news of his betrayal. Surely he didn't want Phil to be able to wander into his tower at any time, that was ludicrous. Yet here he was, either by failure of thought or perhaps the man was just too confident in for his own good.

They reached the room that the golem took him to and it ended up being a storage room of sorts. It was vast and dark, no soul stones that Phil could see were present but there were many boxes that might contain them.

The golem politely stayed at the door while Phil began to search. He went through box after box, but it contained all manner of items but no soulstones. Finally getting frustrated with his search he called for the golem to come in, it did so.

"Where are the soul stones Zarrick keeps here?" Phil asked, figuring he might as well throw caution to the wind at this point.

"This is where he stores Soul stones, although currently all known stones are being used by golems," the golem said and Phil's mood immediately darkened.

He would have to do something he really didn't want to do, though if he'd thought about how Zarrick had reacted last time he saw a soul stone, it made a little sense that he'd use his entire supply, as rare as they were.

He looked at the golem and its construction. He knew the limits of his power and the limitations golems had about violence. It was a limitation that Adam hadn't had, but one Zarrick assured Phil his own golems did. In fact, Phil realized that Zarrick likely didn't know about Adam's ability to cause violence if he chose. It was one of the things that made him unique, and likely had to do with his construction of his soul stone.

A technique lost to time, Zarrick had said, meaning only those that were out in the wild or in golems already were the sole source of getting his hands on one. Sizing up the golem, Phil worked out in his head the best way to rip open its chest and take its soul stone.

He decided to be polite about it and just ask.

"How does one remove a soul stone from a golem without harming it?" Phil asked.

It might have just been a trick of the light or something else entirely, but the golems eyes that glowed a vibrant blue, flickered a moment and he didn't immediately respond. But after just a second or two of waiting it answered.

"Lift here, open this panel and you can expose the soul stone. However I must warn you that doing so will render the golem defunct, if you intend to remove the soul stone powering one," The golem said and again Phil might have been putting his own emotions to it, but it sounded like the golem didn't like his idea.

"Please do so, show me your soul stone," Phil said, and again the golem hesitated.

"You are an honored guest, however I must refuse. Though I may not stop you from doing so, as I am not allowed to cause violence, I will warn you that I will attempt to protect myself as best I can," the golem said, putting his arms in front of himself, blocking his chest.

"Put your hands at your side," Phil commanded and the golem did so.

Reaching out he began to open the chest cavity, but stopped when the golem placed a hand on him. It didn't push or try to stop him, just placed a gentle hand and spoke words that hurt Phil from the inside out.

"Please, I don't wish to die," it said, and Phil heard in its voice the same plea that Adam had, but he stoked the fire within himself and closed off his emotions. He was doing this *for* Adam and he couldn't falter now.

"I'm sorry, but you won't be dead. Just under a new master's care," Phil said in a monotone voice, as clear of emotion as he could be given the circumstances.

He reached out and pulled free the soul stone from its chamber, before closing all of the chest openings. Then seeing several golems, lifeless and inactivated in a far corner, Phil lifted the model over there and put him with his kind.

Then making his way back into the hallway, he snaked back and forth, doing his best to not encounter any more golems. He was lucky though and got to the exit before seeing even one. Opening the door he found Withers and Darius waiting for him.

"I've got the goods, let's get back. I'm not exchanging it until I see the book," Phil said, his voice iron.

"Very well," Withers said, then turning the departed into the abandoned square surrounding Zarrick's tower.

They'd done it, they'd broken into Zarrick's tower and stolen something precious, without encountering the small man and his awesome powers. He couldn't be sure, but it seemed like Withers was walking much faster than before, in a hurry to distance himself as much as possible from the massive tower and what it represented.

They made it back to the hideout without so much as a few words being discussed the entire time. Withers kept his grave shifting between the two of them and Phil was sure something was going to happen. But nothing did the entire time.

Torrents of rain fell in sheets while they traveled in the carriage, but they remained dry, up until arriving. Stepping out into the rain Phil immediately wished he had an umbrella. He hadn't seen any such invention here as of yet, so he was surprised when Withers produced, as if by magic, a black one out of nowhere to cover himself from the rain.

"Got any spares?" Darius asked, not yet stepping out into the rain.

Withers gave him a look but said nothing, walking to his alleyway entrance.

"Guess not," Darius said, stepping out into the rain and pulling his cloak up over his head. "You've got this exchange part handled right? I'm going to go see about finding a place to get warm and dry. Meet me back at my place in a few hours?"

"Sure," Phil said, though a part of him, a small part, wished for Darius to stay just in case Withers tried any funny business.

Walking up to the alleyway entrance, Phil was let in immediately and he made his way to the study, where Withers had already pulled free a book from his shelf and held onto it tightly.

"I need a month," Withers said, looking strained.

"No more waiting," Phil said. "We had a deal and I'm not changing it. No book, no soul stone."

"Perhaps I ought to test the limits of your powers," Withers said. "You feel powerful, but I could be wrong. I'm willing to bet I could take you in a fight."

Phil fished out the contract. "Are you sure about that?"

Withers withered at the sight of it, but still he retained a small measure of his defiant look. "I've not yet broken the contact, that will have no effect on me."

"Here, take this," Phil said, tossing over the soul stone. "Now you have what you wanted, give me what I'm here for."

Withers caught the ball out of the air and cursed under his breath. The contract would now enforce itself, weakening him if Phil commanded it to do so. The leverage was back on his side, but he was putting his trust in a process he didn't understand fully, so it was still a risk.

"Damn you," Withers said, looking at the book one final time before holding it out for Phil to take.

Phil wasted no time, reaching out and taking the book. He leafed through a few pages to make sure it was what he was looking for and sure enough it was the process of creating a golem, with chapters of each of the processes required and elaborate explanations.

"Now that the contract is fulfilled," Withers said, the contract turning to dust in his hands as well as Phils. "How do you think you are getting out of dockside alive?"

Phil tucked the book away in his bag and walked for the door. Several guards appeared and Phil recognized a double cross when it stared him in the face.

"I'll burn my way out if I need to," Phil said, fire already glowing from his right hand. "It won't be pretty and I'll leave you in ruins, Withers. Think before you walk this path."

"I have," Withers said, smiling cruelly. "Give me the book and I'll let you live."

Phil was tired. He was tired of fighting his way through the dockside gangs, tired of all the bullshit he'd had to go through just to get this book, he was tired of waiting. Turning he shot out a powerful stream of fire at Withers, ignoring the goons right in front of him.

The fire must have taken Withers by surprise, because it slammed into the frail old man and slammed him into his bookshelves, causing them to go up in flames a moment later, still Phil kept the fire flowing.

Withers screamed and begged, but Phil was done listening. Even as the blows came upon him, he ignored them, ready to finish the job. It wasn't until a nasty blow to the head broke his concentration that he realized he was under full attack by the goons.

He shifted his flames to burn them up, consuming them like flies drawn to the flame. Destruction and death came easy to Phil now and he leaned into it, destroying the building around him as he made his way toward the exit. Whether or not he killed Withers he wasn't sure, but he was done pretending to be anything but what he was, a powerful Eldritch Knight.

He met Darius at his estate after gathering all his things he cared about from his gang hideout. He'd been lucky enough not to have to kill anyone there, as there was a full on gang war going on after Withers headquarters fell. It seemed like the other members of the Tor'I were dead set on expanding their own territory if and when possible. Phil had created a vacuum of power that was filling itself as he tried to escape the area.

"Time to go," Phil said and Darius nodded.

"I've set everything up here and my manservant will keep the place in order should we need a forward base within the city," Darius said. "Otherwise I'm all set to travel and live out my life with my fellow Eldritch Knights."

There was a touch of something in Darius's voice then, was it sarcasm or something else, Phil couldn't tell. But he chose to ignore it, ready to get out of Dockside before they were forced into more fights that would not end well for the other side.

They made it through the city and got a carriage to get out of the rain as soon as it was possible. It gave them time to talk, but Phil didn't feel like talking much, but Darius was the exact opposite, his chatter never ending.

"What do you think about raising my rank to Master?" Darius asked, the topic of conversation had swung back to his place within the Eldritch Knights. "I mean I'm much stronger than I was before and I was on the cusp of reaching master before. Really I am a master in all but title."

Phil looked at him flatly, but it really looked like he wasn't going to let it go without some input from Phil. So sighing he responded.

"I'll talk with Seph about it, perhaps you'll have to show me what you got first, but I've no doubt you'll be given your proper rank when the time is right," Phil said.

"Good, good," Darius said, rubbing his hands together. "Now about living quarters."

Phil pretended not to hear him and eventually he transitioned to speaking about his time as a member of the Tor'I and how he'd never really fit in with the others. Phil listened with interest, but tried not to show it. There was an odd nervous energy about Darius right now and Phil guessed it had something to do with returning to the Eldritch Knights after so long, so he didn't fault the man.

The rain cut out around the time their carriage made it to the city gate where Phil would take Darius through the portal. Leaving the carriage behind they produced papers and were allowed to leave without much issue. Darius looked impatient the entire time, letting his cloak fall to further fluster the guard by his presence. But in all the process took seconds and they were out on the road heading toward the portal.

The tent city thrived as always, and Phil wondered how many more had joined their cause from its ranks. It was a shame that the other Orders didn't realize the potential of the tent city and its citizens. So many were from far off nations or towns, likely untested for their ascension abilities, leaving a treasure trove to help grow the Eldritch Knights ranks.

Phil casually explained that to Darius as they walked and he seemed taken aback.

"You are taking the lowest of society and raising them up?" Darius said. "And to Eldritch Knights no less? We were once one of the most sought after Orders to join, standing at the head of the pack when it came to offensive power. To think we are accepting just any old peasants now."

"They are going to be your brethren, if you have issue with it already, then I suggest you return to the Tor'I and resume your life as a gangster," Phil said, not missing a beat.

That shut Darius up for several long seconds.

"I suppose it's a breath of fresh air to infuse so many into our powerful Order," Darius said, changing his tune entirely. "I mean, I'm not sure I agree with this half ascension you are doing, but those that can become full fledged Eldritch Knights, I cannot fault their backgrounds. Peasants or not, I will stand among them and fight to regain our place in this world."

"Better," Phil said, sharing a look with him that said more

than his words ever did. Darius took the hint and nodded, accepting that his previous behavior wouldn't be acceptable.

Things were going pretty well, up to the point that they weren't. A large garrison of soldiers were positioned between the road and the portal, something that surprised Phil as that hadn't been a thing since his first crossing through it.

It wasn't until they got closer that he felt the many Ascended among them.

"We should strike hard and fast," Darius said, as they approached the tents laid out on the side of the road.

"Move like you belong and we might just get through this without a fight," Phil came back with, each of them had cloaks that weren't all too dissimilar to several others standing about.

They made their way into the ranks and weren't immediately stopped, a good sign. It wasn't until they were almost through and heading up toward the portal that someone called out to them.

Phil thought about it and stopped, figuring he might be able to bluff his way out of it.

"Don't wander too far that way," the voice called out. "Those golems will rip you to bits, doesn't matter what Order you're apart of."

Phil inclined his head and waited for the man to put his gaze elsewhere, then they began to run full speed for the portal. It wasn't until they'd put a good distance between them that calls of alarm went up and several brave soldiers tried to follow.

Bolts and arrows flew past them, narrowly missing here and there, but all the while they kept running. Then as they reached the portal Darius turned, likely to attack with his fire, but Phil put a hand on him.

"No violence near the portal, these golems will kill us," Phil said, and Darius went pale in the face.

"Rumors are true then?" Darius asked, looking over at the golems before turning to dodge an arrow. "Hope you know what you are doing."

Phil did know what he was doing, having done it so many times before. He activated the portal and moments later, as arrows fell around them, they entered the portal together.

CHAPTER 27
JAMES

With Zarrick gone, Golder was in charge of training James. James on the other hand was trying to get used to the awesome power of the black flame that roiled within him. It called him to action in a way that James had never felt before, but more specifically it called him to kill and consume. He was eating more of his pack meals than he meant to, so hard was the compulsion to do and act.

Getting up he bounced on his feet, shooting off a bar of black flame into the distant sky and screaming as he did so. It felt so intoxicating, he needed to fight, to do something. The chaotic magic that grew inside of him was nothing short of marvelous, but James knew he needed to learn some control.

It was as Pete had said when trying to prepare him for what it meant to take on both light and darkness. The darkness would call you to do terrible things, but the light would do the opposite. Except now it appeared that James had only the darkness to deal with, his own inclinations toward good and bad being heavily tainted by this new power.

"I can see you practically blistering to use your new powers, so let's spar a bit and get you using your new powers," Golder said, sitting up from where he'd just finished a meal of his own.

James could hardly contain himself as the man pulled out a pair of daggers and took a battle stance. He was fast, this much James knew already, so he'd have to do something big right off to keep himself from being knocked out immediately. Summoning forth his fire he prepared to blow it outward all around him a second after the fight started.

As James thought, Golder disappeared one second and appeared within striking distance the next, but James unleashed his powers and Golder's eyes went wide. However the man was fast, disappearing again and reappearing on the edge of the area they were fighting, where the flames were weakest.

But James was ready for him, shooting out a bar of black flame, looking to completely destroy the man if he could. Of course this was meant to be a sparring match, but James couldn't help but want to destroy and take things apart.

Golder surprised him though, but sidestepping the flames just barely and rushing forward, daggers out. James pulled his massive sword up and swung it in an arc, forcing Golder to either duck the blow or stop his advance.

He ducked the blow easily and came into James' defenses, where he slashed his daggers into his shoulders and across his neck, hitting each opening in his armor like it was nothing. James coughed for a second, but his healing factor had him back into fighting shape within moments.

Kicking out, he sent Golder flying backward, but he flickered and appeared before James, dagger trained to take him in the eye.

"If I'd wanted," Golder said, James found it within himself to stop and listen, though it pained him. "I could have killed you a dozen times over. Focus on keeping me back and predicting my movements. Your power is one of consumption, let it burn all around you if you have to, just don't let me get close."

"Got it," James said, then a moment later he shot black flame all around him and out. Then he let his flames consume his sword, sheathing it in flames. And he cut a slash to where he'd guessed Golder might appear, sending a slash of black fire to that location.

It missed, but he kept the pressure going and the fight didn't end for another minute this time, with Golder cutting him several times in the legs.

Golder went on to explain that his strikes, if he covered them in shadow, would be much harder to heal from, so he should avoid getting hit when fighting another Ascended if possible. Then he explained that removing a head or limb was the fastest and most effective way to deal with another ascended.

"Hold on to what you were before," Golder screamed at James as he lost himself to the power for the second time, shooting flames wildly around him as if desperate for something to consume.

"I can't!" James screamed through clenched teeth. "I need to consume! TO KILL!"

Golder appeared before James a moment later and struck him hard on the side of the head. It rang his helmet and brought him back to his senses. He let the flames die down and just tried to be in the moment.

The rocks all around them were scorched black from the training, any vegetation long since consumed by the flames. James breathed hard, harder than he needed to as he tried to keep focus on what he used to be, who he used to be. He was not what the flames wanted, pure chaos and destruction. He was James, a powerful warrior who wanted to avenge a fallen friend. He was alone, he needed the comfort of the flames, he... he needed to destroy.

Another bang on his head got him to come back to and this time he sat in silence of mind and mouth. Pulling free more food he ate to keep himself moving, doing something.

"You've got to not let the power consume what you once were, it is important that you control it and not let it control you," Golder said, James realized the man had a hand on his shoulder and he rolled it to make it fall off, but Golder held a firm grip.

"I'm fine," James lied.

"The hells you are," Golder said. "This power you wield has more of a life to it than any I've heard of, so you need more than anyone else, to master it before it masters you."

"I'm trying," James said, his voice filled with frustration and not a little anger.

"Try harder," Golder said. "And I'm not just giving you tough love here boy. You need to be better, stronger, faster, and in more control than you are now. Zarrick doesn't care for failures and you will be one if you try to take on a dragon with your current control."

James finished eating and cleared his mind. He was a fighter, had always been one and this was no different. He tempered his mind and prepared for the next round. Control, focus, and swift execution of power is what he needed, so he would do it.

Summoning the flames he wreathed his entire body, but he felt no heat from it, just a pull to do more. He mastered himself and forced back the call for himself to do what the flame wanted. Instead he took the motivation to act and tried to give it purpose. He shot out a circle of power around him just as Golder appeared, catching the roguish figure off guard.

The flames pushed him back but he appeared unharmed by the attack, so focusing his mind he chose a location and fired off a stream of black flame, arcing it to cover a greater area.

Golder appeared right at the end of the arc and took another hit, cursing as he disappeared once more. James let the power flow through himself and enhance his abilities. It was only because of this that he noticed a disturbance in his flames from behind and he swung his sword in a powerful arc, turning to slash behind himself.

Golder was there, catching his blow on two glowing daggers, visible strain on his face as he did so.

"Better!" Golder cried out, then he ducked the blow and went up to stab James in his gut. However James anticipated this and surged his flames around himself. Fire leapt up and took the bearded man full in the face, but he was gone just as quick, slipping into a shadow.

"Keep it up," Golder called out, and James shot a bar of flame at his voice's location, only to realize his mistake a moment later when Golder appeared beside him, slashing at his rib cage.

One, two, three, hits made it home before James could redirect his flames to push him back.

"You are too damn fast," James cursed, but he was smiling and felt more in control than he'd been the entire sparring match. Something was starting to click and James was now confident that he could own this power, manipulating it to serve him and not the other way around.

It was during this moment of clarity that James's thoughts turned to Pete and how unfair it was for the game world to have killed him off. James never made friends easily and rarely did he become close to them. The green hats were the exception to the rule, being as close to family as he was ever likely to feel. They'd truly been his found family and he'd lost them all, except perhaps Phil, but in this massive world what were the chances he'd come across his old friend again.

No. He'd found Pete, NPC or not, and he'd made the first true friend since arriving in this world. He had been trying not to focus on the pain that came with the loss, but now he used it to focus himself. No longer would he let others get their way with him, he'd be an unstoppable force of magic and might. He'd be the one to throw down this worlds' government and on top of it he'd figure out a better way.

He'd never really been one to try and play conqueror in the games he'd played, but it was a path he was familiar with. To do it he would need allies and Golder was as strong as an ally as he'd hoped to find so far. But he needed more and he thought he had the right idea of where to start building up a force. He'd carve out a gang of his own in the docksides where he'd killed so many, then he'd do what Pete did for him, making more ascended until he had a force of his own.

"Hey Golder," James said, calling over the short man. "Can you teach me how to ascend someone?"

"Forming some plans of your own are you?" Golder said, chuckling. "It is no small matter, nor is it usually easy, but I can teach you."

CHAPTER 28
PHIL

P hil arrived back at the Eldritch Keep just as repairs were underway from some type of attack. He left Darius then, rushing forward to find Seph and learn what had happened.

"They attacked with a small enough force that avoided our scouts," Seph began to explain, then she went through it all, from Steffans fighting that saved many lives, to how many they'd lost and how they'd begun repairs already, but she worried about morale for the others. They'd lost a few that had been ascended but not taken on the flame yet. These weren't lost from the battle, but they requested to leave and had been given enough supplies to make it on their own way back to civilization; she hadn't offered to let them use the portal.

"Good thing too," Phil said. "There is a force outside the portal now, I think they were getting wise to what we were doing, recruiting from the tent city."

"That or it's just a force from the front resting and resupplying," Seph said. "The peasant wars, according to my informants, had reached a fever pitch and threatens to fall upon the walls of Kothar within the year."

"Perhaps you're right," Phil said, liking that explanation more than his own. "I can't believe I wasn't here to help, I should have never left."

"Did you get it?" Seph asked, as if his words reminded her why he'd been gone in the first place.

Phil pulled out the book and handed it over. "I did," he said. "I just hope it was worth all the trouble I went through to get my hands on it."

Seph said nothing, just fingering her way through the book and her face lighting up as she did so. "With this," she finally spoke after a solid minute, "we will be able to do it! I'm positive!"

"We've much to do, but there is something I have to say to everyone," Phil said, standing and motioning for everyone to gather around. With a little help from Seph and Steffan, a large group had gathered around with Phil, Seph, Steffan, and her sister Mercy in the middle.

"I speak to you now as the head of the Eldritch Order!" Phil said, speaking loud enough for all of them to hear. "I'm not one to speak flowery words to get your attention, nor will I try. I will speak plainly to you as I've always done."

"What happened to us will not be tolerated!" Phil shouted the words and let the green flames around him begin to spark and roil. "No longer will we wait for attacks to come to us. We will show them our strength by taking the fight to their front door. We will march on the walls of Kothar and we will tear it down if needs be. We will send a message to them, we won't be easily defeated, we won't go quietly into the night, we refuse to be forgotten!"

A cheer rose up as those that remained understood the power of Phil's words and what his words suggested. Seph nodded her approval, putting a hand on his arm.

"We will make them take notice of us," Seph said, smiling. "Give me one month of preparation and they'll regret trying to snuff us out."

"One month," Phil agreed. "Then we bring the fight to them."

After the crowd dispersed and Phil found food to eat, he bumped into Darius and waved over Seph.

"This is Darius-," Phil began to say, but Seph interrupted him.

"I know who he is, slime ball of the Order, you should be dead," Seph said, her words venomous. "But so should I." Her words lost some of the heat as she spoke those words. "I welcome you back, Eldritch Knight."

"About that," Darius said, looking around awkwardly as he fixed Phil with a look. "I'd like to be considered a Master now, Phil said he'd be willing to spar with me to show you that I am ready for the title."

"It is Phil who must be convinced," Seph said. "But I will stand as witness if you wish to challenge our new Leader of the Order. Perhaps he should put his armor on first, to keep things fair."

"Give me a moment," Phil said, jogging off and getting himself ready. Steffan followed him, helping him into his armor as he understood the annoyance of getting armor on by yourself. With his help it took only minutes and he returned with his sword and spear, ready to fight.

"This is a friendly sparring match," Seph was saying, but Phil barely heard her focusing instead on his opponent. "Avoid killing blows if you can and if you do happen to kill your opponent, know that I'll deliver a swift death to you afterward."

That bit caught Phil's attention, but when he looked over to Seph he saw her attention was fixed on Darius and he knew the words must be meant for him. Did she fear that he was strong enough to match Phil now? That seemed preposterous, but Phil was aware of his shortcomings as much as his advantages. He wasn't invincible, but he was much stronger than any other Eldritch Knights, according to Seph, that they'd had for over a hundred years.

This gave him an edge, but skill was different from raw strength, and he was sure Darius had loads of skill to show off.

"Understood," Darius said, flames already swirling around him in tight controlled bands of energy. He was already showing more control over his flames than Phil could manage without the aid of his amulet, but Phil summoned fire to his right hand and readied his shield on his left, it sparked to life a moment later.

"Don't go easy on me," Phil called out and Darius just nodded, lowering his helmet and cracking his neck to the side.

The first six bars of flames, Phil anticipated, but the other half dozen caught him off guard as they swung around and turned to hit his back. He only managed to defend himself by surging his power and consuming the flame into his own. But he didn't wait for Darius to throw his next attack, realizing immediately that the sword wielding Darius was likely more suited for distance fighting, Phil rushed in to close the distance.

His spear hit open air as Darius withdrew backward, but he could go only so far until he hit the ring of spectators, so he was forced to fight Phil or flee.

He fled to the side, shooting several bars of green flames as he went, trying desperately to keep a distance between them. Phil used his own flames to cut off his retreat, the intensity of his flames a match for Darius's own.

Suddenly Darius found himself surrounded by flame and Phil at his back, so he turned, raising his sword, sheathed in fire. Then suddenly a shield appeared on his arm made completely of fire as Phil speared low for his open side. It caught the weapon, repulsing it as if the fire were made of iron.

That was a neat trick that Phil needed to learn, but right now he had to focus on his attack. He sheathed his spear in flames and struck again, the sheer force of it throwing Darius backward.

But then several blades of fire came from Phil's face, he raised his shield, repulsing each one in turn. The battle continued on for another several minutes before either side began to tire, the extreme use of flame making Phil realize just how hard it was to keep up the pace he'd set.

Back and forth they fought, Darius proving to Phil that he had what it took to be called a master, but still he let the fight continue. Darius never seemed to tire and his work with manipulating flames into objects was on an entirely different level than what he'd been able to accomplish. At one point he created a small herd of four mixana beasts made of flame and threw Phil to the ground, his sword posed to strike a death blow.

But Phil had easily rolled and deflected his attack, slow as it was, before calling a stop to the match about a minute later.

Seph looked impressed and if nothing else that would be enough to tell Phil that he was worthy to be called a master, but he'd seen first hand his power so he made his decision.

"Darius," Phil said, still catching his breath as he spoke.

"You are a Master of the Flame if I've ever seen one. Congratulations."

Darius smiled and looked as if he were about to say something, but then thought better or it and just continued to smile.

With the sparring out of the way, Seph and Phil got Darius situated in a hut before going off by themselves to go over the runic formations to bring Adam back to life.

"It is very complex, but I think given enough time I'll be able to manage it," Seph said, then showing Phil some of the runes she asked, "Do these formations make sense to you?"

"They do," Phil said. He'd been studying runes since Adam fell, learning as much as he could with every spare moment, and he'd discovered a funny thing about runic formations and the like. Most of them followed a similar pattern as programming, but with so much more type identifying than he'd ever seen in a programming language.

It was enough to give him hope that he would be able to work it all out once he truly learned the language and the syntax of how the programming was done. Because if there was one thing Phil was decent at, it was programming.

"I think once I've learned all of these," Phil said, pointing at some modifier runic formations and marks. "I'll be up to speed enough to really help. This isn't too different from the work I did before coming here."

"Truly?" Seph said, intrigued by this. "I wouldn't imagine you as an academic, more of a brute from what you've shown me."

"I do tend to brute force my way through things, it was a

trait that I had in my work too, but I was very much an academic," Phil said, smiling at her as he looked over more of the runic formations.

She had several books on the formations and basic constructs, one of which Phil referenced to figure out a particularly difficult string of runes.

"So you really think we'll be ready to face them in just a month?" Phil asked, after getting stuck on another hard runic formation.

"I think time is not on our side, but a show of force might be enough to get the king to pressure the Council to allow us to return to avoid a drawn out conflict as another war approaches. They will know that they need us if they are to survive the peasant wars," Seph said.

"What can you tell me about the peasant wars?" Phil asked, having learned very little but heard quite a bit about them.

"Not much, only that they have no ascended but seem to be fighting with some advanced weaponry that can take down an ascended. Who is behind it truly, I can't say, but someone is helping them and they want to tear down all that the Orders had built. All of the branches that have gone up against the peasants have failed horribly, that much I know for certain. Only traditional soldiers have had any progress but they claim the peasants are far more armored and trained than they ought to be, defeating them almost as much as they engage them."

"Sounds like a shift in the power structure of the world is happening, wonder what they've discovered that has been giving them an edge?" Phil pondered aloud.

"Something to do with shield they carry, very little word escapes as most of the ascended that go to fight die, but a few have spoken of shields that negate their powers, leaving them open to attack by long range weapons unlike anything Kothar can bring to bear," Seph said and suddenly Phil had a pit in his stomach.

What if they have guns, he thought. Could this entire peasants war be funded by Earth as a way to destabilize the powers of the world before they take over themselves? They have the knowledge to make guns and with a bit of luck he was sure they'd be able to find some material that would give them an edge over ascended, but wait the only Earthlings he'd met had been Paladins, so why would they give something to a warband that could hurt them just as easy?

No it didn't track, but it was also true that Earthlings were not known for getting along well with others, much less themselves, so perhaps it was the other faction that that bitch paladin had spoken of when they'd tortured him.

"You alright?" Seph asked, Phil had lapsed into silence as he thought things through and she'd noticed the concern on his face.

"I might have an idea of who is backing this peasant war, but I sure hope I'm wrong," Phil said, shaking his head. "My people, I've told you little about my past, but I came here from another planet, a migration is what I think Kotharians call it, or at least the treefolk did."

"I'm familiar with the legends, but that's all they are, legends," Seph said, looking at him with raised eyebrows.

"They are fact, Seph," Phil said. "I'm proof of it. We were told it was a fake realm built just for us, but in fact we were transported through space and time to this land. Millions of my people have come here, so many in fact that I fear what they will be doing to this world, because we've had advanced technology for so long, there is no doubt in my mind they will bring some of it here with them, or at least the knowledge to recreate it."

"I'm not familiar with that term or at least how you used it, technology?" Seph asked, clearly confused.

"They have advanced military capabilities, weapons that could drop a man from twice the distance as an arrow and hit with the force of a concentrated blast of Green flame. Now imagine they create weapons that can do that but several hits of it every second. It would be enough to overwhelm even an Ascended I would think," Phil said, unsure of how else to put it.

"I can't imagine such a force," Seph admitted. "But whatever is to come, we must first worry about ourselves and our survival. Come let us try some of these runic formations of the body we've created for Adam. There is much work to be done and little time."

"Alright," Phil said, standing but unable to fully push the ideas from his mind. Such a force would change the very layout of power in this world, making magic second to technology. But what if they were able to combine the two? That truly brought a measure of dread into Phil's soul and he shuttered to imagine it.

Several days later and Phil's head was full to bursting with new knowledge on runes and their formations. He needed something physical to cleanse himself and Seph had mentioned that he ought to speak with Steffan and do some training with him. So Phil set out to do just that, finding him sparring with his sister, who'd also recently received the Green Flame by slaying her own Mixana Beast.

It was amazing how much had happened that Phil had missed, but it was also concerning as Phil personally felt like perhaps Seph had pushed them too hard and too fast. His feelings were somewhat right, considering they'd lost two potentials to Mixana beast mauling's, meaning they weren't ready to face the true might of Mixana.

But so many more had succeeded, leaving them with more Eldritch Knights than Phil wouldn't have guessed would have been possible in so many short months. His adventures away from the Order had truly changed the face of the Eldritch Order. Most looked to Seph as if she were in charge, which Phil couldn't fault them as she'd been the only one around, but he had to start shifting that to himself if he were to truly be the head of the Eldritch Order.

Phil watched the two train a bit further, before calling it to an end.

"I'm going to spare against the pair of you, feel free to bring your best to the table," Phil said, trying to sound confident, but they were both skilled fighters and two on one was never an easy fight.

Steffan turned a glare toward Phil, but his face softened as he looked at Mercy. "Take a break while I fight him," he said, and Mercy nodded, moving off to go rest.

"No," Phil said, trying not to be a dick but not liking the attitude this young Eldritch Knight was giving off. "Mercy get back here and face me along side your brother. We need to learn to fight together as much as we do in single combat. You will face many powerful foes and learning to team up to bring them down will be important."

Phil did his best to explain his reasoning, though he knew he shouldn't have to, but he had been absent in Steffan's training so he gave him a little leeway. If he were to still be a Pale Rider as Phil hoped, he'd need to rein in his attitude and learn to follow orders.

"Very well," Steffan said, punching out with his sword arm and igniting the blade of his sword. "I'll take him head on, you hit him from his flanks."

Mercy nodded her ascent and her spear ignited with fire as well, both were proving themselves at least competent in using their green flame to shroud their weapons. Phil had no weapons on him, but that was as planned.

He held out his hand and focused, forming a spear of green flame that rippled in his grip but would be sharper than any weapon he currently owned. Taking the spear in his good hand, he twirled it and activated his shield. This got a look from Steffan, who didn't look like he approved of a shield being used, but Phil wasn't to the point where he could replace his arm just yet—though he was close and he'd been working on that in conjunction with working on Adam.

If he had his way, he'd be able to do the impossible and connect his paths directly to his new golem-esk arm, giving him access to his full power once more. As it was now he'd never be a true master of the flame, luckily for him he was still a match for almost every ascended he'd met so far, these two included.

Steffan went on the offensive immediately, slashing and cutting wildly, while Mercy rounded to attack from behind. Phil let loose a swish of fire that forced Mercy back into his viewpoint, before slashing out at her with his spear, forcing her even further into the front of him. Meanwhile Phil expertly blocked incoming attacks with his shield, repulsing the blows as much as blocking them, thus causing Steffan no end of annoyance as he had to keep himself from staggering back when he landed particularly heavy blows.

But they were talented and working together Phil was limited to stay mostly on the defensive, slashing great swaths in the air to keep them from flanking him, while slowly turning backward and making a wide circle so that his feet kept moving.

It was Mercy that drew the first successful attack, slashing low but feigning high first, and catching Phil unawares. The hit bounced off his leg armor; they wore similar, if much more basic, armor of grey and green, but the design was distinctly different from the suit Phil wore, which he knew was meant for the Pale Riders specifically.

His moment of thought led to the next successful attack, Steffan hitting him with a clever burst of flame in the chest. Phil focused up and slashed with renewed vigor, scoring a slash against Steffan's armor that left a molten looking cut that would need to be fixed later. Cursing his overzealous attack, he was careful when he swept his legs out, tripping Mercy and aiming a spear just to the side of his face.

Steffan lost his shit after that, despite Mercy being fine, he attacked with a new found zeal and determination that immediately put Phil on his back step, but only for a moment. Mercy didn't enter back into the fray so it was about time to show Steffan who the true master and head of the Eldritch Order was.

Slashing with his spear, he feigned an attack, then hit him full in the face with his shield, slamming his head backward. Then he followed it up by allowing his spear to dissipate and punching the Knight in the chest, slamming him all the way back and to the ground.

"There is always someone stronger," Phil said, his grin hidden by his helmet. "Next time you lose your cool, remember defense is just as good an answer to overwhelming odds as offense. You both did good, take five while I speak with Steffan."

Mercy nodded, listening to his word as fast as she'd listened to her brothers only minutes before.

"Are you still interested in walking the path of the Pale Riders?" Phil asked, expecting he knew the answer but wanting to hear it from the boy. They would be leaving sooner than later to go seek out the beasts that would allow them to have an additional bond of sorts and he needed to know the number he'd be bringing."

"I'm not," Steffan said, not surprising Phil in the least. He'd watched Steffan over the past few days, how he avoided Phil and spoke much to Darius now that another Knight had arrived.

"You intend to walk the path of a Flameborne?" Phil asked, helping Steffan up, despite him looking like he wanted to kill Phil.

"I do," Steffan said, his voice still filled with malice.

"I can respect that, but you need to learn something," Phil said, leaning in to say the next part. "I am the head of the Order and I cannot tolerate disrespect being openly shown. You don't like me? I get that, but you will show me respect or you will not be a part of this Order. Do you understand?"

Steffan was quiet for a moment before looking down at the ground and speaking. "I understand. I will be better."

"Thank you," Phil said, his voice still low and hushed. "Now rise up and be the proud Eldritch Knight I know you are. Don't cast your eyes down when you can look up and meet opponents head on."

"Right," Steffan said, his voice a little less filled with malice than before. "I'll go see about patching my armor."

Phil nodded his head and went to go speak and train with more Eldritch Knights. He had recruiting to do, he wanted at least ten Eldritch Knights, approximately one third of their number, if he could get them as Pale Riders. There were many more half ascended and they even had limited access to the green flame, thanks to some experiments that Seph had been doing, giving them just enough to manifest a flame in battle and make them appear to be full-fledged Knights.

It was more parlor trick than offensive fire though, but still they were trained up and taught to use weapons with their half ascended strength, making them a match for two or three people at normal strength. Plus they could heal, not as fast as fully ascended, but still a small cut would heal in a manner of minutes instead of days.

"This here is Milo, Jasper, and Bram," Torin said, introducing him to the three others that had told Torin—his newest favorite Eldritch Knight as he'd decided to become a Pale Rider with him—that they too would like to be Pale Riders.

"Bram is a damn good rider too, he used to ride horses quite a bit before we got run off," Torin said, his accent one that stuck out to Phil with its lazy way of speaking.

Phil, remembering what passed as horses out here from his very first time waking up in horse shit, just nodded along. If he could ride what they called horses, then whatever Phil was after shouldn't be so hard. From the descriptions in the books they were more goat than horse, but very few of the illustrations looked like anything Phil had ever seen before.

Horns, teeth, and cloven feet, but in a body built for a freaking bull. No doubt they had a passing resemblance to a Mixana beast, but where the Mixana was more buffalo in appearance, the 'Capravax' as they were called in the writings were hard to handle even after the bonding. But regardless several saddles had been made up, per designs from books and he now had four willing souls to take the journey with him. Less than he wanted, but he would be happy to have them along when the time came.

Ned and a dozen of his kind were also going to be going, saying they wanted a chance to help and see if they could bond the beasts as their nature allowed them access to the green flame in a different, more natural way.

Phil was all for this and said as much when Ned approached him. After some casual conversation finished Phil jumped into telling them truly what it meant to be a Pale Rider.

"According to the histories, we will be a powerful mobile force that leans more into mastery of weapons than the flame, not that we ignore its use, but rather focus on how that flame can be used to enhance our weapons natural strikes and even, as you've seen me do in training, replace our weapons completely with green flame. We all have a ways to go, but you four will be the first to tame a Capravax and ride into battle at my side," Phil said, finishing his little speech.

"Hell yeah," Toris said, pumping a fist.

A softer-spoken man, Milo, spoke up next. "Torin mentioned one on one training with you to help us master our weapons?" Milo asked, his voice like a throaty whisper, perhaps he had damage to his throat or perhaps he just spoke that way.

"Yes, as you will be the first, I want you to be our best and brightest, so I will be taking over your training, effective immediately," Phil said.

Between Phil, Steffan, Mercy, Seph, and now Darius, their training of all the Knights had been accounted for, but Phil was going to step away from helping the general group and focus on his Pale Riders. He had armor that needed to be fashioned and the smiths in the tree city were already working full-time to provide them with the very best arms and armor.

"And what about additional pay," Jasper said, he had a more playful tone to his voice and Phil knew him as a jokester of types. "Torin said you'd be paying us?"

"Hey, I said no such thing," Torin shot back.

"It's what I heard," Jasper said, shrugging his shoulders and looking around the group.

"Believe it or not," Phil said, smiling at their antics. "You will be getting paid, all of us will, you serve the Order but not for free. Right now you are being paid in experience, armor, and weapons. But eventually, soon even, that will be replaced by coin."

The Eldritch Keep had a treasury for such likelihood and Phil couldn't imagine anyone going without pay for too long before they looked elsewhere to employ their skills.

"Once we've gotten the Order reinstated and are back in the good graces of the King, I believe there will even be honest work for you all to do so you can make additional coin," Phil said, seeing Jasper brighten at that.

Even Bram smiled, a toothy grin since he'd lost his front two teeth and spoke with a bit of a whistle when he did speak, which wasn't often. "Good to hear it," Bram said.

Phil smiled, happy at having his Pale Riders ready to do combat and soon they were sparring, testing the limits that each of them had. Torin was by far the strongest, a large man with golden locks and piercing purple eyes. Bram was shorter than most men he'd seen, but still an inch taller than him, with his missing teeth and dark hair he stood out amongst the ranks. Mile and Jasper were two of a kind, one larger and muscled— Milo—where Jasper was wiry but of the same height. Despite his wiry frame he was probably the fastest, something about how his use of pathways really gave him an up when it came to speed.

Milo was strong and fast, where Torin was just strong, but he excelled equally in using his green flame, something Torin struggled with. In all he had work ahead of him, but they were all four talented recruits.

CHAPTER 29
JAMES

Several days went by and James trained relentlessly with Golder, getting stronger and stronger with each passing hour. It helped that Golder seemed unwilling to take it easy on him, so in just a matter of days, he felt as ready as he ever would be to face off against the dragon that awaited him. It just so happened that Zarrick returned around that same time.

"Is he prepared?" Zarrick asked Golder.

Golder looked James up and down for a long few seconds before nodding his head. "He is," Golder said. "I've never seen someone progress as fast as he has, it is truly remarkable."

"Is he now?" Zarrick asked and a look of disbelief crossed his face, but it faded back to his normal half angry half bored expression a moment later. "Show me."

"Right," James said, cracking his neck to the side and beginning another fight with Golder, throwing flames out seemingly wildly, but he had a plan.

Golder did as he did, disappearing and reappearing to cut him down, but James anticipated his moves, slashing with his sword and forcing him to retreat back, nearly taking him with a bar of black flame in the process.

This got a dry chuckle from Zarrick, but James didn't pay any attention. He'd been getting better but so far he hadn't actually won a match against Golder, but this would be the time he came out on top.

Turning to see behind himself, Golder appeared a moment later just as black flames consumed the area. But Golder did something with his daggers, clanging them together sharply and the flames disappeared all around him. It was an odd move that he hadn't used before and suddenly James realized something important.

Golder had been teaching him everything, but he hadn't taught him or showed him all that he could truly do. Suddenly James felt less confident about winning the match when two bars of shadow came racing for his head. He dodged and dispersed both, but it put him on the defensive as Golder did an all out attack on him.

The match ended shortly after, with James panting for air as he tried to keep up with the insane speed Golder showed off.

"He is much improved indeed," Zarrick said, nodding his head slowly as he took in the pair. "For a moment I thought he might best you, old friend."

"Take more than some fancy black flames to take me down," Golder said, his words practically a growl.

"But I almost had you," James said, feeling much more like himself than he had in the past several days. "You are one impressive fighter." James bowed his head in respect to the smaller man, knowing full well that he was the better fighter among the pair of them.

He itched to ask Zarrick for a battle, but he doubted the old man would put up much of a physical fight, likely relying wholly on his magic to combat him. And if James' sense of the man was anywhere close to his true power, then he wouldn't want to tangle with him at all. Not that James was afraid of impossible odds, quite the opposite really, but he'd had his fill for that day.

"What now?" James asked, eager to move onto whatever the next phase of his training might be.

"Now you kill a dragon," Zarrick said, smiling wide, though his eyes didn't match the expression on his face, all doom and gloom.

"I'm ready," James said, standing tall and adjusting his black armored helmet to better see out of its visor.

Zarrick led the way into the wilderness and after another day of travel, something close to fifteen hours of walking, they reached a massive cave, not so dissimilar from the one where Zarrick had given him the black flame.

"Inside you will find your prey, an old black dragon, do not underestimate it and remember to sheath your blade in black flame or it will just heal from your strikes," Zarrick said, taking a seat on a small rock with Golder standing at his side.

"Just go right in and kill the dragon?" James asked. "No plan or anything?"

"It is your challenge, if you wish to have a plan, then come up with one," Zarrick said, brushing him off and barely looking up from where he sat.

James looked at them both for a moment longer before shrugging and turning toward his challenge. Just kill a dragon, how hard could that be? All manner of games and stories were based around the idea of a dragon slayer, he could do that, though he'd really wished he knew more about what to expect from the best.

Deciding he ought to try his hand at sneaking, he slowed

his steps as he entered the quiet cave, listening for any sign of the dragon that lurked within. Step by slow step his heart began to race faster and louder. Stay calm, he told himself, he paused to let his heart catch up to his feet.

After a moment of waiting he'd calmed enough to keep going, the inside of the cave was dark and wet, but he found that his eyes, since accepting the black flame, worked fine in the darkest of nights, so the cave wasn't much different. He saw more in outlines and vague black and white colors, but still he could see all the same.

It wasn't what he could see, but what he heard next that gave him pause, a mighty rush of air as if from something giant sleeping ahead. His armor made more noise than he liked, but there was no helping it, so he moved forward, not as quiet as he'd like, but as stealthy as he could manage.

He rounded a bend in the cave and the darkness began almost too much for even his eyes, but just barely he made out the outline of not one dragon, but several. A massive one, likely the oldest by the look of it, surrounded by smaller ones.

By small though, James was referring to their comparative size, for the small ones were each of them big enough for him to ride atop if he wanted. All plans and ideas fled his mind as he counted the dragons as they slept. One, two, three...fourteen, fifteen, sixteen, plus the big mama dragon makes seventeen of them.

How could he be expected to kill one let alone seventeen? Surely Zarrick was playing some bad joke on him, he determined he would turn around and ask Zarrick that very question, when a noise from behind him caught his attention.

He turned and found himself face to face with the eighteenth dragon, a bit larger than many of the smaller ones, but not nearly as big as the massive one in the center. Its eyes glowed a deep black in his odd black and white vision, but he didn't even need to see it anymore, he could smell it, feel its hot breath on his face through the helmet.

There was something wrong though, why hadn't it attacked yet? James lifted his sword and let flames cover his blade. If nothing else he'd be ready for battle. That was when the dragon let out a mighty roar of challenge and began to circle James.

James did a quick check over his shoulder, all of the dragons were awake now, but none had rushed forward to join the fight yet. Then he felt it, some kind of connection with them, he knew suddenly that he would only have to fight one of them. That he was meant to prove himself as much a dragon as they were and that if he wasn't up to the task then he'd die this day.

James rushed forward just as the dragon slashed out with its spiked tail, cutting rock as easy as a knife cutting through butter. His sword hit flesh and the dragon cried out, covering James in black flames that burnt his flesh in a way he'd never experienced.

He pushed out his own flames and the relief was immediate. Staggering for several long moments, the pain so intense as he healed from his burns, that he could do much more than stay on his feet. So it was that the dragon's tail caught him in the chest, renting his armor and throwing him into a nearby wall. James lost all the air in his lungs, but even so he was battle ready only moments later, heaving in large breaths of air.

The dragon shot more fire, its flames a match for James's in every way. James did likewise, meeting force with force. Neither seemed likely to win this competition of flames, but James came up with an idea first, breaking off his flames and rolling to the side.

He then redirected his flames toward the roof, knocking a large stalactite from the ceiling just above the dragon. It smashed down, doing no more damage than a rock falling on James would do, but it bought him time to get into position.

Covering his blade with as much black flame as he could manage, he slashed down on the dragon, cutting deeply. The dragon roared once more and the fight was back on in earnest. Slashing, burning, cutting, stabbing, and more became James's only conscious thoughts as he gave himself fully over to the battle.

A part of him thought he might not be able to win, but a greater part, fed by the flames, laughed aloud at the idea of losing. He'd take this fight and win it like every other fight he had coming in his future. Nothing, dragon or not, would hold him back.

A sudden gust of wind from the dragon's wings caught James off guard, throwing him backward. The dragon was flying above his head now, readying itself for a dive bomb atop him. James stood his ground and raised his weapon in challenge. The dragon came as swift as a diving bird of prey, all predator.

James laughed out loud as he saw his opening, the dragon extending its next too far as it came down. However the black flames that followed made his ability to follow through with his new plan a bit tricky.

He covered his entire body with black flame, holding back the damage from the dragon's flame just as its maw closed around his left arm. James let it happen, taking the momentum of the dive and letting it flow through him. As he was swung violently down, he swung his weapon one handed for the Dragon's exposed next.

The black flamed blade came down with crushing force

and cut deep into the neck. With a final grunt and a feeling of extreme satisfaction, James finished the deadly blow, taking the dragon's head clean off.

The fight had been long and hard, taking every little bit of himself to accomplish it, but he'd done it. Suddenly a new awareness hit him and suddenly he wasn't alone in his own mind.

The dragon's spirit merged with his own, speaking of destruction, power, chaos, and the need to destroy. It spoke of a long legacy of such actions and how James would be a herald of a new age of Dragon Warriors, hell bent on spreading the message of the great black dragon, the one that resides below.

Chaos will rule and destruction is nigh.

As James felt himself grow ever more powerful, the black flame inside of him solidifying and becoming more a part of him, something formed out of nothing. A link of chain and a dragon's head amulet appeared out of thin air around his neck. The spirit as it finished its final merger with James, whispered that this amulet would give him a great well of power. That it was a representation of the Black Dragon's Order.

James appeared outside of the cave, dragging the remains of the dragon behind him. It seemed a waste to let it rot away in the cave, he figured dragon hide had to be worth something, cut up as it was or not.

Both Golder and Zarrick greeted him with eyes as wide as saucers. But that could have been because of the herd of dragons that followed James out of the cave, none of them attacking, just watching. James felt a kinship with them now and had an idea of their minds.

They wouldn't attack unless James asked them too, but there was nothing to be gained by that, so James just sat beside the fallen dragon and waited to hear what was next. Zarrick walked up on him and eyed the dragon's corpse.

"Planning on using that?" Zarrick asked. "I could fashion some pretty powerful armor with it, and that tail could be a great sword that would have no rival."

"Do as you want with it," James said. "Save some of the meat for me, I'm hungry."

Level up, motherfuckers, James thought as he felt around within himself at his new enormous power.

CHAPTER 30
PHIL

Phil stood over the body that was meant for Adam, everything that could be done had been. It was a simple matter of adding the Soul Stone into the chest and waiting to see the activation. Holding the Soul Stone Phil felt a sense of peace wash over him as he lowered it down and placed it inside.

"Now what?" Phil asked when he didn't immediately wake up.

"There is a priming period, but it doesn't say how long it'll take. I guess we just wait," Seph said, it was the two of them alone in a Phil's hut turned workshop. The night sky was full of light, moons glowing brightly. And there was a stillness to it all, as if the very night itself were holding its breath with them.

They waited for nearly six hours, Phil refusing any meals or interruptions as he waited. The time was nearly upon them, the month almost expired, but Phil didn't want to do anything until he was sure Adam would be okay.

"Why is it taking so long," Phil asked, looking through the book and reading over the passage on activation once more. They'd said all the right words, constructed the body correctly.

The pathways were all correct, if they weren't then his prosthetic wouldn't be working as well as it was, giving his left arm the ability to call forth flame once more as well as activate his shield. He'd worked on it in-between the hours of working on Adam with Seph, the Runic Formations were truly like coding and he had the hang of it now, proving himself a true academic in Seph's eyes.

The arm had been his personal project, a way to prove that he knew what he was doing and it had worked, so why wasn't Adam coming awake as he should?

"Perhaps we should call it a night," Seph said. "Get some rest and let's pick it up in the morning. We have many many lines of runic formations to go through to ensure we didn't mess anything up."

"Fine," Phil said, more than a little angry at the idea of giving up when he'd felt they were so close.

The next two days were spent going through every single line and rune, and they determined that it had all been done according to the book. There were places Phil suggested they could improve things, but they dared not go off script and risk it not working. And yet it still wasn't working.

"I need to leave and seek out the Capravax with those I've chosen," Phil said, his chest going cold as he considered leaving his friend behind. "Put him somewhere safe and we will figure it out after we return. There has to be a way to activate him, something hidden or kept from the book. We will figure it out."

Seph nodded as Phil reached down and touched the soul stone one more time. A sudden surge of peace hit him and he knew his friend was still there, just not able to connect with this new body for whatever reason.

Phil and Seph went over their plan once more. Seph would

take the full force and might of the Eldritch Knights to the city of Kothar in one week, enough time for Phil to gather the Capravax and return with speed. They would rally the tent city folk, offering all of them a chance to fight and be a part of something greater.

They'd discussed it and gotten the tree folk on board with them bringing a mass of people through their land and to the Eldritch Keep, where a city would begin to be constructed. They'd welcome all those that had been cast aside, training only those that could be trusted, but giving aid freely.

This alone ought to make the Kothar royalty think twice about exterminating them. With a sizable enough population and healthy hunting grounds as well as a growing agriculture they were fully prepared to offer a safe haven for those who wished for it. A place separate from the Peasant Wars that were moving closer and closer as the months progressed.

Seph and Phil agreed that it wasn't a perfect plan but it would put pressure on the Kothar's ruling class and the Council of Orders. Phil gave another speech, he was getting better at it, but still he preferred not to speak to everyone at once, enjoying being able to connect on a more one on one level.

After finishing his rousing speech, he found Milo, Jasper, Bram, and Torin.

"You four ready to leave?" Phil asked, directing his question at Torin, the one that spoke for the group most of the time.

"We are," Torin answered. "We've each got the saddles that you had made up and saddle bags to hold our belongings once we have steads to put them on. A shame we don't have horses to carry our stuff until we find these Capravax fellows."

"We could always ask the tree folk to carry everything,"

Jasper said, laughing as he spoke. "They are basically horses, right?" He elbowed Milo who looked practically mortified and said nothing.

"None of that," Phil said, seeing Ned approaching from behind. "The tree folk as you call them are my closest allies and fought at my side long before we pulled you all from the tent city around Kothar. Show them the respect they deserve."

"Yes, sir," came a volley of replies from each of them, even Milo. Jasper was no longer grinning and kept his eyes toward the ground, avoiding Phil's gaze.

He'd get over it, Phil knew. Jasper was like that, he'd go too far on something, get censured, then full shitty for a time before bouncing right back into being a jokester again.

"Will we be skipping training today?" Bram asked, his words whistling as he spoke, still missing several teeth. Phil had to figure out a way to get some kind of dentist to help the man out, but he knew so little about teeth, he'd honestly hoped that his missing teeth would have grown back. Phil's own teeth had shown the ability to repair themselves, even growing a new one when he'd lost one to the fight of his life where he'd lost his left arm.

Arms were a bit harder to grow back though, as time had shown since his loss of his left arm and it never actually grew back as he'd have liked. Instead he'd been forced to wear a prosthetic, but now the one he had was as good as his original, but far less sensitive to hot and cold or even the touch of flesh.

It would do for what he needed though, Phil thought as he summoned his flame to his left hand, feeling the nodes connecting with the artificial ones he'd created in the arm. It allowed him to fully access his lost power and bring to bear his full strength once more. He even had ideas for splitting the paths and perhaps adding a way to multiply the power output of his left arm.

It required a tiny trickle of power to move it around, but he was able to do all the things he'd used his left hand for previously, which wasn't too much. He could pick up items, throw a ball, and more.

"Fancy new arm," Jasper said, finally coming out of his rebuked state. "Any chance you can make me a pair of legs that walk on their own?"

"Your legs look fine to me?" Phil asked, looking at the man with an odd expression of amusement mixed with a touch of annoyance.

"Yeah but if I had a spare I'd be able to rest my real ones while the fake ones walked my happy ass alongside you lot," Jasper said, laughing at his ill executed joke.

"Yeah," Phil said, blinking a few times before looking over to Torin. "Let's move out, no training until we stop to rest for the night."

The journey began with little fanfare, the rest of the Eldritch Knights were preparing to march into battle while the Pale Riders went to find their mounts so that they could be of the most help during the battle.

"My wife is going to be thrilled to hear I've made it this far with the Eldritch Knights," Torin said, smiling wide as he walked beside Phil, who'd been mostly silent as he went over what could possibly have gone wrong with Adam's construction.

"You're married?" Phil asked, surprised. "I didn't realize. Where is your wife?"

"Living inside the city," Torin said. "I got her enough coin to get her and the two little ones over to a place called Dockside, where Seph helped them meet a contact to help find them work and a place to live. Nice lady, that Seph."

Dockside was not likely a safe place at the moment, but Phil didn't see as much, seeing how proud Torin was to have gotten his wife and kids into the city. He supposed that it must be nicer than staying out with the tent city and the dangers that came with living outside the walls.

"Ain't you worried she'll be taken advantage of?" Jasper asked, appearing to be serious for once in his life, but I could see the hint of a grin just a hair's length away from appearing on his face.

"My boy is nearly a man, Tor will keep them safe, he's a proud lad," Torin said. "Mean to have him tested to be a Knight like me after we settle this whole Council business."

"We'd be proud to have him," Phil said, putting a hand on Torin's shoulder and patting his back.

The day's travel ended after fifteen hours of walking and running. They'd taken a slower pace to allow the tree folk like Ned to keep pace, but they still had a few more days to travel before they'd reach the place noted in the books, high up in the mountains where the air thinned.

Through the next few days he got to know each of his Pale Riders more and more. It was nice to get one on one time with them, the Order having grown so fast he'd not had a chance to meet with many of the new Knights personally.

They trained at night, traveled during the day, hunting for meat on occasion when they needed to, but mostly stuck to the hard tack biscuits that were the normal travel food. At some point they found some fruit and Phil showed them the trick of creating more from the seed of an already eaten plant, thus multiplying their yield.

Torin had learned the process already, but played along,

before informing Phil in private that they learned as much from Seph and it was why they were able to produce so many viable crops in a short period of time. Phil wondered at whatever marvels Seph had taught them, but he smiled internally at the thought that he was a part of a larger community that was thriving under his leadership and that of Seph's.

Together they would do great things.

They spotted the first of the Capravax the next morning, and based on the descriptions it truly was one of the beasts they sought. Phil pointed it out on the horizon, the beast much more goat looking than horse.

"Those horns look dangerous," Torin said. The beast had two sets of horns, one pair curled and another set that were shorter and pointed straight out.

"They do indeed," Phil said, pinching the bridge of his nose as he recalled what they were meant to do to bond with the creatures.

It roughly said that they needed to be consumed in fire, a process that binds their spirit with that of the caster, but also destroys the body of the Capravax. Somehow that seemed like it would be unhelpful, killing the Capravax and all, but Phil trusted in the words of those that came before him.

Phil went on ahead with his Pale Riders, leaving Ned and the rest of the company to stay behind for now.

They neared the first one, and it gave out a cry of alarm that definitely sounded more goat like than horse. Suddenly over the horizon came an entire herd of Capravax, varying from small to larger enough to hold a Koth man atop their backs.

"I'll go first," Phil said, eyeing the largest and closest of the Capravax.

He rushed forward, his power lending him the speed of the gods. With each step he prepared his flame for the task of consuming the Capravax, hoping that it was the right move.

Right as he neared though, new figures came over the horizon, people, though they wore thick furs against the cold of the upper mountain, they were very recognizable as plain old humans.

Phil broke off his attack, but the large Capravax had already begun to charge at him, so he refocused himself. Then a whistle filled the air and the Capravax broke off its charge, snorting and huffing in disapproval.

Phil's companions caught up with him, and Ned and those left behind also appeared to be moving up to give him backup as more and more fur clad folks appeared over the horizon.

He counted a dozen or more, at the very least.

Three approached him at speed and he readied his green flame just in case. It turned out not to be necessary as they carried only heavy wooden staves and made no move to attack as they neared.

"Why have you trespassed on our herds?" A deep voiced man speaking in clipped fashion asked. It wasn't all too different from the way the tree folk spoke and suddenly Phil saw a striking resemblance between the tree folk and these mountain herdsmen.

They didn't have sap shells, so that was different, but neither did Ned or those that came with him anymore.

"I've come to do as Eldritch Knights have done in the past, claim a Capravax as my steed," Phil said, deciding honestly was going to be the best policy for this lot.

The three that approached were all dark haired, with eyes

the color of an orange, very distinct with their narrowed features and close set eyes. They had furs covering most of their body and their skin was a lighter color than Ned and his kind, but still it was like they could be cousins or something, so similar they were in every other fashion.

"Your kind has not visited our borders for some time," the lead man said again, then pausing as he nodded in our direction. "I am Gur'Cah and these are my people, the Cah'tur. We welcome a chance to open ties with your people once more. What have you brought to trade?"

It was Phil's turn to panic as he mentally went through what he could offer these people. Sure they had supplies but what truly could they want for out here in the high point of the mountain.

"My name is Phil, Leader of the Eldritch Order," Phil said. "We have many gifts to offer, perhaps you can tell me what you require and we can help you obtain it?"

The negotiations, as they were, took another ten minutes or so until they agreed on trading a half dozen Capravax for an assortment of fruits and vegetables. They, apparently, lived mostly off of the meat of the Capravax and other wild game, so fruits and vegetables were a rarity for them.

"May I speak to you?" Ned asked, his clipped way of talking so similar to the newcomers that it drew Gur'Cah's gaze.

"Of course," Phil began to say, then turning he saw that Ned was looking at Gur'Cah and not him.

Gur'Cah nodded his ascent and they walked off speaking in hushed tones. Phil overheard a portion of it, but it sounded like Ned was just introducing himself using his traditional name.

Another pair of the newcomers led over the Capravax

they'd picked out for them, six of the largest in their herd, big enough to be ridden.

Phil had asked if they knew about the process, but they claimed they knew little as it wasn't something the Eldritch Knights ever did with them watching.

Following the book's instruction down to the letter, Phil readied his flame as the largest of the group stepped forward, ready to fight by the look on its massive face.

Fire shot forth and Phil immediately felt something, a kinship as his flame connected with the spirit of the Capravax. But it wasn't going to go without a fight, that wasn't in the nature of the Eldritch Knights nor the beasts that shared the flame from the Mixana beasts.

It shot through the flames, hitting Phil hard in the chest with a glancing blow as Phil turned to the side at the last second. Bringing up more flames, Phil consumed the beast even as it attacked furiously. Striking here and there, Phil took blows that would kill a normal man, but he held strong.

Finally with a final mewling sound, the Capravax went down in a smoldering heap of ruined flesh. According to the book he had access to he now needed to fully burn it away while the connection formed. So he increased his flame, sweat covering his forehead as he forced out every bit of his power into consuming it.

Phil couldn't see much else, but he imagined he was putting on quite the show for those watching.

The connection he'd felt between this Capravax beast was different than what he had with the merging of spirits with the Mixana beast, but it had tunes that were similar. He felt a rush as the Capravax's spirit collided with his own, violent and agitated by its death.

He held firm and mastered it, forcing his will around it

until it settled within him, adjacent to his core but not a part of it. Then the process was over and Phil was left confused.

The books spoke of being able to call forth the beast at any time, but he'd just killed it and burned away its corpse. Then he felt the urging from the beast to be let free and he followed his instincts, pushing at the soul sitting adjacent to his own.

It moved like his magic and when he released it, flames appeared in the form of the Capravax, but after a moment the flames died away and before him stood a full and living Capravax.

Looking it up and down, Phil marveled at what he'd just been a part of. Somehow he'd used his magic to summon forth a physical beast to ride into battle. He strapped on the saddle and saddle bags, before mounting up on it.

"Do as I've done, trust your instincts," Phil said. "I'm going for a ride."

And ride he did, moving at speeds even he couldn't manage as his Capravax jumped, ran, and dodged through the mountain tops.

"I need a name for you," Phil said aloud despite being very much alone where the air thinned and snow still stuck to the ground. He had a general idea of how to get back, but he was certain that the Capravax knew exactly how to get back. It was like he could sense the beast's surface thoughts.

"What about Cappy?" Phil asked, reaching down to pet its fur.

The Capravax shook its head in annoyance, not liking the name at all. Then Phil had a thought, he was a Pale Rider after all and that had Earth specific implications. But he doubted that the Capravax would want to be called mors, which was the Latin word for death. His sister would remember but he only knew what little Latin he did because of her.

Damn, he really thought he had a cool name for his mount but he couldn't remember what in the hells the Latin name for it would be. So instead he came up with his own name for it, Reaper.

"How do you like, Reaper?" Phil asked and the snort of annoyance wasn't as loud this time. It was almost like he could tell the meaning the word had and he liked it.

It was around that time that he recalled the Latin word for death being mor or mors, which after all wouldn't have been a good name. Reaper fit well enough for what he wanted from the steed.

He took Reaper out a bit further before turning back and checking on his other Pale Riders. They'd all successfully tamed their mounts. Phil swelled with pride as he saw them all mounted up and ready for battle.

The Pale Riders would ride and nothing would stand in their way.

CHAPTER 31
JAMES

James wore his new armor well, a cloak hiding most of it as he neared the arena that he knew all too well. Emotions of every kind rolled through him, but he focused on the one he cared most about, vengeance.

"You can't come in here," some nameless face said, but James just shouldered his way past. No guards came to greet him yet, there wasn't a fight going on but according to Golder the mages would be here for some kind of meeting and despite his warnings, James decided he'd waited long enough.

He had something to do first, going down to the prison area, he dispatched all the guards he saw with ruthless attention, killing each one with a single well placed blow with his new sword. It was made from the Dragon's tail and according to Zarrick, would be harder than any metal you could get your hands on.

It cut through metal easily enough, that much was true, James thought, as he looked down at the final fallen guard. He'd barely gotten out a cry of help before he fell, dead and lifeless on the ground. James no longer worried about looting them or collecting coin. Zarrick had given him the best gear and more coin than he knew what to do with, all for some later promised favor.

"You're free," James said, swinging the gate open and looking at the first cell filled with bewildered looking Kotharians. Large and muscled each of them, they didn't wait for a second invitation, bolting for the door and toward the surface immediately.

One by one he opened and cleared twelve cells, with anywhere from two to a dozen prisoners each.

Now to do the part he was most excited about, dealing with those pesky mages and their magic.

He reached the upper area, the only area he hadn't checked yet and found four men in blue robes waiting for him.

"Are you the messenger that Zarrick said we were to meet?" An elderly man said. "It is quite unusual to keep us waiting, Zarrick or no Zarrick, we've got business that needs attending."

He barely got the chance to finish his sentence before James casually inserted his sword into the man's throat, then wiping it out to the side, he took his head off as he would pull the wings off an insect.

The other three men were quick thinking, despite their age and sparks of blue followed, throwing James backward for only a moment before black flames covered his entire body.

"Black flames?" One of them shouted. "I've never seen such a thing, hurry and kill him quickly!"

He died next, his barrier of blue collapsing under the weight of James's Black Flames. His sword shattered the next barrier just as monsters began to appear all around him.

Hands pulled at James, but he was an unstoppable force, breaking and burning his way through the illusions to get to his prey. Nothing could or would stand against him!

That was when two large sparks of blue smashed into him and suddenly he was having a hard time thinking.

"Bind him quick, no not the Litemar binding, use Gheltings technique, ah damn he's already awake," Came frantic voices. If not for them arguing they might have got off whatever the hell they were talking about, but as it were, James let loose a wave of black fire and screams filled the room even as he stood among the burning arena.

"That was far too easy and not as satisfying as I'd hoped," James said, all four were down and dying from the overwhelming flames he was producing.

He thought he heard one of them scream why or something close to it, so he elaborated to them while they died to his flames.

"You imprisoned me," James said simply. "But that wasn't enough, you had to take from me someone I cared about. You remember the priest Pete? I forget what you all called him, but I've had enough of losing people I care for. You all broke me and you get to pay the price."

They were dead by the time he finished his small rant, but he didn't care, he let the flames warm him as he decided that the arena couldn't remain standing. With black flames so powerful that they metal began to bend, James filled the arena stands with fire next.

He hoped everyone was out, but he couldn't bring himself to care if they weren't. It was time to end this part of his life and move on to what was next.

Down with the government that allowed this kind of barbaric treatment of prisoners. Down with everything, James thought with a smile as he left a burning wreckage behind him.

Golder had given his specific instructions to be as careful and secretive as possible, but as James checked behind himself, black flames roaring up into the night sky, he knew Golder wouldn't be happy with him.

Golder was furious as it turned out and James found himself having to summon up his black flame in his defense as Golder began smacking him around.

"You fool," Golder spat the words. "Is that your idea of subtly? Everyone is talking about the mysterious black flames now, you might have undone several years of work." He spoke through clenched teeth as he prepared another attack, but Zarrick appearing in the training ground inside of the massive black tower, stopped him short.

"He is chaos, did you expect any less?" Zarrick said, humor evident in his voice. "Our plans move forward, are you ready to enact phase two of my plans?"

"No," James said, then leaning down to better be on height with the small man, he said it again. "No, I'm not. I've got my own plans now, give me a few weeks to finish up my work, then I'll be ready."

The flame burned hot inside of him, giving him courage and power. He was not one to be pushed around by some shrimp of a mage. He'd killed four of his kind as easy as squashing a bug, perhaps he could do the same to Zarrick?

"Defiance will not gain you much," Zarrick said, but then he seemed to consider something and continued. "However in this I will grant you a reprieve. Go and spread your chaos, but return in three weeks ready to follow my Orders. Do not make me seek you out, for you will not be a match for my power, trust me."

Golder stiffened suddenly as power swelled around Zarrick

and James felt the vastness of it. Nothing like the four mages he'd fought against, this power was overwhelming as much as it was attractive to James. Yes, he would stay on this one's good side for now. He needed to figure out how to harness such vast power after all, for his own paled in comparison.

Which was saying something considering James now thought himself more powerful than Golder. Sure the smaller man had more tricks and he was a master of his techniques, but if put up against each other in a contest of pure power, James would put his money on himself every single time. He'd proven as much when going against four so-called mages, their barriers and zaps of power were nothing when compared to his vast well of flames he pulled from.

James had no doubt that when the time came for him to do whatever dirty deed Zarrick required, that he'd be a match for it, or rather whoever it ended up being. For he had no doubt in his mind now that Zarrick was just raising him up to put someone else down.

But why didn't the small statured man do the deed himself, James found himself wondering, but when no easy answer came to him he just shrugged. He had the finest loot, more coins than he knew what to do with, a quest to complete and best of all, power in which to accomplish said quest.

"If I'm not needed," James said, he couldn't help but let a touch of arrogance enter his voice, the flames within him pulling him to be someone different than he had been before.

"Go, but remember that some caution is okay," Zarrick said, laughing as he did. "The world might not be ready for a Dragon Order just yet."

"Sounds like a 'them' problem," James said under his breath as he turned to leave.

He'd learned on a few more arena prisons and he would go

set them free, but this time he'd search them for any signs of Ascended. He would start building his own force and Order, Zarrick and Golder be damned.

"What do you think you are doing?" Golder screamed at James as he returned from his two week vengeance spree.

"My job," James answered the shorter man, grinning down at him.

He'd destroyed four of the major arenas, found two that could be Ascended and took only one, a man named Felton Crand as his disciple. He was dark skinned but as big as any Koth James had come across. What was more, he didn't have a mouth on him like that Bradnon fellow that James had accidently killed when he said something a bit too close to home.

James had more plans, killing government officials and the like, but instead of going straight to that he needed to build a force of his own. So with Felton's help—a gang member from out of the city until recently—he would do just that. The fact he'd been from out of town explained his lack of Ascended testing being done on him, or so he said as much.

He'd spend the other free week setting up a gang of his own, he'd named them the Black Dragoons, not exactly subtle but better than nothing. As a Dragoon, Felton was tasked with gathering intelligence, coin, and recruiting thugs to join the lower ranks. They set up a warehouse in the dockside, the place where such activities wouldn't be easily detected because of the lack of guard presence in the area.

It had felt right being back in his original stomping grounds, building something more. As it turned out, the dockside area was abuzz with activity if you knew where to look or how to look. Apparently an entire gang or two had dissolved recently, so the Black Dragoons weren't the only new upstarts.

They were however the only new upstarts that had two ascended on their side, Felton and James cut a bloody swath through many of the newer gangs, until two of the more well established ones finally, just the day before, had come to the table to talk territory lines. James had been surprised by that turn of events, what was more he was shocked to find two Ascended at the head of the last two major guilds.

According to them there was a third member of what they called the Tor'I, an elite ascended that ruled the dockside. And then they gave him an invitation to join said organization. James jumped on the opportunity, despite being confident he could just kill both the gang leaders and be done with it. He set up Felton as their head, and even had some black armor crafted for him and taught him a thing or two about what it meant to be a true Black Dragoon.

He hadn't gifted him with the flame yet, apparently it was a process that involved a pricey tonic and then he only had a limited amount of time before he'd burn up unless he killed a dragon. Unfortunately the dragon herd was far enough away that even James couldn't feel them, so he'd have to go through that portal and he didn't trust himself to remember all the phrases that had been used.

He'd need Zarrick to grow his forces, but before that he really needed to find more Ascended, which is why he returned in truth. He had a few ideas of where to find them, but he wanted to see if Zarrick was onto him yet, or if he even cared he was trying to grow his Order.

"You think you are so clever, you think we don't know what exactly you've been up to or what your end goal is?" Golder said through clenched teeth.

James ignored him, continuing to walk to where he knew Zarrick would be waiting for him in his office. That didn't cool Golder's mood a bit and James almost thought he was going to take a swing at him. It was refreshing to hear that they did, at least thought they did, know what he was up to. It meant he wouldn't have to hide it and perhaps Zarrick would respect his show of power.

He reached the door and knocked, though he could feel the powerful aura of the small man inside.

"Come in," Zarrick said a moment later.

"I'm here as ordered," James said, Golder trailing behind him, red in the face.

James grinned at the shorter man's indignation, but one look from Zarrick wiped the look off his face.

"You think you are fine to just go out and try to build up your own little gang, eh?" Zarrick said, more serious than James had ever heard him before.

James started to speak, then thought better of the words he was about to utter and tried again. "I'm merely going what I feel is right for my own path. I thought you'd be happy that I plan to spread the Black Flames influence."

"How you even found a single person to Ascend that hadn't been placed into an Order already, boggles the mind, but I hear you found two and killed one. What a waste. Now I've heard rumors that the Eldritch Order has grown by several dozen members, you both are turning into more trouble than I cared for," Zarrick said.

"The Eldritch Order?" James said, liking the sound of it. "Is this who I'm meant to exterminate? I love kill quests."

"Matter of fact, yes," Zarrick said. "I've a mission for you. There is a leader of these Eldritch Knights, a man of great power. He holds an amulet, you need to convince him to give it to you. If he won't, then you will kill him and we will wait for the next Eldritch Knight to take it up and repeat the process until I've got the amulet in my hands."

"Sounds easy enough," James said, picking at a piece of food in between his teeth. "I'll have your little amulet delivered within a week. Just point me at the man I need to deal with."

"There is an opportunity coming up, according to my spies, just make yourself ready and resume your training with Golder," Zarrick said. "He looks like he could use a bit of a physical release and you are just the punching bag to take it."

Golder was suddenly smiling as wide as James had ever seen, and that didn't bode well for him. James tried to keep up his relaxed look, but he was tensing over the idea that perhaps Golder was going to show him just how much he still had to learn after all.

CHAPTER 32
STEFFAN

No force waited for them as they left the great portal gate and moved toward Kothar. Of course there wasn't anything to stand before them, Steffen thought, smiling wide. Phil, his former master, had said there would be, but he seemed to be wrong as much as he was right.

Darius, Steffan's new master, walked beside him and he truly respected the man and his abilities. Mercy had still chosen to study under Seph, but Darius had taken over all of his training and taught him more than he'd ever hoped to learn about the green flame and what it could be used for.

The moon was high in the sky as they moved in force toward Kothar. The plan, as it was now, was to stay about a mile out from the main walls, close enough to rush in if needed, but far enough to let Steffan work. He was going to go speak with the leaders of the Tent City and offer them a way out of squalor and starvation.

He had no doubt that most wouldn't take him up on the offer but he had to try. Moving out ahead of the group he walked the mile or so to the edge of the tent city, everyone knew him here now and no one messed with him. Often he'd recruited people, giving them a new lease on life, so he did get some attention, just none of it negative.

He reached the headquarters of the largest gang easily, not a one of their thugs trying to stop him from coming, lest they grab hold of his attention and burn up. He'd only had to kill a few to get that point across, the stories took on lives of their own after that.

"I'm here to talk with whoever is leading this group," Steffan said, he'd grown tired of remembering the names of the man or women who was currently in charge, it changed weekly.

"Madam Du-," one of the thugs began to say, but Steffan cut him off.

"I don't care what her name is, take me to her or risk my wrath," Steffan said.

At first he thought the man might challenge him and he used his ability to feel outward, his was weak and not reliable, to see if the man had potential. Seph and Phil were much more skilled in detecting those who had power or potential, but Steffan was getting alright at it.

Sure enough this one had potential, though he couldn't tell how much or if it had been tapped yet.

"Fine," the thug said, but Steffan raised a hand.

"What's your name?" Steffan asked, startling the thug into a few seconds long silence.

"Chadwick, uh, sir," Chadwick said, standing tall before Steffan. He'd obviously heard that those he took an interest in were rewarded, though what rewards those entailed were likely not easy for their common minds to figure out.

"Well Chadwick, you are coming with me, you are my man

now, got it?" Steffan said, sparking some green fire in one hand to unnerve the man even more.

"Y-yes, sir," Chadwick said, showing more sense than Steffan would have guessed.

"Show me to your former leader," Steffan said, gesturing that Chadwick should lead the way through the tent maze.

They passed through many security checkpoints, Chadwick waving them all away, and all were happy to oblige him when they saw who walked at his side.

"Well met, I'm Madam-," the leader began to say, she wore better than most clothing and a fresh scar on his left cheek.

Steffan cut her off as well. "Your name is of no consequence," Steffan said, brushing her words aside with a gesture of his hand. "You know who I am, that is what is important."

"I do," said the woman, but she was not happy to be spoken to like this, several of her thugs had some huge stones, reaching for weapons in his presence. She raised a hand of her own, stopping them before they made a mistake that would get them all killed.

"Then listen and listen well," Steffan said, launching into the words Seph had prepared for him. He laid out what was going to be happening soon and how all of the tent city was being offered a place where shelter and food would be plentiful. That all they ask is that all abled bodies men and women stand and fight on their side. Then he added that there would likely not be any fighting, but it was the sheer numbers that they were looking for.

She asked if they'd be provided arms or armor, Steffan told her that weapons would be provided, but no armor. This seemed to settle her a bit and she nodded several times before surprising Steffan by agreeing to the plan he'd presented.

She then went on to explain that she had united the gangs

and currently she had, using her name before Steffan could cut her off again—Madam Dun—, control over much of the population. She also informed him that she knew what he was about, taking those who could be ascended and raising them up into power. She wanted access to this power as a condition of their agreeing to go along with the plan.

Steffan tried to reach out and see if she was even a candidate, but his power failed to detect anything. Either way she might be a candidate for half ascension, so he agreed and the work of getting the various tribes under the direction of the gangs began.

Hours had passed and still they weren't as far along as Steffan would like, what was worse there seemed to be some activity at the gate. He was on his way to check it out now, keeping his armor hidden under a cloak and moving through the crowd like a shadow in the waning light of the day.

He neared the wall, where the tent city went right up to it and made an interesting discovery. Guards were out in full force and inviting people into the city, entire crowds were disappearing into the open gate and on the other side was a force of armored soldiers. He could barely make out the glint of their armor, but he was sure that was what they were.

The city was trying to empty out the tent city to move a force of soldiers out into the open. The wide road would be enough for them to do that, so why, Steffan wondered, had they begun to empty out his potential new citizens?

They must have an idea of what they were up to, it was the only explanation that made sense. Turning he disappeared back into the crowd, ready to escape to Seph once he'd made his way through the crowds. Unfortunately a guard called after him, he'd gotten too close too fast and one had taken notice of him.

"Halt!" Came the call, but Steffan was already moving, swiftly cutting through the crowd as at least one guard ran after him. If not for the mass of people, he might have broken away and got free, but as it was the guard followed in the wake he created, catching up to him seconds later.

Steffan turned and punched the guard square in the face before he could say another word, laying him out flat and calling more attention to himself. Now everyone was giving him room, so he threw off the cloak and showed himself for what he was.

"Stay back or die!" Steffan yelled, turning to run again, but then two figures were sprinting from the open gate and moving at speeds that surprised even Steffan.

"Get clear," Steffan called, as the peasants made room around him he knew it wouldn't be enough and people were going to die. But he had to save himself and get the intel to Seph, so he ignited his inner flame and flared it around himself.

A moment later two figures stopped before him, one a Paladin with golden armor and another slim man with great ornate robes on, wielding a bone white staff.

"It appears one of the bugs we are after has been caught in our web," said the skinny of the two, a priest most likely. As if in answer to Steffan's thoughts, his form shifted and darkened to a translucent purple and tendrils of power swished around him seemingly on their own accord.

"Come quietly and no one needs to be hurt," Came a deep vibrating voice from the Paladin.

"I'd rather die," Steffan said, following up his words with a ball of green fire meant to catch the paladin off guard.

Instead the large man flicked an impossibly large sword off his back and deflected the ball of green flame as if it were nothing.

"So be it," the Paladin said, golden flames appearing all around him as his form tensed from the effort.

That was a good sign, Steffan told himself, he wasn't a master of the flames, but obviously a weapons master of some type. That was when his partner attacked, shadowy tendrils reaching out to tie up Steffan.

His sword appeared in his hands in a flash, burning bright green as he slashed and cut away the tendrils of power. Only one or two got through, but it was enough to slow him down as the priest began to summon more.

"It ends now," the Paladin said, raising his massive sword and rushing forward in a blur.

A blast of fire rained down in front of the Paladin and Steffan let out a sigh of relief. He cut free the last few tendrils and looked for the location of the attack. Far in the distance running as fast as the wind, came Darius, Seph, and Mercy, with their forces gathering in a wide line behind them.

Darius, the true master of the Flameborne path, had attacked from such a distance and with such force that it blew the paladin back, true mastery being shown and inspiring Steffan to do more.

Flaring out his power he lashed out with all he had, he had to prove himself worthy of the power he'd been gifted. Screams went up as flames lashed and consumed, but the Paladin and the Priest were ready for it, going on the defensive.

The Paladin charged in again, this time making it through the flames with his entire body covered in golden fire. Steffan met him sword to sword, letting the blow slide off his blade.

He had to avoid taking the full brunt of this Paladin's attack as he was clearly stronger physically.

But his techniques were poor when it came to true power, so Steffan flared his fire and slammed the Paladin in the chest with a semi formed flame Mixana beast, a technique that Darius had been trying to teach him.

Then forming a dagger of flame he hit him right in the panels between the armor and the Paladin yelled in surprise, but Steffan wasn't done.

Before he could draw his blade across the armored man's neck, several shadowy figures appeared around him, grabbing hold of him and stopping him in his tracks. He flared his flames but they didn't go away.

"Time to die," came the priest's voice, wicked sounding as ever.

But it wasn't Steffan's time to die, he had friends and he no longer was standing alone. Before the Paladin could recover himself to give the death blow, Mercy appeared like a speeding arrow, the wind around her whistling as she struck with her thin fast blade sheathed in green flames. Her hair whipped out behind her and on her face was a look of perfect calm and serenity.

Steffan could have hooted he was so happy to see her, but instead he cut himself free of the shadowy constructs just as Mercy lay into the priest, distracting him and weakening his magical forms.

She'd drawn blood from several places and the priest looked completely astonished to be fighting a mere child and losing.

But the Paladin had recovered and Steffan would never let his sister fight alone if he could help it. He rushed forward and back to back they fought off their opponents.

With two Eldritch Knights fighting them directly and more

on the way, the two who had been so confident before started looking for ways to escape. If only the two Eldritch Knights would let up for only a moment, then perhaps they could use their speed to put distance between them.

Steffan read all these thoughts off their faces and smiled at having them on the backstep. He pushed their advantage, but Mercy caught his eye and shook her head. She was right, they had to get back to the group and save as many people as possible.

Steffan let them go, both the Paladin and the Priest fled a moment later and the first battle of the day ended with no deaths.

Returning through the crowds Steffan reported to Seph.

"They are willing to join us, but the city is also offering them refuge, we won't get as many as you hoped, but we should start distributing weapons all the same," Steffan said, seeing Seph's face and not being able to read her expression in the slightest.

"See to it," Seph said, turning to Darius. "I want formations and clean lines. We want to present the worst possible scenario for the enemy, for the first strike often comes before any blood is shed."

Steffan turned and noticed a force of soldiers were coming out of the wall and a thought struck him. "Why do they move out of the safety of the walls, wouldn't it be better for them to stay safe behind them? We have no siege weapons," Steffan asked, looking at them perplexed as a multitude of soldiers mixed with Ascended began to form ranks outside the walls.

"Politics," Seph said, chuckling a bit as she spoke. "The king won't risk us damaging his precious wall right before a possible attack from the peasants army. Hell the fact that any soldiers have joined the councils cause surprises me, but they will be nothing compared to our forces, no matter their numbers."

"I don't understand politics at all," Steffan admitted, his view on life and living much more straightforward without need for such lies and half truths.

"You'll learn one day," Seph assured him, a kind smile on her face as she took him in. Then as if flicking a switch, she looked up and narrowed her eyes. "Who is that?"

Steffan turned to see a lone man moving through the ranks of army gathering before them, he wore all black armor and Steffan could feel his power even from a distance. Whoever he was, he wouldn't be an easy target to kill.

"You feel that," Darius said, shaking his head as he returned from wherever he'd gone. "His aura feels as powerful as Phil's, maybe more so."

"He is broadcasting it in a foolish manner, we now know who must fall first, I will take care of him and Darius you will fight by my side. Together we can take him."

"If you say so," Darius said, he did not look convinced. "Where is Phil and the Pale Riders? They promised to be here today and we won't be showing our best without him."

"We don't need him," Steffan began to say but stopped what else he had a mind to say with a look from Seph.

"He will be here," Seph said, nodding her head and looking as confident as ever.

***

Battle lines were being established and Steffan found himself with Mercy. They had a few spare minutes and he could tell she wanted to talk, so he motioned for her to come over to the side and speak with her. She did so, sitting on a rock beside him.

"What's up?" Steffan said, looking proudly at his little sister and all that she'd become.

"So much has changed," She said, looking distantly into the remains of the tent city, now abandoned as the two halves were split off and taken to either side of the armies arrayed against each other.

"If this works, we won't be outsiders any longer," Steffan said, putting a hand on her back. Her armor was so small and she looked so fragile, but Steffan knew that was so far from the truth. She was a Knight of the Eldritch Order and as such she wielded a power that could lay waste.

What was more, she had shown an amazing skill at the sword, though she tended to use a thinner, faster blade than any others. It was constructed for her by Seph, always watching and understanding what they needed before they did.

She truly should be at the head of the Order, not Phil. But Steffan knew he was just letting his personal issues with the man get in the way. He should be grateful to him, but he seemed to spend so much time away, just like his father had. It hurt to think about so he pushed those thoughts away.

"Do you really think so?" Mercy asked. "I'm so happy having a place where we fit in, but I worry that we've chosen a side that will end badly."

"I will not let anything happen to you," Steffan promised.

Mercy looked up at him, her eyes sparkling with half formed tears. "Same," she said, side hugging her brother, their armors clinking together.

Then they were back up on their feet, putting helmets on as they readied for the battle that would soon be upon them. A battle that would decide the fates of the Eldritch Knights and prove to the other Orders that they would not be forgotten or killed quietly in the night.

"Looks like they want to talk," Seph said, motioning to a group of three figures walking into the dead man zone between the two forces.

"What about?" Steffan asked, unaware of any reason to talk when their motivations seemed clear enough to him. They needed to fight and then beat their opponents.

"Come with us and find out," Seph said. "But keep quiet and let me do all the talking."

Steffan nodded, walking to the side of Darius as Seph led the way to talk.

Two bright armored Paladins, and an old man in blue robes met them in the middle of the field. Steffan was distracted by the odd calm and quiet that had come across both sides of the battle, still before the storm.

The old man spoke first, his tone anything but welcoming.

"Where is your leader, the young man from before," the elderly man said.

"He is predisposed, you will speak with me about your plans to surrender and the terms of said surrender," Seph said.

All three present from the enemy's side looked at her with wide eyes and slack jaws for several long moments before regaining themselves.

"You've stolen the words directly from my mouth," the elderly man said. "If you disperse and retreat now, we will gladly speak with you about the terms of your surrender and the abandonment of this unsanctioned Order you are so intent on forming."

"The Eldritch Order is one of the Original members of your council, do not deny such a fact," Seph practically hissed the words, her temper already reaching its limits.

"Times have changed and they will not be changing back," said the old man.

"Then perhaps I should kill you here and hasten the battle?" Seph asked, her hand going to her sword hilt, tapping it with her index finger.

Steffan smiled at that, all three were surprised once again and power began to swell around them.

"I am no mere illusionist, women, you will learn some respect," the elderly man said, his power swelling in his hands for an attack, Steffen was sure.

But Seph just took her hand off her sword and spoke in a low calm voice. "And I'm no mere Eldritch Knight, I am Crimson Death, last Grandmaster of the Eldritch Order and your match, sir," Seph added the last word with a hint of sarcasm and a smile spread over her lips.

As she was the only one wearing red armor her name made some sense. Steffan had wondered what that was about, but he'd just checked it off as a stylistic choice, not something to do with armor.

"Impossible, you fell at the final battle, I saw it with my own eyes," the elderly man said.

"Did you," Seph said, a flame appearing in her hand, as green as ever, but suddenly she spoke some mushed words and drew out some lines in the air with her finger. Her flames turned a tint of red and Steffan had to take a step back, what had she done he wondered?

All three of the enemy present took a step back and the Paladins, helmets off, looked terrified but it was the elderly man that sputtered out the first words and the final words of their little meeting.

"V-very well, if you will not listen to reason, you will be

made to," he said, turning his back to Seph and walking away stiffly.

The red flames died out the moment he turned and Steffan noticed Seph visibly slacked as if she'd done a great feat of strength.

Darius must have noticed too because he leaned and spoke to just her, but Steffan heard.

"Not up to the same strength as you were in our younger days, eh?" Darius said, putting a friendly arm around her, which she promptly shrugged off and began to march back to their forces.

CHAPTER 33
JAMES/STEFFAN

James watched in disgust as some old men went to speak war in his place. He was the main character of his life and this quest had been given to him by Zarrick, he ought to be the one out there speaking with them. But no, they hardly wanted him there and only the word from Zarrick had kept them from trying to arrest him themselves.

So he watched and waited for them to finish their petty words. Lately he'd felt like nothing could satisfy him other than battle and death. If he were being honest with himself it was a bit odd, but he enjoyed the strength and power embracing the feeling gave him, so he let it happen.

He knew that he was slowly being changed by the power, but for whatever reason he didn't seem to care. Golder had warned him of such changes if you let the power master you instead of mastering it, but what did it matter. He was getting all he ever wanted, the thrill of battle, the vengeance he sought after, and eventually he'd be the king of this land.

That of course would have to wait until he could find more

Ascended, he'd sensed several potentials from the common peasants they'd pulled into the city. He'd already told his second to spirit away as many as possible to his dockside warehouse, which should be easy enough as they were already sending all the newcomers to dockside.

They didn't know what they had or they were just too weak to sense the potential of so many willing candidates, and based off of the ones he'd met, it was most definitely that they were too stuffy to give peasants a chance.

James had no qualms about social status, he valued power and strength and he could grant that to even the weakest among them. His mind snapped back to the present as a cry for battle was given. James ushered himself past the lines of Ascended in the back of the ranks, pushing to be at the front lines where the soldiers would be fighting.

He would be the first to draw blood, that much he would make sure. His sword, the tail end of the dragon turned weapon, was light in his grip, despite the large size of it. With it he would kill them all, end this silly order of Eldritch Knights. But he had to remember not to kill any of the actual knights until he found their leader.

He had his eyes on two men that had gone to the middle, surely one of them was this leader that Zarrick was being closed lipped about. But neither of their powers were much better than the old folks that pretended at being powerful. He was looking for someone of equal strength and whoever that was hadn't appeared yet.

But he could be cautious, perhaps hurting his precious Eldritch Knights would bring out the main boss of the fight.

The march became a run and James let his mind focus on the incoming battle. He distanced himself from the soldiers, running on a head to gain speed. He didn't like the idea of squashing so many bugs under foot, he would go straight for their backline of ascended.

He reached the soldiers in the front, a frightened looking mess wielding spears and jumped. He soured over the spear head, going a bit further and higher than he'd planned. It was as if he were flying, but he needed someplace to land that wasn't occupied, so he threw out black fire, throwing several soldiers to the side and burning others.

Landing hard, he rolled and bisected a man spearing forward toward him. The man was fast, but not as fast enough. James turned as he died on the edge of his blade, shooting black flame into a trio of armored figures in white. They met his flames with green flames of their own, but like so many around him they weren't strong enough.

His fire blasted through and took them off their feet. Before he could follow up and end their lives, the heat of battle chasing away all thoughts of mercy, he was met by a red haired woman, her entire body sheathed in red and green fire. She looked like a walking holiday card or something.

"Come to die?" James asked, shouting over the din of battle all around him. His forces had met their line and were pushing inward through the weak forces of the Eldritch Knights.

A spearman went for James' exposed back and his spear broke on his armor. Turning, James laughed in his face before consuming him with black fire.

"What technique taught you to use black flames?" the red haired woman asked.

James answered by shooting black flames all around her. Somewhere nearby someone screamed a name in earnest and he learned the name of who he was fighting.

"Seph!"

James turned to the trio that he'd knocked off their feet and saw a boy there next to a diminutive little girl, each in armor but too small to be amidst battle. Somewhere deep inside he felt pity for them, but it was quickly drowned down by the thrill of battle as red flames appeared all around him, causing him real pain for a moment.

Then suddenly he was fighting for his life against four opponents. The red demon was slowing already, her flames more green than red now, but the three he'd written off as weak were showing particularly good weapons training, forcing him back several steps.

He shot flames at the smallest one, a girl if the armor was any sign, but the boy, not as large as a full grown Kotharian, leapt in front of the attack, bisecting it with his sword, dissipating the flames. He showed particularly good skills, James thought, wishing he could turn these fighters to his side, but he doubted they could take the black flame after accepting the weaker green fire inside themselves.

Back and forth they fought, James toying with them as the red demon lady overdid it and collapsed mid battle. He thought he might be able to finish her off, but the small girl moved with unreal speed, drawing the first blood on him when he approached.

Then came the flames from the last man, who'd been wielding a spear the entire time, positioning him in ways for his partner to strike out. It turned out he wasn't such a pushover, his flames leapt up around him and started to smash into James, doing actual harm to him as he was forced to abandon his attempt at ending the woman.

Suddenly three figures made of flames appeared around James, a trick he'd seen others do with their power, but not one he'd mastered himself. They superheated the air around James and suddenly he was having difficulty breathing as they struck him again and again.

Steffan tried to get a strike in, but the air was too hot for even him as Darius showed the full extent of his powers against the black flamed monster in front of them. Seph had given her all and somehow had fallen unconscious mid battle, without making much progress against the black knight.

Sure she'd struck him and obviously hurt him, but he wasn't slowing at all, if anything he was getting faster. Suddenly Steffan was knocked off his feet, along with Darius and Mercy, as black flames poured out all around them.

If not for his quick thinking, sheathing his body in green flames, he was sure he'd have died, so powerful was the heat. Darius had been concentrating hard and not being able to protect himself, he lay unconscious a few feet away, but thankfully Mercy was already on her feet, her sword raised and ready.

Steffan got back to his feet just in time for the black knight to slam into his sword first. He was strong, much stronger than even the Paladin he'd faced, so he let the blow glance off his sword before forming a flaming dagger to go for his gut.

But the attack didn't work, instead a knee hit him hard in the stomach and sent him reeling backward. Struggling to breath, he looked up to see Mercy get thrown back as well, no match for the terrible black knight they faced.

She was fast though, back on her feet and appearing before Steffan in a defense pose, breathing hard. Slower than he'd have liked and with pain running up his chest as his body struggled to heal himself fast enough, Steffan stood.

"Together," Steffan panted the words, pain still shocking his mind as it refused to go away.

Mercy nodded her head ever so slightly and they both took defensive stances. Steffan could do nothing but keep his eyes on the black knight. Everything around them raged in the heat of battle and he even thought he heard horns in the distance, but he couldn't be sure, so focused on not dying and keeping his sister alive.

"You are no match for me, children," the black knight said, a hint of humor in his voice. "Where is your leader, I seek him and no other."

Of course this monster was looking for Phil, Steffan cursed Phil's name and the black knight, the impossible foe that could turn aside blows with his armor alone. Another spear cracked against his armor as a half ascended that Steffan had trained himself tried to come to their rescue.

The black knight's arm shot out and grabbed him by the throat, then with a twist of his wrist the man's body went limp. Steffan tensed, but held his ground. They had to wait for him to come to them, they'd not survive an offensive attack, but defense offered them something.

Mercy cringed and nearly rushed forward, but Steffan put a hand on her and shook his head 'no'. They had two people to protect and one of them was moving. Steffan noticed Darius stirring from the side, but so did the black knight. He shot forward with his sword raised.

"Together!" Steffan cried out, but they wouldn't be fast enough, or at least he wouldn't. Mercy got there seconds before him, stabbing out at the black knight's legs, her thin blade finding an opening and drawing a spray of blood that had the black knight faltering. However he also attacked in the same moment, black fire consumed Mercy, throwing her smoldering body back some ten feet.

Steffan abandoned Darius and made it to Mercy's side, she was breathing but unmoving. Rage deeper than anything he'd ever known boiled up inside of him and he turned on the black knight.

Green flames formed around him, so hot that it burned his flesh, but he ignored the pain, for it was nothing compared to the pain he felt for his sister.

"You're dead!" Steffan screamed the words and fire leapt from his very voice striking the black knight.

He was a Knight of the Eldritch Order walking the path of the Flameborne and he would show this black knight what that meant. Ball after ball of flames hit the black knight as Darius recovered and looked around confused. But whatever Steffan was doing it was already fading, his power unable to keep track with his rage.

His flames died out, but he kept throwing the balls of green fire, over and over again, until his body was so exhausted that he fell to his knees in front of the black knight. He would die now, he knew this, but not before he drew blood from this monster.

He slashed out with a half formed flame dagger, nearly passing out from the effort, but the black knight slapped his hand aside.

He watched as the blade descended on his head. If only he'd been stronger, faster, more powerful, were his last thoughts as the blade connected.

Except he found he could still think and he opened his eyes, ashamed that he'd closed them in the end. Before him burned a man in white armor wielding a spear of pure green flame. At first he thought Darius had come to his rescue, but as the white armored man kicked the black knight back some twenty feet into a tumble of people, Steffan knew only one person strong enough to do such an attack.

Phil had returned at last and damnit, Steffan was happy to see him for once.

"About time," Steffan managed to say before his mind and vision were overcome by blackness.

CHAPTER 34
PHIL/JAMES

"Darius, get the wounded and protect them," Phil shouted orders here and there. This was a nightmare, their lines were broken and only his charging in with his mount had saved them from being overwhelmed.

His other Pale Riders had left, charging the sides and flanking the enemy forces, Reaper having gone with them after a quick order from Phil. He should be fighting atop Reaper, he knew, but this black knight had nearly killed all those he cared about most and he needed his personal attention.

"You are the leader, I can feel it," came a voice that was oddly familiar, almost as if speaking from a past life, but for whatever reason he couldn't place it.

"I am the leader of the Eldritch Order and your doom," Phil shouted back, twirling his staff and reading himself against the massive Kothar man, for what else could he be with that kind of size.

They clashed in a spray of black and green fire. Phil had to admit something after only a few back and forth exchanges with the man, he was stronger and his flames hurt like hell. But that didn't mean he was the better fighter.

Phil stabbed forward only to have his spear miss and an elbow smash into his face. Okay maybe he was the better fighter as well, Phil thought as he focused on maintaining his weapon and throwing a stream of fire at the black knight.

"I have no quarrel with you," Phil said in a moment of stillness between their clashes.

The black knight laughed, something that stunk at the edge of his mind, if only for the sounds of the battle he might be able to place the voice.

"Give me your amulet and I'll leave this battle, easy as that," the black knight said.

Phil still couldn't place the voice but he'd heard it before and it was so familiar. Why couldn't he just place it.

"You work for Zarrick," Phil said, shaking his head. "I was wondering when he'd come for it, but I won't be giving it up. Whatever he needs it for, he best be willing to kill me for it."

Phil knew that upon his death it would return to the last bastion of Eldritch Knight power, their keep, so even in death he could thwart Zarrick's motives.

"I'll enjoy killing you," came the reply and the battle was back on in earnest.

The black knight was stronger and his flames were much more potent than they had any right to be, but he wasn't faster than Phil, so he used his only advantage while maintaining his flames in a defensive aura around himself.

It was a shame he had to be enemies with this fighter, the way he moved and fought seemed so familiar and he had amazing potential. Whatever beast the black flame came from, perhaps a dragon based on his armor's design, was powerful indeed. It was almost like he had the same potential as...

Was this man human, no it couldn't be, he was easily the size of an average Koth, but his power and potential were off the charts in a way he'd only seen one other place, the night the paladins had attacked from Earth.

He felt a moment of panic as he recalled the loss of his arm and how hard it had been to kill her, and this foe was easily her match in every way. Would he have what it takes to kill him, he'd grown so strong since that last fight he reminded himself.

But still the fight raged on and it became clearer and clearer that he wasn't going to be able to do it alone. Looking around he saw where Seph had fallen and he wished with all his might that she recovered quickly.

As if sensing that he needed help, Steffan appeared at his side awake once more, striking out. It made an opening for Phil and his spear slashed through the dragon style armor and left the man coughing blood through his helmet.

"Damn that hurt," he yelled as if confused. "Stay out of our fight, boy!" A narrow beam of black fire struck Steffan before Phil could defend him and he hit the ground hard.

Phil couldn't spare a look to see if he still lived, so fast and furious were the attacks from the black knight. It took all he had to parry the blows and keep himself from losing ground. For if he fell backward he would break the line that was keeping Seph and others safe to recover.

Phil had no other choice, if he was going to win this he needed power beyond what he had access to. He reached up and grabbed hold of his amulet, suddenly power swelled around him and his vision turned a shade of green.

He fought hard against the arrogance that filled him as his power reached new heights. He slashed out with his spear, the black knight was nothing compared to him now, his blow hit his chest and drew blood while throwing him back several feet.

TIMOTHY MCGOWEN

Then the black knight laughed and grabbed hold of an amulet around his own neck, suddenly he was moving with a familiar speed and power.

He was the head of whatever Order he was a part of and had access to a well of power as well. All of this hit Phil as a realization but he had to keep fighting, his power wouldn't even last as long as it had before, for it took time to recharge.

Moving with blinding speed the two fought like super-heroes, each punch, kick, and slash, digging huge grooves in the ground and cutting nearby soldiers into two. So much power concentrated in a single area, if felt like the pressure of it all would be enough to break the world.

It was Phil who broke first, one moment his power was there surging and the next he was left feeling weak and power-less in comparison. The black knight glowed with potential power and he struck Phil hard enough to rupture several organs and shatter bones.

Phil coughed up blood in the handfuls as his body tried to put him back together. He barely made it to his feet when the black knight appeared in front of him.

"So weak," he said and suddenly Phil knew where he'd heard that voice before, during so many digital conferences and the few times they'd gathered in person per his sister's insistence.

Tank or James rather, stood before him wreathed in power and deadly intent.

Before he could say a word, blood still pouring out of his mouth and keeping him from speaking, James raised a black blade and swung down on Phil.

Something blurred beside him and a clang went out as something struck the side of his blade, making it barely miss its target. Phil looked up to see one of the golems of the portal

302

fighting back James with such precision combat and skills that it boggled his mind.

James obviously lost his amulets power then, as he stumbled backward and coughed several times. The golem turned to Phil and spoke, suddenly the world went still with realization.

"I am glad to be alive," Adam said in his usual voice, but then he bent his head to the side and another familiar voice appeared.

"Daaamnn flesh bag, you look messed up. Thanks for getting me into this place, I honestly thought you'd forgotten about me for a while. Pretty cool moves right? I downloaded the internet before we left Earth and since I have a body now, I can do martial arts. Hooowaaaayy!"

Phil blinked repeatedly, confused at the strange turn of events, but Adam or Eve or whoever they were spoke up again this time in Adam's voice.

"I apologize for that, it would appear that there is a side of me that is quite eccentric. Are you able to stand, or should we try to retreat?"

"We don't need to fight," Phil began to say, but James rushed in and Adam met him blow for blow, moving in ways Phil had only seen in old kung fu flicks. It was truly amazing the ability to fight Adam was showing, but as skilled as he was, James was faster.

However Phil had an idea, spitting out more blood he wrenched his helmet off and stood tall.

"James," Phil managed to say though it pained him to speak.

The black knight stopped mid swing, but Adam didn't stop, smashing upward and knocking off his helmet. James fell to a knee in front of Adam, his eyes never leaving Phils.

Adam finally paused, turned to Phil and spoke in Eve's

voice. "James is here too!" Then she reached forward and hugged the kneeling knight. "It's me Eve." Eve added when James kept staring at Phil, eyes locked and some internal conflict raging within him.

James pushed Adam or Eve, whichever was in control at the time, back and turned to pick up his helmet. Only then did he break his stare with Phil, utter confusion on his face. Just when Phil thought he might talk to him, he turned and ran.

Why was James running, he didn't really know, but what he did know was that if he stayed there any longer he'd be compelled to kill one of his last living friends. He needed to work out his own demons, but first he wanted to pay Zarrick a visit. That terrible little man had given him this evil power and set him on a path against his friend.

The battle rages on around James as he ran, but he had no desire to participate anymore. He felt so numb and a little dumb for trusting so easily. How was it that Phil was surrounded by friends that he wanted to protect and love, but James was alone with two short evil men.

James almost turned back at that thought, but he stayed his course. He needed to speak with Zarrick, but he feared he wouldn't be strong enough to take out the little man, so there had to be another plan. Perhaps he'd disappear into the dockside and build up his gang while working out his own emotions.

Yeah that sounded like a path that would keep him alive. He'd do that, have what Phil found and when the time was right, he'd strike down Zarrick, the traitorous bastard, and join

Phil. The Green Hats would ride again, they even had Eve, somehow in the body of one of the portal golems. Phil had always been a tricky man, of course he'd find a way to get Eve into the game.

One thing was certain, he had to spread his flame and grow more powerful or else he'd fall to Zarrick and his plans.

Phil watched his friend go and although he wanted to go after him, there were more important matters at hand. The battle around them wasn't going well with the biggest hitters of the Eldritch Order sitting out the fight.

"Rally the men, I'm going in!" Phil yelled, raising up and nodding to Adam that he should join him.

Steffan, Mercy, Darius, and even a sickly looking Seph all looked at him as if he were crazy, but Phil had plenty of strength left to turn the battle. He rushed out and with his trusty golem at his side, they turned the tide of the battle.

It wasn't all that hard, the half ascended had been doing their part, they just needed a bit more leadership. The horde of untrained tent city villagers were the most distracting part of the battle, they stayed back and tried not to do any actual fighting.

But beyond all that Phil was able to bring the battle to a close, the forces of the council retreating as one by one, Phil bested their best Ascended. Without the black knight on their side, they truly had no chance against his force. His Pale Riders did wonderfully to help turn the tide as well, flanking and bringing low the enemy wherever they went.

Phil called for a retreat of his own forces after the enemy

walled themselves up and they began to tend to the wounded and dying on the battlefield. It wasn't until an hour or two later that he finally got to go check on Seph to see what had taken her out of the battle. When he got there he was surprised to see her still on her back and her breathing labored.

"What's wrong, what happened, why aren't you healing?" Phil asks, unable to hold back his passion as he knelt beside her.

"I've been meaning to tell you," Seph said, her words barely a whisper and hoarse from coughing up blood. "I've pushed myself too far too fast. There is nothing left for me but death, I was happy to have fought at your side."

"You've destroyed your core?" Darius asked, looking down with concern.

"Several times over," Seph said, trying to chuckle and failing to do so. "I was already working with several cracks when I met the boy, my life span severely shortened." More coughs. "I'm a candle that has burned too low, let me die with my favorite students around me. Phil, Mercy, Steffan, come close."

They did so, Phil so shocked that he didn't know what to say, the right words wouldn't come. Instead he held her hand as she drifted into unconsciousness. She continued to breathe for several seconds longer, but eventually even her raspy breath stopped and she died.

Phil cried over her dead body and thoughts of vengeance against the world poured through his mind, but he couldn't bring himself to utter a single word.

It was the small girl, Mercy that spoke first, putting a hand on Phil's shoulder.

"She wanted the Order to be strong, she wanted us to be unified. She got to see her dream come true, now we have to honor that memory and keep the Eldritch Order together at all costs."

"We will prevail," Phil said, looking to the strong Eldritch Knights around him. "Together we are strong."

The End of Book 2
Return for the next Book to see how the adventure ends for Phil and the Eldritch Knights.

LEAVE A REVIEW

Thank you for reading. Please leave a review.

Check out my website at AuthorTimothyMcGowen.com

If you really liked the book, please consider reaching out and telling me what you enjoyed about it at, Timothy.mcgowen1@ gmail.com.

Join my Facebook group and discuss the books at: https:// www.facebook.com/groups/234653175151521/

Join my Patreon at: https://www.patreon.com/ TimothyMcGowen

ABOUT THE AUTHOR

 Timothy McGowen, a Kansas-based author, cherishes the joys of family life with his wife and two daughters. His journey in the literary world began in grade school, and it's a passion that continues to flourish. Inspired by the imaginative realms of Terry Brooks and Brandon Sanderson, Timothy endeavors to follow in their footsteps, crafting stories that resonate with fantasy and adventure enthusiasts.

Prior to dedicating himself to the art of storytelling, Timothy honed his skills as a Software Developer, an experience that not only enriched his technical knowledge but also subtly influences his narrative style. This unique blend of technology and creativity is evident in his work, where he seamlessly integrates elements of Fantasy with splashes of Sci-Fi and the innovative concepts of LitRPG/Gamelit.

Timothy's passion for both reading and writing books is the lifeblood of his creative journey. For those who share this enthusiasm, he warmly invites you to join his newsletter. Stay updated with the latest news and embark on an exciting journey with each new book release.

facebook.com/timothym.mcgowen

x.com/TimothyMMcGowe1

instagram.com/timothy.mcgowen1

LITRPG GROUP

Check out this group if you want to gather together and hear about new great LitRPG books.

(https://www.facebook.com/groups/LitRPGGroup/)

LEARN MORE ABOUT LITRPG/GAMELIT GENRE

To learn more about LitRPG & GameLit, talk to author and just have an awesome time by joining some LitRPG/Gamelit groups.

Here is another LitRPG group you can join if you are looking for the next great read!

Facebook.com/groups/LitRPG.books

List of LitRPG/Gamelit Facebook Groups:

- https://www.facebook.com/groups/LitRPGReleases/
- https://www.facebook.com/groups/litrpgforum/
- https://www.facebook.com/groups/litrpglegends/
- https://www.facebook.com/groups/LitRPGsociety/
- https://www.facebook.com/groups/AleronKong/

www.ingramcontent.com/pod-product-compliance
Lightning Source LLC
Chambersburg PA
CBHW020842020726
47497CB00005B/1210